Bryce had stretched his hand out, so that the tips of his fingers were only an inch away from her shoulder. One inch.

She didn't move a muscle. "What?"

He remained motionless, too. His long fingers didn't close the distance between them, but they didn't retreat, either. It was like a freeze frame, the two of them suspended in time, only an inch apart.

She asked again, because the tension of that inch was unbearable. "What?"

"Nothing," he said, his voice oddly vague. "It's just—"

She was acutely aware of her heartbeat, which seemed to be the only part of her still moving. One inch. If she leaned his way even the slightest bit, their bodies would connect.

But she couldn't. The distance between them, even if it was only an inch, was his distance. He had put it there, and only he could take it away.

"It's just that… If you wanted my respect for what you did today—for what you're trying to do with your life… You've got it."

Respect… Numbly she thanked him, said goodbye and climbed out of the car. Respect was cold, completely without passion. You respected your congressman, your pastor, your fifth-grade teacher and your elders.

Respect had no power to do the only thing that mattered. It could never close that final, fatal inch.

Dear Reader,

What is the mystique of small towns? So many stories are set in them, including this one. They must have something that speaks to our deepest fantasies.

I grew up in Tampa, Florida, which, though not New York or L.A., hardly qualifies as "small." But I, too, feel the small-town magic, lean longingly toward the peace and charm. Is it the sweet air? The big sky? The unlocked doors, the homegrown stores, the creeks and glens and quiet places?

Yes, all that. But perhaps there's something even more profound. Perhaps we're all yearning to connect—and to believe our connections are "forever." Maybe it's appealing to think that, even if we are shy or injured or just born loners, the close bonds of a small town could save us from ourselves. They could pull us in, banish isolation, promise permanence.

Heyday is that kind of town. Bryce McClintock left in scandal and disgrace fourteen years ago, vowing never to return. But when he finds he has inherited one-third of his father's estate, he must come back to the town that officially labeled him The Sinner.

He tells himself it's temporary. Just until he can sort things out. But that's before he meets the stray dog and the crazy tenants. Before he discovers he's got a new niece he didn't know about, and a new job he doesn't want. Most of all, that's before he learns that Lara Lynmore, the one woman who ever got under his skin, has come to live in Heyday, too.

Bryce is about to find out one more thing about small towns— and about true love. Once they claim your heart, they never really give it back.

I hope you enjoy this story.

Warmly,

Kathleen O'Brien

P.S. I love to hear from readers! Write me at P.O. Box 947633, Maitland, FL 32794-7633. And visit me at my Web site, www.KathleenOBrien.net.

The Sinner
Kathleen O'Brien

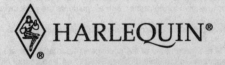

HARLEQUIN®

TORONTO • NEW YORK • LONDON
AMSTERDAM • PARIS • SYDNEY • HAMBURG
STOCKHOLM • ATHENS • TOKYO • MILAN • MADRID
PRAGUE • WARSAW • BUDAPEST • AUCKLAND

ISBN 0-373-71249-9

THE SINNER

Copyright © 2005 by Kathleen O'Brien.

This edition published by arrangement with Harlequin Books S.A.

www.eHarlequin.com

Printed in U.S.A.

Books by Kathleen O'Brien

HARLEQUIN SUPERROMANCE

927—THE REAL FATHER
967—A SELF-MADE MAN
1015—WINTER BABY*
1047—BABES IN ARMS*
1086—THE REDEMPTION OF MATTHEW QUINN*
1146—THE ONE SAFE PLACE*
1176—THE HOMECOMING BABY
1231—THE SAINT†

HARLEQUIN SINGLE TITLE

MYSTERIES OF LOST ANGEL INN
  "The Edge of Memory"

SIGNATURE SELECT SPOTLIGHT

HAPPILY NEVER AFTER—coming in August 2005

*Four Seasons in Firefly Glen
†The Heroes of Heyday

Don't miss any of our special offers. Write to us at the following address for information on our newest releases.

Harlequin Reader Service
U.S.: 3010 Walden Ave., P.O. Box 1325, Buffalo, NY 14269
Canadian: P.O. Box 609, Fort Erie, Ont. L2A 5X3

CHAPTER ONE

"NO KIDDING, th-that's your job? You get *paid* to guard Lara Lynmore's body?"

Bryce McClintock flicked a look at the name tag of the stammering young man next to him. Ted Barnes, Assistant Event Manager, Eldorado Hotels. Ted was a just-barely-twentysomething kid whose silver, European-cut suit said he wanted to be all Hollywood glamour, but whose freckled face said he'd just stepped off the bus from Iowa.

The way the kid's mouth hung open as he looked at Lara Lynmore gave him away, too. Real Hollywood types took celebrities for granted. And Lara Lynmore wasn't even technically a "star" yet. Although ever since her first leading role, as Bess, the doomed black-eyed beauty in the high-budget movie version of "The Highwayman," had premiered this summer, she was getting pretty close.

Close enough to have attracted about a million innocent, panting fans, like this guy.

And one stalker, an obsessed former stuntman named Kenny Boggs.

Kenny wasn't just annoying. He was dangerous.

Bryce had seen the irrational, increasingly hostile letters the stuntman had sent to Lara Lynmore after she rejected him. He'd heard the threats on her answering machine. Kenny meant business.

Bryce had seen way too many creeps like Boggs—for these past eight years in the FBI they'd been his whole life. That was why he'd quit. That was why, as soon as he could find someone else to take this idiotic position of guarding America's sweetheart, he was headed straight for the Bahamas, where his biggest problem would be figuring out how to beat the house at blackjack.

However, Ted wasn't to blame for Bryce's career problems. Ted was just a sweet sap who was going to break his corn-fed heart trying to Be Somebody, and then slink home to marry the patient girl who would never guess that every time her sensible husband made love to her, he'd be thinking of Lara Lynmore.

So instead of telling him to buzz off, as he had planned, Bryce just nodded. "Yeah. I'm her bodyguard. But it's no big deal. It's just a job."

A sighing silence. Though Bryce didn't want to take his eyes off the crowd for long, he glanced over at the kid one more time. Was that drool he saw shining at the edge of his open mouth? *God.*

"Movie stars are people, Ted. They're pretty, but they're just people."

Ted didn't even blink. "Not Lara," he whispered. "Lara Lynmore isn't just people. Look at her."

Bryce didn't have to look at Lara to know what Ted was talking about, but he did. And he saw what he'd seen every day, every night, for the past six weeks. A twenty-six-year-old brunette with the long-legged, ripe-breasted body of a wet-dream goddess and the sweet, wide-eyed face of the girl you'd loved and lost in high school.

It was that off-kilter combination that got you. Bryce was tough—he prided himself on it—but even he wasn't so tough he didn't feel it. It was like a one-two punch, sharp and below the belt.

Today Lara was giving a speech to the ladies of the Breast Cancer Awareness luncheon, so she wasn't wearing her usual party-girl getup—no dagger-cut necklines, no sequins, no peekaboo lace.

Which wasn't to say *no sex*. She looked sexy as hell in a feminine rendition of the riding clothes seen in *The Highwayman*. A pair of tight-fitting white breeches, a cardinal-red jacket, a white ruffled kerchief at her throat pinned by a simple sparkling diamond. A red ribbon gathered her long, dark hair at her neck and let it spill down her back all the way to her fantastic butt.

Bryce shifted and tightened his jaw. Ted from Iowa might be right. Lara Lynmore really wasn't just an ordinary person. She was dangerously potent, the female equivalent of heroin. People who ventured too close could get addicted, get crazy, get hurt.

Bryce wondered what Ted would think if he knew that, just last night, Bryce had taken a willing Lara Lynmore down to her lacy under-nothings, right there on her living room sofa—and had chosen to stop there. To walk away empty handed.

He'd think Bryce was nuts, that's what he'd think.

Bryce half thought so himself. He still wasn't sure what had stopped him. God knew this job had teased every one of his hormones into a raging fury. It was like some kind of torture, standing within inches of this high-octane beauty 24/7, trying to keep those hormones on a leash. No wonder they'd ended up panty-dancing on the sofa last night.

Maybe what had stopped him was the thought of Darryl, Lara's lawyer. Darryl, who had roped Bryce into this bodyguarding gig by playing on an old law-school friendship. *Just for a little while,* Darryl had begged, just until California's best professional bodyguard was free and could take over.

You're the only one I can trust to control this until the professional can take over. It's serious, Bryce. This nut wants to kill her.

A few days, like hell. That had been six weeks ago. Finally, last night, just in the nick of time, just before the panties came off, the new bodyguard had called to say he could start tomorrow.

Which meant Bryce just had to get through today, and then he was home free.

And, thankfully, today looked like a piece of cake. He'd already vetted the help, everything from the waiters and chefs to good old Ted here. He'd made the setup crew change the position of Lara's podium—they'd set it up in the center of the dais, but he needed it closer to the wings, where he'd be stationed.

And then, making himself truly popular, he'd made them remove the first row of tables, which were much too close to the dais.

That had improved the situation, though even now, things were a little too tight to be ideal. But when he looked out and saw the hundreds of pink hats and light-blue, yellow and pink party frocks in the audience, he felt better. The Breast Cancer Awareness luncheon was an ocean of estrogen punctuated by a few slim, white-clad waiters circulating gracefully among the tables.

A cocky muscle man like Kenny Boggs would stand out in this crowd like a circus clown in a cemetery.

"And, in conclusion—" Lara's voice sounded good over the microphone, which accentuated its throaty undertones. "I'd like to thank all of you for—"

Bryce had seen a copy of her speech. Three more sentences, and they were out of here.

Suddenly, without apparent reason, his heartbeat quickened, instinct sending a jolt of adrenaline through his system. Something was wrong.

His eyes narrowed, scanning rapidly over the smiling crowd. Damn it. Every instinct he owned was telling him something was wrong. *What was it?*

It was… Scanning… Scanning…

It was that waiter. That waiter near the front, the one who was just a little broader in the shoulders than the others. The one who had a tray in his hand, but was walking between tables instead of slowly rotating around just one, as all the other waiters were doing, picking up uneaten fruit tarts.

Bryce edged forward for a better look. What in hell was the guy doing? His serpentine movements were bringing him ever closer to the dais. Still, it wasn't Kenny. Kenny Boggs had blond hair, and this guy was…

Shit. Bryce came out from behind the curtain just as the waiter looked up. It *was* Kenny, what a fool, what a maniac, here of all places, even with dyed hair and a uniform he should have known—

Their eyes met for one broken edge of a second, but it was enough to warn the muscle-bound psycho that he'd been made. His huge shoulders clenched.

Bryce moved forward, reaching for Lara, who hadn't noticed anything yet. "Get back," he barked. She looked over at him, horror instantly digging a jagged furrow between her lovely brows. Her grip on the podium tightened. She looked as if she weren't sure which way to run, as if she were frozen.

Kenny wasn't frozen, though. All in one lightning movement, he dropped his tray with a clatter and began to run toward the dais, a large knife gripped in his left fist, point down.

At least it wasn't a gun.

Still—Bryce knew about crazy people. Often they were able to beat smarter, stronger, saner people because they didn't think in predictable patterns. They didn't fight according to even the most subconscious of rules. Sometimes they didn't feel pain. Sometimes they liked it.

Bryce had his gun out before Kenny took the first step, but everywhere he looked women were screaming, scurrying around the tables like squealing mice. If Bryce shot and missed Kenny, the bullet might bury itself in the crowd, in one of those terrified, well-meaning ladies in their stylish pink hats.

Some of them were even scrambling closer to the

dais instead of toward the exits, as if fear had robbed them of their sense of direction. They stumbled on the short rise of stairs, on the hems of their expensive dresses. It was pure pink-and-blue chaos.

Damn it, damn it. He didn't dare shoot.

Kenny moved fast, but Bryce got to Lara first. He shoved her toward the wings, even though she still gripped the podium so hard he could hear her fingernails rip on the wood.

"Ted," Bryce called roughly, and thankfully the lovestruck Assistant Event Manager was still there—and still thinking. Ted caught Lara as if she were a well-tossed football. He wrapped his skinny arms around her and began to drag her behind the curtain.

Bryce was the only thing that stood between Kenny and the curtain. Kenny rammed into him, shoulder first, trying to go right through him. But Bryce held his ground, and Kenny cursed with a hoarse fury that made Bryce's blood run cold.

"You can't keep me from her, you bastard," Kenny said, or maybe it only sounded like that, Bryce wasn't sure. His voice was crazed, his syllables more like the grunts of an animal than a human being.

"She's mine," he said, slashing wildly. "Mine, mine—"

Bryce kept the knife blade away somehow. Should he have holstered his gun? It was more of a liability now. The fight had become primal, hand-to-hand. He could smell Kenny's breath. Foul. It seemed to carry the stench of his psychosis.

The struggle lasted about ten seconds. He felt Kenny's knife finally find a home, sinking into the flesh of his upper arm as if it were a piece of pie.

The cold blade radiated fire out in all directions. And then it hit bone. Bryce's vision exploded, red and starry, but he refused to faint.

The split second it took Kenny to work the knife free was the second Bryce needed. Ignoring the pain, he dropped his gun into the sweaty inch between their bodies. He jerked Kenny around so that the gun pointed toward the back of the dais, where no one could get hurt if something went wrong.

And then he pulled the trigger.

Kenny frowned, and for a minute Bryce thought maybe, somehow, he had missed. He had his finger on the trigger again, ready to pull, when Kenny's mouth opened and blood spilled out like liquid words.

Kenny shook his head, as if rejecting the truth, but his body knew. He began to slide to his knees. Some absurd instinct made Bryce catch him under the arms and break his fall, lowering him toward the floor, careful of crooked legs and lolling arms.

Kenny's abdomen was pulpy, red, and sickening. Bryce looked at it only a second before training his eyes on the man's face. Kenny's breath was coming in small, choking spasms. He stared up at Bryce and clutched his arm, as if he needed comfort. Bryce found that he couldn't pull away. He didn't even try.

"Lara," Kenny whispered, sounding, here at the end, as innocent and adoring as wide-eyed Ted from Iowa. His fingers opened and shut rhythmically on Bryce's coat sleeve. He shut his eyes and said her name one more time, tight with agony, blood bubbling between his lips. "Lara."

His hand fell away.

With a fierce suddenness, the sounds of the real world came rushing back into Bryce's ears. He felt wobbly and wet, as if he had just surfaced from a deep sea dive. Still, he struggled to his feet and took a step. He must have lost a lot of blood. He felt strange, as if he were about to fall asleep, or as if he had just awakened.

He was surprised to see he still held the gun. Its warm weight was like a living thing in his hand, black and smoking, temporarily docile but always dangerous.

He fought the urge to toss the gun aside, aware that the police would want to look at it, do tests and take prints and label it as evidence. He couldn't let the curious onlookers touch it.

He stared down at Kenny Boggs, weaving a little, casting a moving shadow across the silent body. It all seemed so bizarre. Somehow he had never believed it would come to this. He hadn't ever really believed it would end in death.

Bryce had never shot a man before. Maybe, he thought suddenly, he should have mentioned that to Darryl before he accepted this mission. He hadn't shot any of the criminals he'd investigated during eight years in the FBI. He hadn't shot the thug who stole his Lexus from his apartment parking lot, or the creep he'd found in bed with his girlfriend. He hadn't even shot his father, whom he had hated more than anyone else on earth.

But he'd shot this guy. This total stranger. He didn't seem to be able to force that to make sense. Kenny was crazy, of course he was, as crazy as a rabid dog, but he had died with Bryce's bullet in his stomach and Lara Lynmore's name on his lips. Even now, that just wouldn't make sense.

"Bryce!" Lara came running out from the wings, stumbling gracefully. Ted must have wrestled her to the ground back there, because her bloodred coat was torn, and her tight white pants had dirty circles on the knees. Her brown hair flew around her shoulders, matted and dusty, but still flattering, as if she'd just come from Makeup, where they'd transformed her into the perfect heroine in distress.

Bryce turned away, suddenly unable to bear the sight of her.

She called his name again, catching on the *y* subtly, so that the sound hinted at a deep, inarticulate need. He'd heard that sound before. It was exactly how she'd called out to her lost highwayman in her big death scene. *Brava, Ms. Lynmore.* He half expected the delighted director to appear and yell "Cut!"

When he heard her first soft sobs, he started to walk away, toward the other end of the dais, where he now saw the uniformed cops appearing.

"Bryce, come back." But he didn't turn around. Kenny's bloody body lay between them, and it was a gulf he knew he would never be able to cross. Not today. Not ever.

"Bryce."

He almost paused. She sounded so alone.

But what a joke that was. Lara Lynmore, budding starlet, was never alone. Already a dozen people were rushing past him, eager to comfort the beautiful woman who was crying so prettily, acting as if her heart would break.

Of course she was. That was what Lara Lynmore did. She acted.

CHAPTER TWO

LARA RODE THE GLASS ELEVATOR up to her third-floor apartment, clutching her bag of new shoes as if it were the Holy Grail. It was ridiculous to be so proud of something so simple. But this was the first time she'd ventured out of her apartment alone since the shooting, and even if it was just to the Jimmy Choo store, it still felt like a victory.

Her mother had wanted to go with her. She always wanted to—not because she thought Lara still needed protection, but because she enjoyed the adventure. If none of Lara's fans recognized her right away—which happened very rarely these days—Karla Gilbert would be sure to do something to draw a crowd.

"Look, Lara," she'd say loudly enough for everyone standing nearby to hear, "it's just like the scarf you wore in *The Highwayman*." It was childish, but Lara had learned not to mind. Her mother's vicarious pleasure had always been by far the most uncomplicated reward of this strange and exhausting career.

Today, though, Lara just hadn't been up to all the fuss. Today had been a test, to see if she could shake off the depression and anxiety that had been smothering her for the past eight weeks.

And she had passed the test. She leaned against the cool elevator walls and closed her eyes, squeezing the Jimmy Choo bag to her chest.

Now if only she could pass this next test, too. She thought of the long yellow packet, the letter from Moresville College, that lay at the bottom of her purse, like a bomb waiting to explode, and shivered slightly. This test would be so much harder.

But she couldn't wait any longer. She'd agonized over this, she'd worried and prayed and dreamed, until she had thought she'd go crazy. But the time for fretting and planning was over. Now that she knew she was strong enough to face the world on her own, it was time for action.

Today was the day.

The first day of the rest of her life. She almost smiled, thinking how perfectly that old cliché fit the moment. A small squeeze of excitement tightened her chest, but it was brief. Almost immediately the anxiety returned.

She caught a watery reflection of herself in the elevator's glass cage, pale and incomplete, broken by the green ferns of the three-story atrium that slid down as she ascended. Who was this plain young woman? Without makeup, without the elaborate hairstyling, without the expensive wardrobe, she looked just like any other woman. Nothing special. Not even as pretty as the ladies who sold shoes in the Jimmy Choo store, or the stylish professional women who moved through the elegant foyer below.

Certainly not the kind of woman men died for. If only Kenny Boggs had seen her like this, maybe none of the horror would have happened. A vision of his bleeding body superimposed itself onto her reflection, and she closed her eyes, suddenly sick.

How could he be dead? How was it possible that a human being had died merely so that she could live? Who was she? What made her life more valuable than his?

Logically, she understood that there were rational answers. Kenny Boggs had tried to kill her. People had a right to protect themselves. But the emotional truth was more complicated, like a dark, twisted knot inside her heart. The questions remained, ghosts that followed her around, pale and quiet in the daytime, stronger and louder at night.

But she repeated the mantra she'd used every sleepless night for the past eight weeks. Kenny was dead. She couldn't go back and change the past.

Now all that was left was to change the future, if she was brave enough to do it.

The elevator finally stopped. She walked to her own door, took a deep breath and put her key into the lock. She was ready, her speech prepared, her shoulders squared—so why were her knees suddenly just a little too soft? She wasn't afraid of her own mother, was she? Surely, after the initial shock wore off, her mother would—

But this was just more worrying. More procrastination.

She turned the key. The rest of her life lay, green and

shining, like Oz, just across the long bridge of this one conversation. She couldn't afford to lose her nerve now.

"Mom? I need to talk to—"

But for a second, as the door to her apartment swung open, she froze. Had she opened the wrong door?

She didn't recognize anything in this room.

Except her mother. Karla rushed over, cupping Lara's chin in her hand and kissing her on both cheeks, an affectation she had picked up recently, as if they were from Italy instead of Mobile, Alabama.

"Oh, good, Lara, you're here! Ignore the mess in the living room. Remember, it's a work in progress. It's going to be magnificent! Maxim, she's here! Show Lara the plans!"

Lara touched her mother's hand. "Plans?"

Her mother adjusted a strand of platinum-blond hair behind her delicate ear and knitted her freshly waxed eyebrows. "The decorating, darling. Remember? I told you last week."

Lara shook her head slowly. She didn't remember anything about decorating. And besides…this was decorating? The living room looked as if it had been ransacked.

Her mother laughed merrily. "Oh, Lara, you never listen to me. I must have talked to you about it ten times, and you said it was fine. You've been needing to do something with this place, and now that you're—"

Maxim came over, wearing an olive-green suit with gold braids at the shoulders. He had redecorated Karla's apartment last year, while Lara was in England filming *The Highwayman.* Lara had met him once or twice on visits home, and he'd scared her to death. With his black eyes and black moustache, he looked like some sadistic headmaster at a horror-movie military school.

"You must change. You must change everything." He drew his imposing black brows together. In spite of his outrageous clothes, Maxim defied every stereotype about the effeminate interior decorator. He didn't just re-decorate your rooms, he went to war with them. "Ev-erything."

"Hi, Maxim." Lara tried not to resent his presence. But the timing couldn't have been worse. And it cer-tainly pointed out that her mother, at least, wasn't trapped in a mental maze of guilt and bloody memo-ries, trying to make sense of Kenny Boggs's death. Her mother was moving on, picking out paint and fabric and furniture.

Of course, she hadn't been on the dais that day. She hadn't seen Kenny's body.

Lara forced a smile. She was always pretending these days, trying to be like other people. "Maxim…I think maybe we should put the redecorating off a little while. I need to talk to my mother—"

Maxim growled. "You cannot put this off a minute. Not a second." He let his black gaze sweep the room angrily. "There is no style here, there is no ambiance. There is no *you*. Not the real you."

If only he knew how true that was. The real Lara hadn't ever set foot in this apartment. The real Lara hadn't been seen for years. In fact, in some ways, she felt that the real Lara hadn't yet been born.

"Maxim has such wonderful things planned, Lara.

All white, very modern. With little explosions of color, like…" Karla put a pale pink fingertip against her dazzlingly white teeth. "Oh, show her the lamp, Maxim."

"Yes. The lamp is the masterpiece." Maxim picked up a long, cherry-red, twisted-glass thing from behind the sofa and held it out like a javelin. It was at least six feet long. It looked like…Lara searched her memory for what it reminded her of….

It looked like a Twizzler.

Maxim ran his hand along the twisted, ropy surface lovingly.

"Picture," he commanded. "It glows, top to bottom. Very red. Dramatic. It stands behind a virginal white sofa. The sofa has purple pillows. Perhaps one is yellow, to startle the eye. And then…" He held the Twizzler erect. "Fire!"

Lara hesitated, wondering whether Maxim might be insane.

"Oh." Without warning, his face crumpled. Even his moustache seemed to wilt. "You don't like it?"

"Yes, of course," she assured him, though it shocked her to see how vulnerable he was under that military surface. How could she have forgotten the one immutable truth of Hollywood? Everyone in this town was playing a role, apparently even Maxim. "It's…unforgettable." He frowned, unconvinced, so she went on. "I love it, honestly. It's just that I really need to talk to—"

She suddenly felt a hand on her shoulder. She looked over to see Karla plucking at the cotton sleeve of Lara's T-shirt and frowning.

"My God, Lara," her mother said. "Please. Tell me you didn't wear this out shopping."

Lara stiffened, but she kept her voice calm. "Yes, I did."

"Oh, honey, noooo." Her mother sounded as distressed as if Lara had confessed to walking naked down Rodeo Drive. "And no makeup? No mousse?" She fingered Lara's hair desperately, as if she could salvage her after the fact. "Oh, honey, honey. Not even any lipstick?"

Lara tried to keep smiling. "It's okay, Mom." She held up the shoe bag. "As you can see, they were willing to take my money, anyhow."

"But what if people had seen you?"

"People did see me. Lots of people. No one turned to stone."

"But I mean, someone *important?* God, what about the paparazzi?"

"Mom. I'm not that big a deal. I went, I shopped, I came home. I'm not Elizabeth Taylor. I don't exactly stop traffic."

"Not dressed like that, you don't." Her mother sighed. "But when you try, when you do something with yourself, then you're—" She turned to Maxim. "Did you see *The Highwayman*?"

Maxim nodded. "Yes. It was a foolish movie, but her beauty there, it was amazing. When she shot herself to warn her lover, the audience wept. Everyone. I swear this."

Karla turned back to Lara. "You see? It's all in the presentation." She grabbed her purse off the sofa and began rummaging through it. "I know I have a lipstick somewhere."

"Mom, please—"

Karla held out a small, elegant gold tube. "Here. It's a coral, which is really my color, not yours, but it'll be better than nothing."

Lara's jaw tightened, and she felt her heart beating in her ears. "I'm in my own house. Surely it's safe to be ugly in my own house."

"It's not safe to be ugly anywhere," Karla said firmly, clearly not catching the sarcasm in Lara's voice. Karla never joked about beauty and grooming. They were a religion with her. "Not when you're a star. Not when you're Lara Lynmore."

"I'm not Lara Lynmore, Mom. I'm Lara Gilbert. And I'm serious. We need to talk."

"But—" For the first time, Karla's lovely brown eyes registered an uncomfortable awareness. "Can't it wait until after the redecorating?"

"No." Lara gave Maxim a short, apologetic smile. "I'm sorry, but it's important."

Karla bit her lower lip. "But— Wait, that's right, I almost forgot, you need to call Sylvia. She has some scripts she wants you to look at. She thinks one of them may be *the one*." She shrugged as if to say, *oh, well, it can't be helped.* "I promised you'd call as soon as you got back."

"Please, don't keep brushing me off." Lara touched her mother's arm. Though they hadn't talked about what came next, surely her mother had sensed *something.* Surely she knew that Kenny Boggs's death had been a turning point.

"It is very important," she repeated slowly.

Karla frowned. For a split second, Lara thought her mother looked frightened, but she blinked, and the illusion was gone. Irrationally, as if she hadn't heard her daughter, Karla turned her back to Lara. She picked up a card full of fabric swatches and began to flip them with a jerky urgency.

"Nothing's more important than calling your agent." She didn't look up, didn't turn around. "Honestly, Lara, I've told you a million times, if you want to make it to the big time, you're going to have to—"

"But I don't."

"What?"

"I don't." Lara hadn't meant to break it this way, but apparently her mother's instinctive defenses weren't going to allow for a cushioned preparation. And the words were desperate, fighting to come out before guilt and fear and pity smothered them in her chest.

"That's what I'm trying to tell you, Mom. I don't."

Karla still didn't turn around, but her hands had frozen on the fabric swatches. When she spoke, her voice sounded tight. "Don't what?"

"I don't want to do this anymore. I'm quitting. I'm getting out."

"You're…you—"

The fabric fell to the carpet with a ruffling flutter of color. And then, with a soft exhale of the breath she must have been holding far too long, maybe for eight whole weeks, Karla Gilbert slid to the floor, too.

Maxim jumped, trying in vain to catch her, assuming the faint was genuine. The Twizzler lamp dropped from his hands. It must have been a delicate glass because, even though the carpet was soft and expensive, the lamp shattered into a hundred red pieces, which sprayed out like jagged icicles of blood.

The symbolism was a little heavy, Lara thought numbly. The best directors would eliminate it, judging it over the top.

But whatever it lacked in subtlety it made up for in drama. It definitely got its message across.

Lara Lynmore, the world's most selfish, ungrateful daughter, had just broken her mother's heart.

"So, Bryce, tell us. What's it like living in the haunted frat house?"

Bryce looked over at Claire McClintock, the dark-haired, sad-eyed beauty who had married his brother, Kieran. She was pregnant, very pregnant. All through dinner Kieran had fussed over her as if she were made of moonbeams.

"It's okay," Bryce said with a neutral smile. "A little raw, but it has the virtue of being free and unoccupied." Abandoned for at least three years, the frat house had been part of his inheritance. He had laughed when he heard about it. Old Anderson McClintock really had owned the entire damn town, hadn't he?

Bryce looked around the lovely blue dining room. "It's definitely not as elegant as this place."

He didn't add that he was surprised to find the Mc-Clintock mansion decorated in such good taste. The last time he'd been here, the infamous Cindy, his father's fifth and final wife, had been in charge of it for five-

and-a-half whole months, which apparently had been enough to do some serious damage in the vulgarity department. Bryce wondered who was responsible for the new restraint. Had old Anderson tossed out Cindy's excesses when he tossed out Cindy herself? Or was this the gentle Claire's doing?

Bryce had no way of finding out, of course. He'd been gone for fourteen years. A lot of things happened in that much time. One of the things that had happened was Bryce had lost his right to ask questions.

In fact, even Kieran's simple dinner invitation had come as a pretty serious shock. Back when they were kids, and Bryce had been forced by court order to spend the summers in Heyday, the two boys had hardly been close.

Bryce was four years older, and about a hundred years cockier. He had hated old Anderson, who had divorced Bryce's mom to marry Kieran's mother, and he hadn't bothered to hide it.

He hadn't hated Kieran, exactly. He'd actually felt kind of sorry for the kid, who had to live with Anderson all year round, and, after his own mother died, endure the string of bimbo wives, too. However, in Bryce's older, wiser, estimation, Kieran had been an ass-kissing little dork. As he recalled, Bryce had made the poor kid's summers pretty rocky.

And to top it off, old Anderson had died early this year, and in the will, Bryce, who by all rights should have been disinherited like the black sheep he was, had been left a full third of the McClintock estate.

Bryce could imagine how resentful Kieran must

have been when he heard that news. The Sinner, who never went within a hundred miles of Heyday, inheriting equally with the Saint, who had stuck to the old man like a lapdog. Where was the justice in that?

But to Bryce's surprise, when he arrived in Heyday a few days ago, after two months in the Bahamas trying to forget the whole Lara Lynmore/Kenny Boggs fiasco, Kieran had called him immediately. He had even offered to let Bryce stay here, at the old homestead. But Bryce had drawn the line at that. He had a lot of nasty memories of this place. And he wasn't sure how much family togetherness he could actually stomach.

"But what about the ghost?" Mallory Rackham, who sat to his right, looked genuinely curious. "Have you seen him yet?"

Bryce transferred his gaze to Mallory, the pretty young bookstore owner who had obviously been invited to this intimate little New Year's Eve party for his sake. There were only six of them—Kieran and Claire; a smart, sharp-tongued pair of married lawyers named John and Evelyn Gordon; and Bryce and Mallory.

"Not yet," Bryce said. "But remember I've been there only a week. Maybe this ghost is shy."

"Or maybe he's fiction," Evelyn Gordon said as she scooped a bite of the pomegranate parfait Kieran's gorgeous housekeeper, Ilsa, had just put before her. "Teenage frat boys don't kill themselves because their girlfriends dump them. They just get drunk and have mindless sex with the first thing they see wearing a dress."

"Oh, no, he's real," Ilsa said suddenly. She blushed,

as if aware that, as the mere housekeeper, she probably shouldn't have spoken.

John Gordon, who had a mouthful of parfait, glanced up. "Yeah? You've seen him?"

Ilsa shrugged sheepishly. "No. It's just that when I pass by there, I get…" She shivered. "A feeling." She looked across at Bryce and put her hand over her heart. "You are brave to stay there, Mr. McClintock, all alone at night."

Amazing. He had been in Heyday only four days, and already he'd been invited over for a nice fatted-calf dinner, and now the housekeeper was coming on to him. But she was one damn glamorous housekeeper. If his New Year's resolution hadn't been to give up women, he might just have taken her up on it.

He laughed. "The only brave part is living with the mess. You may be surprised to learn that fraternity boys aren't big on cleanliness."

Oh, man, how dumb could he get? That sounded like a blatant request for a housekeeper. Ilsa's blue eyes twinkled at him hopefully. She had just opened her mouth to speak again when Kieran gave her a smile.

"Don't I get a parfait?"

Ilsa apologized profusely and then deposited the last crystal goblet in front of Kieran slowly—a little too slowly, Bryce thought. And was he imagining things, or did her breast brush lightly against Kieran's shoulder? *Wow.* Apparently Ilsa was an equal-opportunity flirt. Any McClintock man would do.

And right in front of Claire, too.

But Claire was leaning back in her chair, trying to get

comfortable, ignoring her parfait and equally indifferent, it seemed, to any threat that the gorgeous Ilsa might pose. Even at this advanced, lumpy stage of pregnancy, she obviously didn't worry that her new husband might stray.

Of course, watching Kieran watch Claire, Bryce had to admit her confidence was probably justified. No matter who was talking, no matter whose luscious breasts were hovering just above his hands, Kieran's gaze lingered on his bride as if she were the sweetest parfait of all.

The rest of the meal was uneventful. Bryce decided Kieran must have briefed everyone on which subjects were off-limits. Anderson himself and all five wives, especially Cindy, the last one. And of course *The Highwayman,* which Bryce had noticed was playing right now at the new multiplex on Main Street. Guns, stalkers, bodyguards, the FBI, Kenny Boggs and, last but not least, Lara Lynmore.

Thank God for the weather! Otherwise, they might as well have been mute.

Actually, that was fairly sensitive of Kieran, Bryce had to admit. Bryce almost hadn't come home from the Bahamas at all, knowing he'd be forced to rehash the whole ugly mess with everyone he met. Over here, Lara was just big enough to still be news, even after two months. In the Bahamas, almost no one had even heard of her.

Over there, he hadn't thought about her at all. Not in the daytime, anyhow. A couple of dreams might have sneaked through now and then, but that didn't mean anything. Random firing of neurons, or too many Bahama Mamas.

Finally the parfait goblets were empty, and it was after eleven-thirty. The New Year was almost upon them. Bryce drank the last of his champagne. He didn't have a New Year's wish, except perhaps that this year would be more peaceful than the last.

Apparently Kieran had a few business details he needed to wind up with Mallory Rackham. Bryce gathered that her bookstore's building was part of the McClintock estate. As Bryce's lawyers, the Gordons were involved, too, Kieran suggested that maybe Claire would like to show Bryce around, help him get reacquainted with the house.

"Just be sure to come back in time for the toast," Kieran added, pulling his wife close and kissing her lightly on the neck.

Claire smiled. "Of course I will. It's bad luck, you know, if you don't say 'Happy New Year' to the one you love at midnight."

"I don't believe in bad luck," Kieran said softly. He took his wife's hand and held it so tenderly Bryce felt the urge to look away. "Not anymore."

"Knock it off, you two," Evelyn Gordon said. "You're going to make me barf up my parfait."

"Would you listen to that lovely mouth on my lovely wife," John Gordon said in mock disapproval. But he pulled Evelyn in and kissed her on that lovely mouth, and suddenly Bryce felt so out of touch with the whole damn world it was like being caught in a Plexiglas isolation tank.

Everyone was in love, it seemed. Everyone but him.

He looked over at Mallory Rackham, who was quite beautiful, but who oddly didn't stir any romantic impulses in Bryce at all. She didn't seem uncomfortable surrounded by all this fog of bliss. She didn't seem to feel left out. She was smiling at the Gordons across the table.

So why did Bryce suddenly feel so strangely alone? And what was wrong with that, anyhow? Alone was a choice. Alone was good.

Maybe it had nothing to do with romance. Maybe it was just that this could have been his family, his real family. This could have been his town. These could have been his friends. And yet too many years, too many emotions, too many bad decisions stood between them.

"Let's go out on the porch and look at the backyard, shall we?" Claire was suddenly at his elbow, smiling up at him. "It's really beautiful on a clear night like this."

She was right. The long, narrow strip of garden behind the eighteenth-century mansion was amazing, an orderly oasis of grace and peace under the deep, starry blue sky.

They walked slowly along the back porch, just beyond the warm yellow rectangles of light cast by the library windows, where the others were working. The weather was perfect, hovering on the crisp edge of frost, so Claire seemed quite comfortable in her green velvet maternity evening gown, and he didn't even really need his dinner jacket.

When they came to the edge of the house, they stopped. He leaned his elbows over the cold, marble railing, favoring his wounded arm just a little, as it was already mostly healed. Claire rested her shoulder against a smooth column.

"It's changed a lot since I was a kid," he said.

"What's different?" Claire looked out into the semi-darkness. "I didn't know the house before I married Kieran. I don't even know when the pool was put in."

"The pool was always here," he said. "At least as long as I can remember. But it all looked very different to me, somehow. It didn't look this—peaceful."

She smiled. "Adolescence isn't a very peaceful time, is it? I mean, it isn't for any of us—but it must have been particularly tumultuous for you."

Somehow he didn't get the impression she was poking around for gossip. She had a peaceful quality herself, kind of like this garden, as if she had been through a lot and found calm on the other side.

"Yes," he said, surprising himself. "I was pretty damn angry most of the time. This garden belonged to my father, and that alone was probably enough to poison it for me."

She just nodded. Bryce looked at her lovely profile rimmed in moonlight, and he decided that Kieran had done very well for himself. A woman who knew when to be silent was rare. A beautiful woman who knew was nothing short of a miracle.

They stood together several minutes. The air was cold and clean and sweet, filled with the scent of unseen winter roses. The light in the pool was off, so the wind-ruffled navy-blue water was lit only by wavering points of starlight. Somewhere a fountain trickled.

Suddenly, Claire made a small noise, something between a gasp and a moan. He looked over and saw that she was clutching the railing with one hand, bending toward it. Her other hand was pressed against her abdomen.

"Are you all right?" He touched her shoulder. "Do you want me to get Kieran?"

She shook her head, but she didn't seem to be able to speak. Her breath was shallow and quick. He put his arm around her shoulder and felt the trembling in her fragile body. Oh, hell. He didn't know anything about pregnant women. What was happening?

If it had gone on a single second longer, he would have scooped her up in his arms and carried her in to Kieran. But just then she took a deep breath and straightened up to her full height, which still didn't reach his chin.

"Sorry about that," she said with a wobbly smile. "Thanks for not sounding an alarm. It's just false labor—it happens every now and then. I saw the doctor this morning, and she says it's perfectly normal. The baby's not due for a month. The doctor says it may be a little early, but it's not imminent. A couple of weeks, at least."

Bryce had removed his arm, but in his mind he still could feel those shaking shoulders. That was normal?

"But even so…shouldn't you tell Kieran?"

"God, no." She laughed softly. "You've seen how he treats me. If I told him about this, he wouldn't let me out of bed until the baby was born. He'd be spoon-feeding me parfait night and day. I'd go crazy."

From what Bryce had seen tonight, he judged Claire McClintock to be a pretty sensible lady. He decided, on the spur of the moment, to trust her.

"Okay," he said. "I won't say anything."

She squeezed his arm. "Thanks," she said. "You know, I—"

But just then the peaceful blue midnight was shattered by the sound of gunfire. Bryce started, his heart accelerating under his dinner jacket, but almost immediately he figured it out. Of course. Up and down these normally quiet streets, people were celebrating, ushering in the New Year with sparklers and firecrackers and half-heard, half-drunken renditions of "Auld Lang Syne."

In the middle distance church bells began to ring.

The library doors opened, and the others spilled out onto the porch, carrying glasses of champagne. They left the doors open, so that the stereo could reach the garden. It, too, was playing "Auld Lang Syne," which in this clear starlight sounded more poignant than anything Bryce had heard in a long, long time.

Suddenly the cell phone in his pocket rang. He glanced at the caller ID, and for a minute his heart began to race again. The area code was 213, the area code for Los Angeles, California.

Excusing himself, he answered it, moving to the edge of the porch so that he wouldn't disturb the kissing and laughing and hugging going on among the old Heyday buddies gathered there.

"Hey, McClintock, this is Joe. Hope I'm not interrupting."

"Of course not," Bryce said. Joe was the police officer who had been shepherding the Kenny Boggs issue through the system. He was a good guy.

Bryce realized that his voice sounded dull, so he put more energy into it. "No problem, Joe. What's up?"

"I just wanted to tell you the final hoops have been cleared. Everything's in order. You can even have your gun back if you want it."

No. He didn't want it.

"Thanks," Bryce said. He paused. "I mean it, Joe. Thanks."

"Forget it. I just— I mean, I also wanted to say…I hope things go good for you there in—what the hell was the name of that burg you came from?"

"Heyday," Bryce said. "Heyday, Virginia."

Joe laughed. "Yeah, in Heyday. I wanted to say Happy New Year, you know. I hope it's a good one for you, McClintock. You deserve it."

Bryce swallowed hard and thanked him, surprisingly touched that Joe had remembered and made the effort. It was only nine o'clock in California.

But when he clicked off and looked down at the silent cell phone in his hand, he had to face the truth.

He knew what he'd really been hoping.

Fool that he was, he'd been hoping that, in spite of everything, Lara Lynmore had been thinking of him.

He'd been hoping that somehow, even out there in Tinseltown where the New Year's Eve parties were just getting started, she might sense that, here in Heyday, it was a cold and lonely midnight.

CHAPTER THREE

MORESVILLE COLLEGE WAS small in acreage, but big on charm. The view people always saw on the post-cards, shot from Stagger Hill just above Heyday, was downright quaint. The school's half-dozen Federal-style redbrick buildings were sweetly tucked into the surrounding flowery woods—they always photo-graphed it in the spring—like so many giant Easter eggs.

Seen from ground level, in the visitor's parking lot at the tail end of the winter break, it looked much more institutional. Bryce locked his car and gazed around. Maybe it was just the absence of student bustle, but he thought the campus looked run-down and tired.

He wondered what that was all about. When he'd last been in Heyday, the college had been thriving, really making a name for itself.

He poked around a little, getting oriented. By the time he reached the office of Dilday Merle, chairman of academic affairs at Moresville College, for their ten o'clock meeting, he was five minutes late. But since he wasn't sure what the hell this meeting was all about, anyway, he wasn't terribly worried.

So, 301…that was the corner office, four big windows with great views. Bryce whistled under his breath. So Dilday Merle had finally made good, huh? Bryce was glad to see it.

Fifteen years ago, Dilday Merle had been the Algebra II teacher at Heyday High. On his next-to-the-last visit home, Bryce, who had fooled around and flunked Algebra II at his own school in Chicago, had ended up attending summer school in Heyday. He'd been assigned to Dilday Merle's class.

The guy had been geeky and ancient even then. Bryce had thought he was a total loser. And he couldn't believe that the slow-witted Heyday kids hadn't already seen the entertaining possibilities for making fun of Dilday's name. Bryce and the dorky teacher had locked horns early, but to his surprise, Dilday Merle had won the battle. Bryce had never stopped being cocky and obnoxious, but he had damn sure learned algebra.

They shook hands now with warmth that was, on Bryce's side at least, quite sincere.

"Bryce McClintock. It's been a long time."

"Yes. It has."

The pleasantries didn't last long. Dilday looked scatty, with thick black glasses overhung by shaggy, unkempt eyebrows and Albert Einstein hair, but he was mentally as sharp as a shark's tooth.

"All right," Dilday said. "Let's get down to it. You know I want something, or I wouldn't have asked you to come over. Maybe you already know what it is?"

Bryce lifted one brow. "Money? I've just been here a week, but so far that seems to be the odds-on favorite."

Dilday laughed. "Oh, no. Money's not my department. Our president, Dr. Quentin Steif, he's the official
back-slapper and fund-raiser. I'm sure he'll be calling
you before long. No, my area is academics. I am hoping I can talk you into teaching a criminology class."

Well, that did cut to the chase. Dilday had always
known how to keep students awake and edgy. Bryce
could feel his curiosity pricking. He sat up a little
straighter. "You're kidding."

"No. I don't have time to kid. One of my criminology teachers quit last week, no notice, along with one
of my special ed people and two British Lit professors."
His eyes twinkled behind his glasses. "You're not by
any chance a big fan of *Beowulf,* are you? I'd gladly put
you to work in the English department, too."

Bryce smiled. "No one is a fan of *Beowulf,* Professor Merle."

"Oh, for heaven's sake, Bryce. Call me Dilday. Or
whatever version of the name you prefer these days. As
I recall, you had several pretty good ones."

Bryce shook his head. "Sorry about that," he said. "I
was seventeen. I was an ass."

Dilday grinned. "Yes, you were." He held out a slim
file folder. "Here, this is the syllabus our last teacher
used. You could adapt it to suit yourself, or you can
work straight from his plans. It doesn't matter to me.
You've got the credentials, and we need a teacher. We
don't pay squat to adjuncts, but you don't care about
that, anyway."

Bryce took the folder but didn't open it. "Hold on. I
haven't said I'll do it."

Dilday didn't look fazed. He just smiled, toying with his letter opener, the same letter opener he'd always used. Its handle was carved in the shape of a zebra. In Heyday everything was zebra-this and zebra-that. It was one of the cutesy affectations Bryce had despised most about this Podunk town. So why did the sight of this particular letter opener suddenly make him feel a little nostalgic?

"In fact," Bryce went on, steeling himself to resist all appeals to the past, both overt and covert, "a list of the reasons why I *can't* do it—not to mention the reasons why I wouldn't *want* to—would stretch out from here to D.C."

"I know," Dilday said patiently. "But you'll do it, anyway, because you're a nice boy. You always were."

"Really? I thought we just agreed I was an ass."

Dilday shrugged. "Ass is attitude. Ass is window-dressing. Ass is, at heart, simply fear in fancy clothes."

Bryce paused a moment, his nostalgic goodwill toward this old man diminishing. "I thought you taught algebra, not psychology."

"Oh, forget about me. And let's, just for the moment, forget about you at seventeen, too. All that stuff is irrelevant now. I've got a crisis on my hands, Bryce. I take it you haven't heard about what happened here a couple of years ago?"

"No. I haven't."

"I thought someone might have told you, since that journalist Tyler Balfour turned out to be your brother. But then—I guess communication between you and Kieran has been pretty spotty."

"You might call it that." Bryce shrugged. "So how about if you tell me? What the hell does Tyler Balfour have to do with anything?"

"He damn near destroyed this college with his muckraking, that's what." Dilday took off his glasses and started cleaning them on his tie.

The gesture took Bryce back fifteen years in one split second. He could almost smell the chalk dust and the cheap perfume of the cheerleader who had sat next to him in Algebra. He had almost had sex with her under the football bleachers one night, but she had chickened out at the last minute.

"No, let me rephrase that," Dilday said carefully, arranging his glasses on his nose again. "He didn't nearly destroy us. We did that to ourselves. Balfour is an investigative reporter for a paper in Washington, D.C. But you can't kill the messenger, can you? What happened to us was our own fault. We had a problem here, and he came to town and found it. Then he went home and published a big exposé and—"

"Hang on," Bryce said. "When you say you had 'a problem' here, what exactly does that mean?"

"It means—" Dilday sighed. "Well, there's no way to sugarcoat it. Some of our female students had formed a call-girl ring, and—"

"My God. I remember that." Actually, Bryce had thought it was hilarious at the time. Rich sorority girls turning tricks in pokey little Heyday for mall money. He had read the first of the series, but then he got caught up in a trial and missed the rest. He'd meant to go back and read it all, but in the end he hadn't cared enough.

Heyday was boring. Even underage prostitution and local politicos caught with their pants down couldn't make it interesting.

And he certainly hadn't remembered the reporter's name. He would never have put it together with the Tyler Balfour who had turned up out of the blue in old Anderson McClintock's will.

"Still…how did that become a big problem for the college? Surely a little bad publicity, a few rotten apples—"

Dilday shook his head. "You underestimate how sensitive these things are. College campuses are supposed to be like protected bubbles, where parents send their children to make a safe transition to adulthood. Whether it's realistic or not, we have an obligation to provide a secure environment. When word got out that their daughters were getting involved in things like that…"

Bryce was finally catching on. "They began to pull them out."

Dilday nodded. "Seventy-five the week the series was published. It tapered off after that, and some came back, but we're still down a net total of eighty students. In a small campus like ours, that's a lot."

"But what does this have to do with me? Surely I can't be held responsible for the sins of my brother. Half brother. Especially one I didn't even know existed until about ten months ago."

"It's not a question of responsibility. I need you, that's all. I need someone with credentials, which, after a law degree and eight years in the FBI, you've got in spades. I need someone who's independently wealthy, who's able to make do without a real salary. And most of all I need someone who has some panache, who might bring in a few extra students."

"Panache?" Bryce crossed his ankle over his knee and lay the file folder on his lap. "That sounds like a euphemism for something. What?"

"You know what." Dilday Merle gave him a straight look. "You are a celebrity right now, Bryce. You just shot somebody while you were defending a gorgeous actress, and you got knifed doing it. That's exciting. They're just kids. They'll eat that stuff up with a spoon."

Dilday's main talent as a teacher had always been his down-to-earth clarity. And he was certainly being crystal clear right now. Bryce had to hand it to him—he wasn't trying to do a smoke-and-mirrors dance about his motives.

"But it won't work," Bryce said. "Even if I wanted to teach your class, which I don't, I won't be in Heyday long enough. The term goes until, what, May? I wasn't planning to stay here more than a month or two at most."

"So stay longer. You own this place, or at least a third of it, right? Stick around a while. It won't kill you. You'll have plenty to do just straightening out your inheritance."

Dilday was right, of course—wasn't he always? In only a week, Bryce had discovered just how hopelessly tangled his ties were to Heyday. He had tenants and mortgagees, employees and sycophants and a couple of enemies. He even had someone trying to sue him over an illegal dumping that had supposedly fouled the soil twenty-five years ago when a dry cleaner had occupied one of his buildings.

Absently he opened the folder and scanned the contents. The absconding Dr. Douglas had put together a pretty good class, basic and easy to teach. All the major theories and paradigms were covered—subcultural, gender-based, social structure, social process, developmental, it was all there.

He remembered this stuff from school, and what he didn't remember he could refresh easily. It looked so orderly, so pure and hopeful here on the page, all well-intentioned and academic. Nothing chaotic and bloody, unpredictable and heartbreaking. It might be a nice change of pace. It might help him remember why he'd gone into law in the first place.

And he would have something to bring to it. Something practical and concrete, based on his years of real-life work. It wasn't just "panache." It was experience.

He glanced up, wondering if Dilday could sense his weakening willpower.

"Just this one, Bryce," the old man said. "I'm desperate. Classes start in three days. And it's only a few months. It might be fun."

Bryce looked up and smiled dryly. Who would have thought that Dilday Merle could, just for a minute, sound exactly like Lara Lynmore's desperate lawyer?

"I give you my word of honor, I'll be looking for someone to replace you," Dilday said. "Please. Just until I can find somebody else."

"You know," Bryce said, wondering why he was

such a bloody fool, but knowing he was going to say yes. "I'm pretty sure I've heard that line before."

THREE DAYS LATER Bryce confronted his first classroom full of students. Thirty-eight of them. Dilday must be in heaven. Three days ago, there had been only twenty. But then the word went out that Bryce McClintock, notorious bad-ass and bodyguard to the stars, would be teaching it and, just as Dilday had predicted, enrollment had soared.

Bryce had expected the first day, at least, to be intimidating, but they looked like nice kids. Some of them weren't even kids. At least two of the male students were in their late twenties, and that woman in the last row must be somebody's grandmother. Bryce found himself curious. What were their stories? Why were they here? What were they hoping he could teach them?

The real surprise was that Ilsa, Kieran's housekeeper, was one of his students, too. She had come up to him just before class and confided in her husky, accented whisper that Kieran had encouraged her to go back to school, so here she was.

Bryce had been friendly but carefully distant. It was actually kind of scary, when you thought about the number of ways in which beautiful Swedish coeds with ulterior motives could easily spell trouble for a young professor who was her boss's brother.

Maybe he was being unfair. Maybe busty, beautiful Ilsa was a dedicated scholar. But somehow he doubted it.

The first half of the class had gone well. The kids seemed to hang on his every word. Only one boy had found the nerve to mention Lara Lynmore or Kenny Boggs.

"Mr. McClintock," the kid said eagerly. "You shot that stalker, and you aren't even like a professional bodyguard. That's like, so awesome."

"No, Mr...." Bryce had scanned his roll sheet calmly. He'd known this question was coming, sooner or later. Maybe it was just as well to get it over with. "Mr. Winston. No, it wasn't *so awesome*. It would have been *awesome* if I'd been able to protect my client without having to resort to killing anyone."

"But—"

"No buts. Shooting is always a last resort. Always. That's true for police officers, bodyguards, anyone. If you're good at your job, you find ways to solve your problems without resorting to violence."

The kid had subsided, smart enough to know he'd been chastised. But Bryce saw that young Mr. Winston's bright eyes continued to follow him with an unmistakable hero-worship. How dumb could you get? This same excited teenager probably would have wet himself after one look at Kenny Boggs's wound.

God. Kids.

He had decided to break the ice with a classic observation-training exercise. He had asked the students to look out the window for five minutes and mentally note as many details as possible about what they saw. People, scenery, cars, weather, whatever.

It was raining, which made the exercise more difficult, more gray and confusing. Most of the passers-by were bundled up in shapeless, hooded raincoats, and dashed through the quadrangle quickly, rushing for cover.

In about two minutes, by prior arrangement, Dilday Merle would come by, stop right outside Bryce's window and stage an argument with a student. Afterward, Bryce would ask his class to reconstruct what they'd seen. If it went according to plan, no two students would remember the argument exactly the same way.

Which was, of course, the point of the exercise. From that moment on these students would be a little more cynical, a little more observant. They wouldn't automatically trust eyewitnesses. They wouldn't take anything for granted, which might someday save someone's life.

He watched with them, leaning back in his chair, tapping his pencil against his desk, waiting for Dilday to come out. He was sorry, for Dilday's sake, that it was raining. Cold January rain in Heyday, Bryce had discovered on the way to school this morning, felt like tiny silver needles pricking every exposed inch of your skin.

But Dilday owed him big-time. A little soggy chill wouldn't begin to pay the debt.

Some of the kids were already getting restless. Bryce made a mental note of their names. If they didn't settle down, they'd never make good lawyers or even law enforcement officers. Short attention spans couldn't make it through stakeouts or endless hours of boring depositions. Heck, they'd never even make it through the dusty tomes of the law library, which were the most stultifying books ever published.

Suddenly a young woman appeared on the far side

of the courtyard, walking toward them through the rain. Bryce looked once—then looked again.

Slowly, he let his pencil fall to the desk. She wore the standard college student uniform—blue jeans and down-lined jacket with the hood pulled up to keep out the cold and the rain. She held an armload of books to her chest, as if trying to keep them dry.

She could have been anybody.

But he knew that walk, trained from childhood to sashay subtly, putting one foot elegantly and directly in front of the other. Head held high, from years of balancing a book there, or a beauty pageant crown. And of course he'd know those long legs anywhere. His hips burned suddenly, as his body recalled exactly how those legs had felt, wrapped around him as they wrangled on the sofa, just seconds away from the consummation they both craved.

He stood up, as much to ease the pressure as anything. He didn't need a closer look—he already knew. That wasn't anybody. That was Lara Lynmore.

The only question was—what the hell was she doing *here?*

He moved to the window. But just as Dilday Merle and his hapless student appeared and launched into their carefully scripted argument, the rain began to fall in earnest. Now half obscured by Dilday, the young woman bent her head to her books and began to jog along the shining silver sidewalk.

The students watched Dilday Merle, but Bryce watched the woman. He saw the hood fall back, exposing dark, nut-brown hair that wasn't quite what he'd expected. He moved closer still, trying to see through the streaks of rain and thrashing branches.

But it was too late. She made a sudden turn and darted into the science building. *Damn it.* He looked toward his classroom door, wondering if he could make it across the quadrangle in time to catch her.

The timer on his watch beeped. The official five minutes of observation were up. Thirty-eight faces turned expectantly toward him.

It took him a couple of seconds to remember what they wanted. Oh, hell, that's right. He was the teacher here. For the next ninety minutes, he couldn't leave this classroom for anything. Not even to chase the wet, long-legged mirage who would might well turn out to be an annoyed eighteen-year-old total stranger majoring in elementary ed.

"So," he said, collecting himself just in time. "Tell me what you saw."

The students began to call out details. Trees, leaves, rain, a kid streaking through muddy puddles on his skateboard, obviously late for class. Someone had seen a cat, though the others booed that report, insisting he was nuts.

Thirteen cars—no, ten—no, eleven cars and three trucks. And, of course, Dilday Merle lecturing some poor boy—no, it was a girl—no, another teacher.

"Did any of you see a woman?" It was stupid, but he had to ask. Surely, if the famous Lara Lynmore really had just loped across the Moresville College quadrangle, someone would have noticed that.

Thirty-eight blank faces stared at him. "You mean the woman Dean Merle was chewing out?"

"No, that was a boy," another kid insisted. "I know him. He's in my psych class."

"It was a girl," a boy with spiky brown hair said. "She was hot."

"God," another student, this one a female, said scornfully, "You're such a sketch, Matt. It was a boy."

"I don't mean the person with Dean Merle," Bryce amended carefully. "I'm talking about another woman. Running down the sidewalk behind them."

Several heads shook. Several students frowned, determined to remember, determined not to fail on this, their very first day.

"No." Ilsa, her hands folded in front of her, the perfect student, looked at him seriously. "I didn't see a woman. What kind of woman? A teacher?"

No, damn it. Young. Sexy. A movie star. A woman with dangerous legs and an angel's face. But he couldn't say that. With all the sexual harassment rules these days, he couldn't even say it had been a *very pretty* woman, or they might think he was a weirdo. They'd think he was a "sketch."

And besides, maybe he'd better shut up.

If he had begun hallucinating, if he was going to start seeing visions of Lara Lynmore every time he turned around, he'd probably better keep that little piece of insanity to himself.

CHAPTER FOUR

THE HIPPODROME SUPERMARKET on the outskirts of Heyday wasn't exactly five-star shopping, but it was open all night, so Bryce made the trip. A disturbingly skinny spaniel had been hanging outside the kitchen door of the fraternity house for the past three days. Its whining was so pitiful Bryce realized he was going to have to feed the mutt. Otherwise, the ghostly frat-boy might end up with a spectral pet.

Bryce hated grocery shopping. Still, if he had to do it, eleven at night was the most desirable time. The brightly lit, cavernous place, which had been total chaos the last time he ventured in, was almost empty.

Half a dozen people, tops. A nurse taking home a frozen dinner after the late shift, a harried father buying diapers, a couple of kids from the college with a cart full of Twinkies and Bud Light, and one red-nosed old guy who was paying for his wine with dimes.

Bryce slung a huge bag of lamb-and-rice nuggets—how horrible did that sound?—into his cart. Then, remembering he was out of coffee, he decided he might as well spare himself a second trip.

Thankfully, his list was short. He hadn't had the

nerve yet to try out the frat house oven, which had about two inches of extremely suspicious black crust under the rack. He would hire a housekeeper eventually, now that he knew he was stuck in Heyday for a couple of months. Till then, he'd just eat out.

Still, he needed to keep the bare minimum on hand. Bread, coffee, beer, an apple or two…

The produce section, which was right next to the beer cooler, was comparatively busy. Two college boys were making a show of suggestively squeezing cantaloupes and alternately moaning and giggling.

Bryce couldn't help smiling. *Morons.* If you added both their IQs together, the cantaloupe would still outscore them.

Predictably, they started flirting with a young woman who stood nearby, studying the bananas, a basket filled with fresh spinach and mushrooms hooked over her arm.

"Hi," one of the boys said, sidling up to her. "Let me tell you about bananas. See, you want to get yourself a nice, firm one. And take my word for it. Bigger is definitely better."

The boy shot a gleeful look back at his friend, still immature enough to be more interested in scoring joke points with his buddy than anything else. "Yeah," he went on, delighted with his own brilliance, "these little stubby ones aren't very satisfying." He wiggled his eyebrows. "If you know what I mean."

The young woman's hands gripped the banana so tightly Bryce was surprised it didn't pop. He figured that any minute she'd turn and shove the whole thing down that idiot's throat. Bryce took his time picking out a tomato. He'd enjoy watching that.

But she didn't do it. Though the punk was waiting for a reaction, the woman just stood there, her hands frozen on the bananas.

Without speaking, she edged farther down the counter. She turned her head away, exposing the graceful, pale nape of her neck between her hairline and her jacket.

Something moved inside Bryce, some primitive awareness that was way ahead of his conscious mind. He knew that neck. He knew that woman.

It was Lara.

Though it was as preposterous as ever, he wasn't really shocked. It was as if he'd been half expecting this for days, ever since that first class, when he'd looked out the window and hallucinated a vision of her.

Idiot kid. If the boy knew he was making a pass at Lara Lynmore, movie star, he'd probably faint headfirst into the avocados. She could have destroyed him with one look. But she clearly didn't have the confidence to do that anymore. And why should she? She'd spent ten months stalked by a madman who had probably seemed, at first, to be as goofy and innocent as this kid.

Bryce walked up and put his hand on the boy's shoulder.

"Hey, pal," he said politely. "Do something for me, would you?"

"Huh?" The kid looked up, too surprised to be hostile. "What?"

Bryce gave him a cold smile. "Shove off."

Before the kid could react, Bryce picked up the greenest banana on the display. "And take your banana with you. It won't be ripe for years yet." He picked up the kid's slack arm and slapped the banana into his hand. He raised one brow. "If you know what I mean."

The kid's friend snickered—he got it, anyhow. And the dark flush creeping over the banana-boy's smooth cheeks said he got it, too.

"Sure, man, whatever. Hey, I didn't know she was with you."

And then, desperately trying to look cool about it, the boys sauntered away.

Bryce took a deep breath and slowly turned around. He came face to face with a snub-nosed, freckle-faced, jean-clad young woman. A typical, grungy coed who just a month ago, according to *Vanity Fair,* had been Hollywood's Sexiest Newcomer.

"Lara," he said. "Lara Lynmore."

"No." She spoke softly, shaking her head. "Lara *Gilbert.*"

She looked so young without her makeup. Her eyes were so dark, so haunted, and her face so pale. He didn't have the heart to say what he'd been planning to say.

Instead he simply took her basket of vegetables and plopped it into the cart next to his dog food.

"Okay then, Lara Gilbert," he said. "Come on, I'll buy you a drink. You've got a hell of a lot of explaining to do."

LARA WONDERED where Bryce was taking her.

At this hour on a winter's night, a little town like

Heyday was fast asleep. Pointy stars glittered like frost on the black sky, unchallenged by man-made lights. The fields they passed were empty—even horses and cows knew when to hunker down.

Ahead of her, Bryce's expensive sportscar seemed almost ghostly as it glided down the tree-lined road. Silver metal skimming across glittering snow at the edges of the road, flickering in and out of shadows, brushing past bony black fingers of oak and elm.

He had slowed down once, as they approached a roadside diner. But at that very moment the diner's marquee lights blinked off, and the clock in Lara's car changed to midnight. Now what? They were almost ten miles outside the Heyday city limits, halfway to Grupton, the next little town. Was there anything out here at all?

Suddenly his turn signal began to pulse red, warning her that he was about to pull off the road. She looked to the right, surprised to see that a long, low building had sprung up out of the shadows.

Absolutely Nowhere. That's what the small red neon sign said. The name definitely fit.

Amazingly, at least five other cars were nosed up to the long brick building, looking as if they planned to stay all night. On closer inspection, the place was bigger than she'd realized. The part that fronted the road was small, just an average hideaway bar, but behind that the building stretched out in a long line of brick motel units. Another red sign flickered in front of the first one. *Vacancy.*

Bryce parked first, then waited so that they could

walk in together. A gentlemanly gesture, but his un-smiling silence sent a different message. Lara's stom-ach tightened as she brushed past him through the door he politely held open.

Inside, the bar was much more civilized than she'd expected. Booths lined the perimeter, each with a red tablecloth and a red-globed candle. Huge, framed maps decorated every wall, each with a red arrow pointing to some famous city, and the helpful words, "You are NOT here."

She had to smile. Of course you weren't in Paris or London or New York. You were *Absolutely Nowhere*.

And there wasn't a single zebra in sight. Obviously they were no longer in Heyday, either.

Bryce led her to a booth in the corner, as far away as he could get from the other couples in the room, most of whom were huddled in pairs, twining fingers, nuz-zling necks. With surprise, Lara recognized one of the librarians from the college, who was toying with the ear stud on a man about half her age, a man who didn't look like anybody's husband. They appeared to be about one drink away from renting a room.

Instinctively, Lara didn't say hello. She was still un-comfortable drawing attention to herself, for fear some-one might recognize her. Besides, Absolutely Nowhere was clearly the in-destination for people who didn't want to be spotted by the folks back home.

A waitress appeared, and while Bryce ordered his beer, Lara wondered what to get. She'd planned to ask for a sparkling water, but suddenly she thought she might need something stronger.

"I'll have a rum and Coke," she said.

"With extra ice, please," Bryce put in automatically, but he clenched his jaw afterward, as if he regretted saying anything. As if he would like to pretend he didn't remember that small detail, or anything else about their six weeks together.

But he did remember. Lara hugged that thought.

When the waitress was gone, he leaned back against the bench seat and regarded Lara steadily for a long moment. She fought not to fidget, though she knew she looked awful. That was part of her "disguise," and it had worked well so far.

In fact, she looked less like a movie star than half the people in this room. At least they had dolled themselves up for their late-night assignations. Lara hadn't even combed her hair before twisting it back into a plastic clip. Her old jeans were fraying at the cuff, and she was sure this T-shirt had a paint stain on the front.

For the first time in months, she almost wished she had taken her mother's advice, and never left the house without being painted and costumed and battle-ready.

"Okay, let's hear it," he said. "What the devil are you doing in Heyday?"

His voice was cold. He obviously wasn't going to make this easy. But then, why should he? Back in L.A., he'd made it clear he wasn't interested in pursuing their relationship, and now here she was, living in his hometown. She suddenly realized exactly how strange this must look to him.

"First of all, I'm going to school," she began. She held up her hand to stave off his protest. "Don't laugh. It's true."

"It may be true, but it's ridiculous. Unless—is this some kind of undercover research? Did you land a role as a coed?"

"No. It has nothing to do with films. I'm through with films."

He tilted his head. "Oh, come on."

His tone wasn't exactly insulting. He sounded too amused for that. But even so she felt stung.

She was so tired of having this argument. No one could understand why she'd quit, why even a million dollars wasn't enough to compensate for working at a career you hated. In fact, no one could understand why she'd hated it—wasn't it what every girl dreamed of?

But the *dream* of being an actress was very different from the reality. No girl dreamed of standing around for twelve hours straight, with strangers tugging on you as if you were no more human than a mannequin, arguing about how to hide the fact that one breast was a millimeter larger than the other. No one dreamed of seeing your own head superimposed on some naked body, then plastered all over the Internet, or of the nasty, suspiciously stained letters that flooded your mail for months afterward.

No one dreamed about the claustrophobia of never being private, or the isolation of not knowing who to trust. No one dreamed of a stalker.

"I know it's hard to believe," she said. "My agent doesn't believe it. My own mother doesn't believe it. But I've left Hollywood for good. I'm studying to be a music therapist."

He cocked an eyebrow, a mute but eloquent incredulity.

"This is only my first semester, but I think I might have a talent for it. I've always liked to work with people. The very best times, back in Hollywood, were when they sent me to a hospital, or a nursing home. When I could really connect, and be myself. Of course there are lots of ways to make a career working with people. But music is very special to me. I think I've always understood its healing qualities. Actually, I've used music as a kind of therapy my whole life, to see me through the rough times."

She heard the crack in her voice, and she stopped. She didn't want to get maudlin. He would hate that. Besides, he didn't know a thing about her childhood, about the years before her parents divorced, when tension hung in the air like smoke, hiding terrifying fires she couldn't see, couldn't predict, couldn't avoid. Fires that would flare up suddenly in tears and slamming doors and shattered dinner plates, and in her mother's blistering tirades. "I'll leave. And I'll take Lara with me. You'll never see your daughter again."

Finally, one day when Lara was thirteen, the fire went out. Her father left them both for a young woman of twenty-one. And then there was only the cold, empty air of abandonment, and her mother's determination that they would show him. Lara would be a star.

She tucked the memories back into her subconscious and arranged her face into what she hoped was a calmer control. She even tried to smile. "At least I'm already trained in music. All those years of voice lessons, piano lessons—they might finally be worth something, after all."

His eyebrow rose. "As I recall, they already *were* worth something—like a million per movie and climbing."

"I don't mean money," she said. "I mean personal satisfaction."

He tilted one corner of his mouth wryly. "You may be the only person in Hollywood who thinks there's a difference."

"Which is why I didn't fit in there. Which is why I needed to leave."

"Sure, for a vacation, maybe. A month in the Bahamas. Even I needed one, after the whole Kenny Boggs thing. I can see why you might have trouble getting over that—the guy was a head case. But you *will* get over it. You'll go back."

Before Lara could respond, the waitress arrived and proceeded to drop cocktail napkins on the table. On each napkin was a cartoon of an angry woman. *"Where have you been?"* it read above her scowling face. And below it, the answer. *"Absolutely Nowhere."*

Lara was glad to have an extra minute to decide how to respond to Bryce. Irrationally, she had hoped he would be different, that somehow, in spite of everything, he might sense her sincerity. But he'd merely echoed exactly what everyone else had said.

There, there, they'd all murmured, patting her back either literally or figuratively. *Of course you were terrified, take a break if you need to, come back when you feel better.*

They didn't dare take her decision seriously. They needed her to come back and make them some more money. She'd been shocked to discover how many people had been expecting to get rich on the Lara Lynmore franchise.

"It wasn't just Kenny," she said when the waitress had finished arranging their drinks. "It was a lot of things. I understand why you're skeptical, though. I'm committed to making a new life for myself, but I can see it will take time to convince people."

"About a hundred years." He tilted his beer on the napkin, rotating it thoughtfully. "But let's just say for a minute that you're serious, that you really want to be a…"

He glanced up.

"Music therapist," she supplied evenly.

"Right. Even if you really wanted to be a music therapist, why here? You can't tell me Heyday has the best damn music therapy school on the planet. We don't have the best anything, except maybe the best selection of cheap souvenir zebras."

Stalling, she took a sip of her drink. The first part of her explanation had been difficult enough—but it paled in comparison to this.

"Well, I looked at quite a few schools. Lots of colleges offer music therapy majors these days, and I visited several of them. But when I got here—"

She hesitated. How much could she safely say?

Bryce was still looking incredulous. "When you got here, what? You were overwhelmed by the cultural stimulation, the sophisticated residents, the endless choices of shopping, entertainment and excitement?"

She flushed. Is that what he really thought she was all

about? Shopping and snobbery and utter self-indulgence?

"Actually," she said, "I think I was impressed by the lack of all that. I was drawn to the quiet charm. The peace of the place."

Toying with the damp edge of her napkin, Lara went on without looking at Bryce. "Frankly, I've had all the excitement I can stand for a while. And besides—" She raised her gaze. "I was curious about Heyday. The few things you'd said about this little town had been so emotional—"

He laughed. "Yes, but that emotion was pure contempt."

"Still. It was intense. Obviously your years here had been important in shaping you, and I was curious. I wanted…" She chose her words carefully. "I wanted to know more about you. I—I've missed you. When we were together, it was—I was—"

If only she were better with words. If she were playing a role here, someone would hand her the perfect lines, eloquent, powerful words that would miraculously soften his eyes, gentle his tone, unlock his heart. Instead, there was only this foolish fumbling to make him understand when she hardly understood herself.

But she refused to chicken out and say something noncommittal. She'd spent too many years being afraid to speak the truth, too many years worrying what other people wanted, what other people might think. In this new life, she was going to be honest, no matter how terrifying.

"Our time together was—special," she blurted as

bravely as she could. "I know it sounds crazy, but during those weeks you came to mean a lot to me."

A daunting silence greeted that line, and for a moment she wished she could take it back. But it was true. She'd been drawn to him, not just his virile good looks and strong, hot hands, but everything about him. The calm authority, the rare moments of unexpected kindness, the intelligence, the wit…and beneath it all, the sense of some unspoken pain.

Lara held her breath, suddenly overly aware of the librarian and her boyfriend, who had begun to shuffle out of their booth giggling and whispering and fumbling with their check.

Finally Bryce shook his head slowly.

"That," he said, "is the most ridiculous thing you've said in this entire preposterous conversation."

She tightened her hand on her glass. She reminded herself that she had expected this. Shortly after Kenny's shooting, when she had seen Bryce at one of their many interviews with the police, he had made it clear he didn't think they had a future together. He hadn't said so outright, but she knew he resented having had to kill a man to protect someone as frivolous as Lara Lynmore.

So this was no surprise. She lifted her chin. "I'm sorry you think so."

Bryce sighed heavily and leaned forward. "Look, Lara—"

But he never got to finish the sentence. Just then a tall, skinny man came up and clapped him on the shoulder.

"Well, if it isn't Bryce McClintock," the skinny man

said. "It's about time you paid me a visit. I've been waiting fourteen years to talk to you, son."

Lara looked curiously up at the man, who she guessed to be about forty-five and who seemed to have been made of spare parts. He had a long, basset-hound face, which contrasted oddly with pointed leprechaun ears. But he was smiling broadly, which made him look charming in spite of the fact that it showed off a large gold front tooth.

Bryce didn't look quite as thrilled, but he was perfectly civil.

"Slip," he said, holding out his hand to shake the other man's bony fingers. "You still own this dive?" He looked over at Lara. "Lara Gilbert, this is Slip Stanton. He built Absolutely Nowhere about fifteen years ago."

"Hey, there, Ms. Gilbert," he said. Lara held her breath momentarily, wondering if he might recognize her, but the man couldn't have been less interested. He turned back to Bryce right away. "Yessir, I built this place, fifteen years ago this May, and it surely did put your pa in a pucker cause I wouldn't build it in Heyday. He said he had some land he'd give me cheap, well, I knew what that meant. Swamp land. But anyhow I said what's the point in putting a place like this in Heyday, where everybody knows everybody? You gotta get out of town before you can really let loose, that's what I say."

"And you were obviously right," Bryce said politely. "Things look good."

"Yeah, I stay in the black most of the time. Plenty of people looking to have a little fun, thank goodness."

He tugged on one of his big ears. "But that's not what I've been wanting to talk to you about. I wanted you to know I stuck up for you back then, you know, back when it all happened."

Lara saw Bryce's face tighten, and her curiosity immediately spiked. She had learned his expressions pretty well. This one meant he didn't want to talk about it.

But Slip Stanton obviously wasn't quite as clued in. He kept on going. "Yeah, not that it did any good, but after you left town, I went to see your daddy. I thought somebody ought to tell him how it had really been that night. Hell, you weren't much more than a kid, and the broad was all over you, buying you drinks until you could hardly see straight, much less think straight."

Bryce smiled. "I can imagine how that little interview must have gone."

Slip chuckled. "He jumped all over me, said it was all my fault. And partly it was, I guess. By law I should have checked your ID. I think he would have sicced the cops on me if he hadn't been so desperate to hush it all up. Still, maybe he listened, because it wasn't long before that little chippy was packing up and moving on."

"Yes," Bryce said with a short laugh. "But they all did that anyhow, eventually." He raised his beer in a small salute. "Still, it was a nice gesture, and I appreciate it. Thanks."

"Any time." Slip grinned, his gold tooth flashing in the candlelight. "Not that you're likely to need it again, I guess once is enough for that." He glanced over at Lara. "Anyhow, sorry to interrupt your drinks. Nice to meet you, Ms. Gilbert. And Bryce, now you're back, don't be a stranger, okay?"

Bryce made another noncommittal salute and, combined with a smile, it was enough to send the other man off happy.

When they were alone again, Bryce turned to Lara. "Sorry about that," he said. "I probably shouldn't have brought you here. But Heyday isn't exactly full of choices at this hour."

"No problem. He seems nice. But what was that all about?"

"Oh, God, let's don't get into that at this hour of the night." He looked suddenly tired. "Didn't you say you moved here to unearth the secrets of my past? Well, I'll let you ferret out this one for yourself. It shouldn't be hard. That stale, seedy tale is the only thing anyone in Heyday remembers about me."

She waited. Though she would have liked to hear this story from Bryce himself, she could tell he really didn't want to tell her. She had to respect that. She had no right to crowd or push.

Still, there was one thing she could clear up. "All right. But that's not really true, you know. I didn't just come here looking for gossip."

He frowned. "Well, you couldn't have come here looking for *me*."

"No," she said. "Actually I thought this was the last place on earth you'd be. I know how you've always despised Heyday. I was shocked when one of the other students told me you were teaching a class at the college."

"Yeah, well, God knows it shocked the hell out of me." He took a long drink of beer and, putting the bottle down, gave her a half smile. "So help me out here, Lara. If you didn't come to find me, and you didn't come to snoop into my checkered youth, I'm back to my original question. What the devil *are* you doing here?"

She took a breath. "I guess I needed a quiet place to think things through. To begin to heal after—after Kenny. Heyday seemed perfect for that. I want you to know I didn't intend to come across like some kind of stalker myself—as you said, I had no idea you'd ever set foot in Heyday again. But knowing you had once lived here, that it was your hometown, well, it made Heyday seem a little less foreign than other cities I might have chosen. A little safer."

She looked at him, feeling ridiculously anxious. She didn't need his permission to live in Heyday. He didn't own it. Well, actually, she'd heard that he did own a lot of it. But even so—he couldn't exactly run her out of town.

He had a deep crease between his brows and a tension in his shoulders that told her he wasn't buying it.

"For God's sake, Lara. You're smarter than that. I understand that you're scared, that you need something to make you feel safe. But there's nothing magical about me, or the town where I was born. I'm nobody's guardian angel."

"I know that. It's just that I—"

"Look, this idea that you…care about me. It's absurd. You hired me to carry a gun and use it if Kenny

Boggs got too close, and that's what I did. It was a job, that's all."

"That's *all?*" She squared her shoulders. "Are you sure about that?"

"Absolutely."

For the first time, she felt a touch of anger rising. She knew he hadn't much respected the well-oiled, waxed, tanned and highlighted Lara Lynmore. He had despised her sweet-and-sexy, mega-expensive designer clothes that lured fans into hungry obsession. He'd stood somberly by through the long hours of her late-night parties, refusing to be moved even when she twirled over, tipsy enough to tug his hand and beg for a dance. And though he hadn't said a word as he mutely handed her an aspirin the next morning and turned her over to her personal trainer whose job it was to ensure that the parties didn't wreck her all-important looks, she knew what he was thinking.

He was thinking that Lara Lynmore was a self-absorbed, superficial piece of eye candy.

No, he hadn't respected her. Maybe he hadn't even really liked her.

But he had wanted her. It was dishonest, and pointless, to try to deny that now. Within days of his arrival, every time they were in the same room, the air had sizzled. Within weeks, they had been in each other's arms.

"What about the night of the art gallery opening? When we got home, when you kissed me... If Darryl hadn't called—"

"That night was a mistake," he said flatly. "But even so, it was just sex."

"Just sex? I don't feel like that very often, Bryce. Can you honestly say you do?"

He shrugged. "Often enough to recognize it for what it is."

"And that is?"

"An intense but temporary hormonal flare-up. Quite pleasant, as long as you don't read anything more serious into it."

She felt her cheeks grow hot. Part of her simply couldn't believe he'd said that. Were they talking about the same night? Her veins buzzed a little whenever she remembered it, even now.

But she had no intention of sitting here begging him to admit that their interlude had been something magical. Maybe he was telling the truth. Maybe it had only seemed extraordinary to her because she had so little to compare it to.

"All right," she said, struggling to keep her voice from sounding as hot as her face. "If you say it meant nothing, I believe you. Even so, I would have thought that you might, at the very least, respect my efforts to remake my life. But if you don't, that's not going to stop me, because this isn't, in the end, really about you—or even us. It's about me."

"Lara—"

"Please. Hear me out. I didn't come here to pester you, and I don't intend to. Heyday is small, but surely we can avoid each other if that's what you'd prefer."

She stood up. "And now I think I'd better get home. Because, as ridiculous as it might seem to you, I have an early class in the morning."

CHAPTER FIVE

BRYCE HAD A BAD NIGHT, thanks to the encounter with Lara, which had gotten under his skin more than he would have expected. He kept rehashing their conversation, wondering how on earth she expected him to believe a word of it. Movie star turned music therapist? Trading the red carpet for troubled children and chemotherapy patients? Right. She'd tire of this little game in…he'd give her about another month.

Still, the earnest, needy expression on her gorgeous face—paradoxically more beautiful without its Hollywood glamour—haunted him. She had clearly hoped he'd take her seriously. He had stayed up trying to sort it out for hours, but got nowhere.

And, of course, the dog from Hell hadn't helped.

Not content with his giant bowl of lamb-and-rice nuggets, his bed and blanket and covered porch, the stray spaniel had scratched on the back door all night long. Though the porch was just under his window, Bryce had held firm. No way was he going to end up sharing a bed with that fleabag. But he'd paid dearly for it. He'd hardly slept a wink.

He could have changed bedrooms—the frat house

had ten. But though most of the downstairs areas of the Greek Revival mansion were fairly respectable, the bedrooms were disgusting.

Only Bryce's room, second floor at the back, was habitable. Fifty years ago, it had belonged to the poor student who'd ended up jumping out the window and becoming the resident ghost. Since then, word was it had seldom been used by the fraternity brothers, except for the occasional dare.

Bryce figured he'd rather share a room with a sad little ghost than with the aromatic remnants of too many Jim Beam binges and midnight pizza fights. Besides, the ghost never made a peep. Which was more than you could say for that insufferable mutt, who didn't shut up until dawn.

Bryce might have survived that. He didn't teach on Tuesdays, so he had planned to relax today, anyhow. But then, at 7:00 a.m. sharp, the front doorbell had begun to ring. It was Elton Fletcher, his property manager, something he'd inherited, apparently, along with the rest of this mess.

The boyish-faced man was about Bryce's age, thirtyish, and he was combed and starched and obsessively clean-cut. He was also a serious overachiever. He had brought a twenty-page list of issues he was quite sure Bryce would want to address personally.

He was quite wrong, and Bryce wasted no time telling him so. But even when you weeded out the ones Elton could handle himself, that left at least a dozen questions only Bryce could answer.

So he had invited Elton into the kitchen and let the

man ramble on while he fixed coffee and tried to wake up.

"Okay, then," Elton said after nearly an hour. "I'll tell Mr. Tresnor that the lease is non-negotiable, and that he has seventy-two hours to sign or give notice." Elton scratched neat little notes to himself on a legal pad, then turned back to his list. "I guess that's it, except of course for Mrs. Milligan."

Bryce yawned. "Her lease is non-negotiable, too."

"No, no, it isn't that. Mrs. Milligan is…well, she's different. She doesn't pay rent at all."

"She's not a tenant?"

"Oh, well, technically she's a tenant. One of the seventeen houses you inherited out in Yarrow Estates. She just hasn't paid rent in—" he consulted his notes "—about two years."

That got Bryce's attention. "Why the hell not?"

Elton looked uncomfortable. "It's always something different. One month, she said her sister had been kidnapped, and she spent everything on ransom. Another month, she said someone was shooting poisoned air in through the vents, and she shouldn't have to pay to be assassinated. Last month apparently her Doberman was depressed, and the cost of therapy cleaned her out."

"Good God."

"Exactly. I tried to get Kieran to evict her—he'd been handling things for your father for months—but he said she was either a damn creative woman or a lunatic, and either way he wouldn't dream of insulting her."

Bryce had to laugh. Only in Heyday. "Well, my

brother is a saint, and, as we all know, I'm not. Tell her I don't care about the back rent, but she's got to start paying or get out."

"Excellent. Yes, very wise," Elton said, putting a tidy black check mark next to Mrs. Milligan's name. His tone was so prissy, so righteously pleased to be given the authority to put the screws on crazy Mrs. Milligan, that Bryce almost regretted his decision.

"Is that all?" Bryce wanted Elton to leave. The property manager's Marine-cut hair, his sharp Number Two pencils and the knife-edge crease in his khaki slacks had begun to get on Bryce's nerves. Nobody should look like that at seven in the morning.

Two minutes after Elton's car pulled away, though, the doorbell rang again. Cursing under his breath, Bryce opened it.

He recognized his new visitor right away, though he had only seen the man a few times. Red-haired and freckled, he was a student in Bryce's criminology class.

Harry…Harry…Wooten, maybe? Thirty-eight students made for a lot of names to keep straight, but this guy stood out. He was a little older than the other kids, maybe about twenty-eight or nine, but about ten times more responsible.

"Hi, Harry," Bryce said. He put more welcome into his tone than he felt, just because Harry was such a great student. But he really hoped this wasn't going to become a habit. He liked the kids in his class, but that was the key. He liked them *in class.* "What's up?"

Harry stooped to pet the spaniel, who had wandered

around front, obviously aware that the action was all out here now.

"Hi, buddy," Harry said, scratching the dog's ears. He reached into his jacket pocket and dug around for a minute, eventually pulling out a broken piece of linty dog treat. "Here. Want this? It's old, but it's probably still good."

The dog thumped his tail hard on the ground, sending bits of muddy snow bouncing. As if asking permission, he looked back at Bryce, the whites of his eyes showing while he tried to keep both biscuit and Bryce in his vision.

Bryce scowled. "Don't try to pretend you belong to me. I don't give a damn what you eat." He looked at Harry. "Want a dog?"

Harry gave the dog a last pat, then stood. "Can't," he said, sounding regretful. "I can't afford the three I've already got."

"God. You've got three dogs?"

"No, just one." Harry smiled. "But I've got a wife and a little girl, too, and I can't afford any of them." He came to the bottom of the front porch steps, and stood there diffidently, his hands in his pockets, looking up at Bryce. "That's why I came by. I heard you had inherited this place. It's a great old house, but it's been mistreated for years. I'm a handyman, at least until I pass your class and talk to the police academy. I thought I might be able to give you some estimates on some repairs."

Bryce shook his head. "I'm not planning to do any. Now if you could give me an estimate on demolition, that's something I might be able to use."

Harry stepped back, eyes wide. "You're going to tear down this fantastic old mansion? Why?"

"I guess you've never been inside. The place looks like Animal House. Half the walls are covered in dart holes and graffiti. The carpets reek of booze and petrified pepperoni. The only kitchen appliance that works is a coffeemaker I bought yesterday."

"But that's all superficial stuff. The house itself....it's one of a kind. It wasn't always a fraternity house, you know. Back in the 1800s, it was a private home. The Brennans. Their only daughter was married on this very porch. Look at those columns. And over there. Look at that marble work."

Bryce swiveled his head and tried to see what Harry was so excited about. But all he saw was peeling paint and cracked plaster. Bryce didn't particularly like old houses. His condo in Chicago had been built just days before he moved in. Even in the Bahamas, he had stayed at the newest hotel on the island. He liked fresh, clean things, things that came without the baggage of ancient history, ancestral expectations. Without sappy legends and disgusting odors and stray dogs and ghosts.

It probably came from those summers at old Anderson McClintock's house. You couldn't breathe there, with all those other, dead McClintocks staring down at you over their painted noses—and Anderson himself always trying to break you, own you. Bryce's mother had understood. That was why she had gotten out early, the minute she discovered that Anderson had taken a mistress, before she lost her self-esteem and her willpower.

She had understood why Bryce had hated going back. In that house, she knew that, unless you fought constantly, and fought ugly, you might get swallowed whole. You might, like Kieran, become a smiling, dancing puppet instead of a real person.

"Sorry," Bryce said. "I guess I'm a philistine. I don't see anything. But I'm not completely hell-bent on tearing it down. If someone will buy it from me, I'm happy to let it stand."

"Boy, I wish I *could* buy it. Wouldn't that be sweet? But, like I said, I'm struggling just to make ends meet these days. Terri, that's my daughter, she got hurt in a car accident…" He swallowed hard. "That means my wife can't work. She's worried half to death. And with me taking classes…"

Harry sighed heavily, running his hand through his springy red curls. "I really hoped you might have some work, but…"

Bryce hesitated. He felt himself about to do something stupid. He hardly even knew this young man. Harry's money troubles, his hurt kid and his worried wife…they weren't Bryce's problems. He had agreed to teach Harry criminology, that was all. He hadn't agreed to adopt him.

The spaniel trotted up to him then, licked his hand and lay down at his feet, with his chin on Bryce's shoe. Bryce looked down once, then raised his gaze to the snow-laden gray sky.

What the hell was it about Heyday? He felt as if he had stepped into quicksand and was sinking deeper with every passing day.

"Okay, Harry, look. I'm not into restoration, but I'm into breathing clean air. If you're any good at painting and pulling up carpeting, I'd be glad to give you some work."

"Oh, Mr. McClintock! Jan, that's my wife, she'll be so happy." He beamed. "She told me it wasn't worth it to even ask you. She said she'd heard that you never—" His smile faded, and a flush crept up his cheeks, freckle by freckle. "I mean, you know how people are, the things they say. But, it's obviously not true, so—"

"Yes, it is," Bryce said, moving his foot and letting the spaniel's chin slide to the cold porch floor. No use letting anybody get delusional here. "Whatever it was, Harry, I guarantee it is one hundred percent true."

WHEN SHE GOT BACK to Lazy Gables Ranch after sitting through English, Algebra and Psychology of Music, Lara had to fight the urge to go upstairs to her pretty maple four-poster bed and take a nap.

She was exhausted—the encounter with Bryce had made it difficult to sleep at all last night. But she had a lot of homework to do. As she peeled off her coat and scarf and hung them on the brass coat tree in the foyer, she averted her eyes from the tempting staircase. She hooked her backpack over one shoulder and forced herself down the hall of the old 1800s ranch house, all the way to the huge, bright yellow kitchen.

Oscar Allred, the ranch's caretaker who lived in the apartment over the stables, was already there, washing his hands. The big, scarred oak table, probably original to the house, was set with two blue pottery bowls of steaming soup.

"Oscar, you're an angel," she cried, dropping her backpack onto one of the empty chairs.

Oscar turned from the sink and smiled. He didn't look like an angel—he looked ruggedly human. Just short of sixty, Oscar was blond with silver highlights, lean, weather-beaten and drop-dead handsome, like Robert Redford. Casting directors would kill for this look.

She leaned over one of the bowls and sniffed the air deeply. "Mushroom—my favorite! How did you know I was starving?"

"It's three o'clock," he said. "And you didn't eat breakfast."

She groaned. Ever since she'd moved in, Oscar had been after her to eat better, insisting that she was ten pounds too skinny. She had tried to explain that, in Hollywood, being only ten pounds underweight almost qualified as being fat. He had merely frowned and said, "Even the dumbest animal knows it should eat when it's hungry."

"Okay, you caught me," she said, tugging his sleeve playfully. "I meant to, honestly, but I was late for class. I'll make up for it now, though. That smells divine."

Oscar just grunted. He obviously didn't approve of skipping breakfast, but he wasn't the type to waste words on a losing battle. She wished Oscar could give her mother a few lessons in self-restraint.

Though at first Lara had been uncomfortable with the idea of renting a house that came with a resident stranger, she had fallen in love with Oscar instantly. He was like the father she'd never had—even when she'd *had* a father. Always grounded, always calm, always there. Full of the unadorned common sense she'd been craving all her life.

He put down two glasses of tap water, something Lara wouldn't have dreamed of touching in L.A. But it sparkled like liquid diamonds in the sunlight from the large kitchen window. Heyday had the cleanest water Lara had ever seen.

"Jill Baker from the seniors' home called this morning," Oscar said as he pulled out a chair. "Note's on the front hall table. She said you can start this weekend."

Lara, who had just dragged off her boots and arranged them neatly by the back door, looked up with a smile. She'd talked to Jill, the activities director at Heyday's one retirement home, about leading Friday-afternoon music sessions with the residents. Nothing elaborate, just some sing-alongs and paint-to-music classes. It would be a great way to begin trying out some of the therapies she was learning at school.

But she hadn't been sure Jill would say yes. In a little town like Heyday, a newcomer was kept at arm's length for a long time. Especially the college students, who came and went and didn't always interact well with the "townies."

"She said it's okay? That's wonderful!"

"No need to sound shocked," Oscar observed dryly. "People aren't exactly beating the seniors' home door down, begging to work for nothing."

She laughed as she headed to the sink to wash her own hands. Oscar was probably right. Jill hadn't agreed because Lara was such a fabulous music therapist.

She'd agreed because Lara had agreed to do it for the right price—for free.

Still, she was thrilled, and she couldn't wait to get started. But first things first—today she had a test to study for. They ate Oscar's fantastic, thick brown mushroom soup quickly, and then, obviously aware that she needed to focus on her work, Oscar went outside to check on the fence at the eastern edge of the ranch, over by the river.

Lara watched him go, appreciating the measured dignity of his movements. He never hurried, and yet he got more done than anyone she'd ever known. He was happiest when he could work outdoors. The world seemed to speak to him. The clouds told him how much snow was coming, and how soon. The horses told him when they needed exercise, or another blanket. Once she'd even seen him running his rough hands over a wounded rabbit, as if he were listening with his skin.

It made her feel peaceful just to think of him out there, tending things and making sure all was well.

Her cell phone rang, but she didn't answer it, reluctant to break the good mood Oscar's soup and the news from Jill had created. She knew it was her mother, undoubtedly itching to deliver today's lecture. It might be the standard one: *Throwing Away The Chance Of A Lifetime.* Or her mom might be ready to play the one Lara was really dreading, the guilt card: *How Could You Do This To Me?*

Eventually the ringing stopped. Relieved, Lara washed the dishes quickly and then, spreading her books and papers out on the table, got comfortable in one of the rail-backed chairs. In forty-eight hours, she'd take her first Psychology of Music exam, and she was determined to do well.

No, more than "well." Straight As, that's what she was shooting for. Nothing less would do. She had so much to prove. Some of the colleges she'd talked to had seemed excited about the promotional possibilities of having a celebrity on campus, but as soon as she explained that she would want to attend as Lara Gilbert, not Lara Lynmore, their excitement had faded. Lara Gilbert wasn't exactly the perfect college applicant.

Even Moresville College's dean of admissions, who had been more welcoming than anyone at the bigger colleges, had looked at her transcripts and expressed polite skepticism. All those "private tutors" on location, all those corners cut and concessions granted to get her a high-school diploma while she was busy storming the Hollywood gates.

He had asked her outright, could she do it? It would be hard, harder than she anticipated. Could she make the transition to "the real world"?

She'd vowed that she could, and now she had to make good on that vow. She had to prove it to him, and to her mother, who predicted Lara would come crawling back to Hollywood before the Shenandoah Valley snow was off the ground. And she had to prove it to Bryce McClintock, whose scoffing half laugh had told her that he assumed this was just another game of make-believe, like putting on eighteenth century barmaid's clothes and pretending to be Bess, the landlord's black-eyed daughter.

But most of all Lara had to prove it to herself. Because here was her humiliating secret: it *was* hard. She had discovered that she was spoiled and undisciplined and hopelessly out of touch. She hadn't sat in a classroom since middle school. She was only twenty-six, but she hadn't written a term paper or visited a library or taken a standardized exam in nearly fourteen years.

She'd just finished highlighting Chapter Nine when the doorbell rang. Slipping a piece of loose leaf paper in to mark the page, she got up and went back down the hall to the front door, her socks making soft sounds on the wooden floors.

The express courier stood there, bundled up in a puffy ski jacket and gloves, stamping his feet. She hadn't realized how long she'd been studying in the cozy kitchen, or how cold the afternoon had grown. The sun was low on the horizon, and it cast an orange-gold glow over the hilly path that led to the ranch house. The patches of snow in the yard looked like mounds of melting sherbet.

"Heavy one this time," the courier said as he pulled one glove off and rooted around in his pocket for a pen so that she could sign the receipt. "From Los Angeles, like always. You must have a great mom."

Lara sighed as she saw the thick white envelope. She didn't have to open it to know what it was. The courier had been delivering packages like these to Lara about twice a week, every week since she'd arrived in Heyday. Obviously curious, he'd finally begun to fish around for information, and she'd told him they were care packages from her mom.

But her mom's "care packages" didn't include loving letters, hand-knitted sweaters, chocolates or chicken soup. These envelopes held only one thing. Scripts.

And, judging by the size of today's package, lots of them. Her mother was sure that someday one of these scripts would be irresistible, and Lara would come flying home to accept the part. Karla Gilbert was nothing if not persistent. Lara fought the urge to take the courier's pen and write Return To Sender all over the pretty white envelope.

Instead, she signed and accepted the delivery, as she always did. And just as the courier started back down the hill to his truck, the cell phone in her pocket began to ring.

God, did her mother have the place bugged? Lara flipped the phone open with a sigh.

"Lara, where have you been?" Karla Gilbert's voice was high and tight, the pitch it always adopted when she felt aggrieved. "I've been trying to call you all day."

Lara dropped the package of scripts on the hall table and started back to the kitchen. "I've been in class, Mom. Remember? On Tuesdays and Thursdays I have class until three."

Her mother made an impatient noise. "Oh, I can't keep that straight. Besides, I needed you, Lara, it was an emergency. You know they put the new wallpaper in your apartment today. I spent the entire day at your place, supervising. It looks beautiful. Why you'd want to sell it now, when it is looking better than ever—"

"Mom. You said an emergency. Surely not a *wallpaper* emergency?"

"I was getting to that part. Well, Marina helped for a few hours, but she had to go home, she has a family of her own, you know. And then, I was so exhausted from trying to get the back rooms in order, you know they are a terrible mess. Anyhow, I was so tired that when I walked upstairs I slipped."

"Are you okay?" Lara paused at the kitchen door, suddenly anxious. Why hadn't her mother mentioned this right away? But then, her mom always told every story chronologically, leaving no detail out, no matter how trivial.

"No, I'm not okay. I fell down ten stairs, for heaven's sake. I'm bruised all over my legs, and apparently I threw out my hand to catch myself, because the X-rays showed I fractured one of the bones in my wrist."

"Oh, Mom, I'm sorry! Did you go to the emergency room? What did the doctors say? Did they have to put a cast on it?"

"Yes. They said it was lucky I'm so petite, or it might have been much worse. I might have needed pins and screws and plates, all manner of terrible things."

Lara sat back down at the kitchen table and picked up her highlighter. Her mother wasn't used to suffering in silence, so this might take a while. She remembered when Karla had gone through her first liposuction last year, Lara had hired a full-time nurse to wait on her hand and foot. But the woman's primary job had been to listen to Karla's constant complaints.

"Still, even this cast is very annoying," her mother said when she'd run through the list of could-have-happened disasters. "It's unwieldy, and it looks terrible."

"Forget about how it looks," Lara said. "How does it feel? Does it still hurt?"

"It's awful." Her mother paused. "Honestly, Lara, I think you'll have to come home now, don't you?"

Come home? Pressing the cool plastic highlighter against her forehead, Lara counted to three.

Then she spoke calmly. "Mom, you know I can't do that."

"Of course you could." Her mother's voice escalated into the upper registers again, and this time it had an added tremble. "You just don't want to."

"I have classes. Tests. I can't just walk away from them."

"I don't see why not. There are always other classes, aren't there? I need you, Lara. I can't be here alone, not at a time like this. I can't do a thing for myself. I can't even hook my own bra. And a few minutes ago, I got an itch, right under the cast. I nearly went crazy."

Lara almost laughed. "Mom, be serious. You can't really expect me to drop out of school and fly across the country to scratch under your cast."

Her mother's offended silence was eloquent enough to shame her. Lara put down the highlighter with a sigh.

"I'm sorry, I didn't mean to make light of your problems. But you have to understand that I have obligations here. I can't just ditch them. How about if I hire another nurse for you? You liked that, didn't you?"

"*Liked* it? *Liked* being flat on my back, blinded with pain?"

"I mean, you liked having the nurse. She worked out well?"

Another silence. But Lara could hear her mother breathing heavily. It sounded almost as if she were fighting back tears.

Finally Karla spoke. "I have to say, I honestly never thought I'd be in this position. I have a grown, beautiful daughter, and yet I'm completely alone. If I want the least bit of help, I have to buy it from a stranger."

An uncomfortable heat spread across Lara's cheeks. This wasn't fair. She had invited her mother to come to Heyday with her, but Karla had been so angry she had offered a cold and absolute "no." Lara could go ahead, be a fool, go live in some ridiculous Virginia backwater, but that didn't mean Karla had to trot along after her.

Lara had been so desperate to break free of the octopus arms that seemed to be tangled around her, holding her to Hollywood, that she'd taken her mother at her word.

But she should have known this would happen, sooner or later. Ever since Lara's dad had abandoned them, Karla had shown a nearly pathological fear of being alone.

And no matter what, Lara knew she couldn't buy her own freedom and happiness at the cost of her mother's. She took a deep breath, squeezed the highlighter so hard she was surprised the yellow ink didn't come spurting out, and made herself utter the words.

"Well, I still can't come there, Mom. But if you don't mind the fact that I have to be gone a lot, I'd love it if you'd come spend a couple of weeks here."

CHAPTER SIX

WHEN HE WAS FOUR YEARS OLD, Bryce's mother scooped him up and put him on a train to Chicago, introducing him to the concept of a *normal* city. Since then, he had never failed to shake his head in disbelief when he entered downtown Heyday.

A hundred years ago, this had just been a sleepy little Virginia hamlet called Moresville—or, as the locals liked to say, Boresville.

But then the circus had come to town. And, on their first night here, the animal trainer had left the cages unlocked.

By morning, there was nothing boring about Moresville. Elephants stomped down the streets and crashed through the milliner's window, emerging wearing straw hats trimmed in fake cherries and violets. Monkeys clambered onto grocers' shelves, tossing around heads of lettuce and pelting customers with gumballs. An ancient tiger lay down in the sunny center of the street, stretched out his patchy, dirty legs and went to sleep while startled horses and carriages jumbled together on both sides of him, the worst traffic jam the city had ever seen.

Women fainted, kids screamed with delight, and

men cursed angrily at the animals, who couldn't have cared less. But within hours enterprising merchants had placed chairs and tables and makeshift bleachers along the street. They rented them by the hour to curious gawkers who wanted to watch the clowns and ballerinas and trapeze artists try to corral the animals.

Most of the beasts were caught in the first day or two. But that was long enough to bring in tourists from fifty miles in all directions. And somehow, in the end, an enterprising pair of zebras managed to outsmart everybody. Though the two were spotted frequently, out by the river, in someone's backyard, or even munching on garbage behind the diner, no one ever could get a rope around them.

Newspapers loved the story. *Circus Zebras Have A Heyday In Small Town.* And, somewhere in the chaos, Heyday was born.

Theoretically, everyone said, those zebras might still be out there, or at least their wild offspring. People in Heyday did love a legend. Every few years, some drunk or head case called up the paper, insisting he'd seen the zebras. The last recorded sighting had been during the millennium New Year celebration, when liquor flowed fairly freely.

Now Heyday was pretty much just a kitschy joke. The city government complex, which Bryce's father had built, was the only building with an ounce of dignity in the entire downtown area. Every retail establishment that had gone up in the past hundred years had included a faux circus façade, a circus name or a circus tableau in the window—or all three.

And zebras—good God! Zebras leaped from awnings, hung from the official Heyday banners on streetlights, smiled from the sides of passing utility vans, spilled across every shelf at the five-and-dime. You had your lawn cut by Zebra Landscaping. You filled your car at the Zebra Fuel Depot. You sat on black-and-white striped chairs and ate Zebra hoagies at the Big Top Diner.

No wonder Bryce had always hated to come back in the summer. It was damn embarrassing to have been born here, but at least that was beyond your control. To return voluntarily meant you were soft in the head.

So what did that say about Bryce now? He met the goofy grin of a life-size cement zebra positioned outside the toy store and decided it might be better not to think about it.

He parked on Hippodrome Circle, then walked a couple of blocks to Roustabout Road, where Rackham Books was located. He hadn't seen Mallory Rackham since the New Year's Eve dinner at Kieran's house, but he had liked her. He was glad to see she'd resisted the temptation to call her business "Tiger Tales" or "Sideshow Stories."

He needed a couple of books for his class—as he got deeper into his subject, he realized that, through the years, he'd forgotten a hell of a lot about criminology. Ironic, but true. When you did something every day, you no longer needed to know exactly what it was called or how it was defined in the textbooks.

He'd expected to have to order them, but, amazingly, when he'd phoned, the bookseller on duty had informed him that Rackham Books did indeed carry those titles. Guess not everyone in Heyday was completely brain dead.

But when he opened the door and saw the kid behind the register, he wasn't so sure about that anymore. "Wally," the boy's name tag read. Wally had six silver posts driven through his ear, three through his eyebrow, one through his tongue, with which he toyed while he read a comic book, and God only knew how many in places Bryce hoped never to see.

Wally's hair was half green, half red, and stood straight up in spikes as if he'd just stuck his finger in a light socket. Other than that, everything on the kid was gravedigger black. Naturally, the comic he was reading was called "Nightslayer."

"Hey," Wally said casually as Bryce approached the counter. He let go of his tongue and put it back in his mouth. "How's it goin'?"

Apparently, in Wally's estimation, a customer wasn't anything to get excited about. He hadn't even put down the comic book.

"Great," Bryce said. "You have a couple of things on hold for me. The name's McClintock."

"Oh, yeah, right." Wally bent down, and when he straightened up he had three books in his hand. "Here ya go."

Bryce looked at the titles. *Breastfeeding Breakthrough, From Colic to Diaper Rash,* and *Fairy Tale Nurseries.*

"Sorry," Bryce said pleasantly. "Wrong McClintock. I'm Bryce."

The kid looked down at the picture of a baby nestled against a bare breast. He flushed as red as his hair. "Oh, man. Oops. That's for Mrs. McClintock. She's going to have a baby."

"So it seems." Bryce held back a smile. If he'd wondered whether Wally's unconventional hair and body piercings indicated a truly troubled, antisocial personality, he had his answer. Underneath the hair dye, this kid was as mainstream as apple pie, and a virgin to boot. In ten years, he'd have two-point-five kids, a savings account and a favorite chair down at the barbershop.

Wally shoved the books back under the counter noisily, as uncomfortable as if they'd been the newest nudie magazines. When he emerged, he had Bryce's books in his hand.

"This is your stack." He pointed to the "hold" slip wrapped around the books with a rubber band. "See? Mr. Bryce McClintock."

"Bryce McClintock?" A strident voice rose from the other side of the store. "Did you say *Bryce* McClintock?"

The hair on the back of Bryce's neck began to quiver and stand on end. He knew that voice, though he hadn't heard it in fourteen years. It was the haughty contralto that belonged to Aurora York, the busybody who used to live next door to Bryce's father.

Every summer, she'd made Bryce's life pure hell. A close friend of Anderson, she'd elected herself Bryce's summer mother, which in her mind entitled her to boss and lecture and spy and tattle. For several summers, Bryce had retaliated with such juvenile pranks as having pizzas delivered to her house, depositing dead mice under the seat of her car and cutting the blooms off her favorite roses. Finally, somewhere around the time he turned sixteen, he grew up enough to simply tell her to go to hell.

Of course, he knew now that she had probably meant well, and he'd just been his usual obnoxious self. He set his face in a smile as he watched her come toward him now and stifled a sigh. This homecoming was going to be one long, unappetizing banquet of cold crow.

"Mrs. York," he said politely. "It's been a long time. How are you?"

"I'm fine, of course," she said acerbically. She looked just the same as she had fourteen years ago. She still wore too much rouge on those aristocratic cheekbones, and she still wore a nutty feathered hat over her silver curls. "Surprised to see you back in Heyday, that's for sure. I thought you were busy romancing movie stars and shooting psychopaths."

Bryce lifted his shoulders, then let them fall. "Sorry to disappoint you," he said. "That was a temporary gig."

"I'm not disappointed," she retorted, scowling. "I've thought for years that you ought to come home. Although I certainly *will* be disappointed, if you're planning to make trouble with Kieran and Claire."

He squinted, unsure he could have heard her properly. "Why on earth would I do that? And *how?*"

She hesitated, then cast her glare briefly in Wally's direction. "You probably should go look for that book on bunions, Wally."

Wally made a protesting noise. "We don't have it. I already—"

"Look again," Aurora commanded. Bryce remembered that tone, and he felt sorry for the poor kid. The bad-ass Bryce McClintocks of the world just barely managed to hold their own against this woman. The blushing Wallys didn't stand a chance.

When the kid was gone, she turned back to Bryce, wagging a finger at him. "How could you cause trouble? Don't try that innocent act with me, Bryce. I know what happens to women when you're around. When you were growing up, I watched them circle the house like bees over honey. I can see your father's garden from my window, you know. And believe me, I saw plenty."

"Mrs. York," he said softly, trying to remember what exactly he'd dared to do in his father's own backyard. Not much, surely. Well…there had been the little flute player from the high school band. She had been a very talented girl. "You surprise me. I didn't take you for a voyeur."

She stiffened, but it would require more than that to embarrass Aurora York. "Yes," she said, unrepentant. "And I saw what happened out there just a couple of weeks ago on New Year's Eve, too."

He shifted the books to his other hand. So she still lived next door. How lucky for Kieran. He and his bride would have to be careful to draw the drapes. Or maybe saints didn't have anything to hide.

"And what exactly," Bryce asked carefully, "did you see?"

"I saw you out on the porch with Claire. You had

your arm around her. You were pretty cozy, I'd say. You'd just met her that night, hadn't you? That's pretty fast work, even for you."

She scanned him with her sharp, dark eyes. "You haven't changed much, have you?"

"Apparently not," he said. "And I'll bet you haven't changed much, either, have you, Mrs. York? I'll bet you ran straight to Kieran and told him what you saw."

She tossed her head back, and the green feather on her hat quivered in response, like a living thing. "I certainly did. He loves that gal. They're going to have a baby any day—in fact it's overdue already. He had a right to know."

Bryce's fingers tightened on the books. The meddling old bitch. He couldn't believe he'd just been regretting all those pranks. Obviously, he hadn't been nearly nasty enough. "And what did my little brother say?"

"Oh, you know Kieran. He never can bring himself to think ill of anyone. He said he was sure it had been nothing. But he wasn't sure, not one hundred percent. His housekeeper told me that he checked with Claire about it the next day."

His smile felt fake. "Checked with Claire about what?"

But he knew what. What he didn't know was why it should surprise him that Kieran considered him capable of such a thing. Bryce was never going to live down the past, not here in Heyday. Which was why Kieran's little happy family charade hadn't fooled Bryce for a minute. *Happy family* and *McClintock* were mutually exclusive terms.

"Checked with her about whether you'd made a pass at her," Aurora said smugly. "Of course she said no. What else could she say?"

He leveled a cold gaze at her. "She could say it was preposterous."

"Not with you, it isn't. After all, the last time you were in Heyday, you—"

He had to get out of here. He opened his wallet, threw four twenties on the counter and turned back one last time to Aurora.

"Then she could say it was a nasty business, spying on people and trying to stir up trouble. She could say it was a damn shame that St. Kieran didn't trust his brand-new, pregnant wife more than that, whatever he might think of his black sheep brother."

WEDNESDAY AFTERNOON WAS Lara's only window of free time in a hectic schedule of classes and volunteer work, and she often used it to just wander the charming countryside around Lazy Gables and clear her head. Even in this rainy, gray winter, the Shenandoah Valley was beautiful, with its rolling hills and unblemished meadows. She could only imagine how lovely it would be in spring.

This particular Wednesday, she needed the soothing hand of nature more than ever. By this time tomorrow, her mother would be here.

Karla was set to fly into Richmond at noon, which Lara cynically assumed was a deliberate attempt to get her daughter to skip class. But Oscar had insisted that he'd pick Karla up and bring her back to Lazy Gables Ranch just in time for Lara to get home at three-thirty.

She'd thanked him with a hug. He was the most amazing man. Apparently he hadn't needed a blueprint to see where the land mines were in this particular mother/daughter relationship.

So this was Lara's last afternoon of complete privacy, and she intended to use it well. Luckily, the weather had cooperated. The big sky was a dark, powdery blue, with an elegant row of white clouds on the horizon. It was like strolling under a Wedgwood bowl.

It had snowed a little last night, not enough to blanket the valley, but enough to decorate tree limbs and fence posts with a frosting of crushed-diamond white. She walked slowly, drinking in the crisp air and listening to the clear notes of the hermit thrush as they gathered in the bare-limbed trees.

When she reached the river's edge, she stopped, as she always did, mesmerized by the water, which was so cold and clear she could see the silvery blue rocks and green pebbles on the riverbed below.

The wind was sharper here, but the view was so perfect she wished she could stay forever. Pulling her cap down over her ears, she eyed the huge beech tree that stood beside her. Its long, bare branches swept close to the ground.

The perfect climbing tree.

The very idea made her feel excited, and irrationally guilty.

Back when she was eleven or twelve, she remembered, she used to love to climb trees. But then, at thirteen, she landed her first tiny part in a movie, and suddenly she wasn't a kid, she was a commodity. If she had broken a bone, or scraped her face, or bruised an arm, she would have been replaced. So of course her mother had swaddled her in cotton, kept her indoors and monitored her every move.

Looking back, she realized that was the exact moment at which her life had seemed to change. From that day on, she hadn't been able to twitch a muscle without considering the implications. She couldn't cut or dye her hair, as her friends did, or buy fake nails or sneak out for a temporary tattoo. She couldn't pierce her ears, much less her navel or her nose. No sports or roughhousing, no late nights or junk food. She couldn't even go to the beach—the next audition might require a magnolia-fair Southern belle.

As her roles got larger and more important, her mother's protective smothering became the least of her worries. By the time she landed her first leading role, in *The Highwayman,* her legal contract had expressly forbidden engaging in dangerous activities, or immoral behavior, or anything that might jeopardize the motion picture, or even make the audience think ill of her.

It had been like living in a straitjacket.

But she wasn't under contract now. For the first time in almost fourteen years, she was free.

She tucked her ponytail up under her cap, buttoned her jacket, wrapped her hands around the lowest limb of the beech tree, kicked her feet against the trunk—and began to climb.

Her palms stung a little, but her body swung up and over, and suddenly she was astride the branch. Hanging on to the thick trunk, she rose carefully, glad that her years of ballet lessons had taught her the art of balance—and the ability to arrange her feet in ridiculous positions.

She climbed slowly, one branch at a time, gathering confidence as she hoisted herself ever higher. A few sparrows darted away as they saw her coming and landed on the next tree, where they continued to watch her curiously.

Finally, about four branches up, she stopped at a large, comfortable limb and sat again, her bottom nestled securely in the crook of branch and trunk, her legs dangling free, as if she rode a pommel horse. She peeked once, and registered that the glittering river was not so very far down—but then, lifting her face to the pure, cold wind, she stared up at the sky, which seemed intense and very near. She felt a solitary snowflake kiss her cheek.

Just then the wind gusted, and the branch swayed—almost imperceptibly, but it was enough to make her stomach leap. She held tightly to the wood between her knees and laughed out loud, exhilarated. It was a little like flying.

It was hard to be sure how long she stayed there, with the wind burning her cheeks, but eventually she heard the sound of voices below her. Someone else had come to look at the river, to glory in its winter purity, just as she had done earlier.

Two people, a man and a woman. She was a little too high to hear their words, but there was no mistaking their body language. These people were deeply in love.

The man, who had blondish hair the color of dark

sunshine, wrapped his arms protectively around the woman. She wore a bulky winter coat and scarf, so it was hard to be sure, but she seemed young. And she just might, Lara thought, be pregnant.

The woman leaned back against the man, as if his hard body were her home, as if she fit there the way the water below them fit into its riverbed. He bent down and kissed the crown of her head, and then her temple, her ear, her neck. His hands began to stroke her rounded belly—oh, yes, the woman was pregnant, and the man loved it, cherished it.

The woman's head fell back as his hands rose to touch her breasts. And that was when Lara began to climb down, taking the branches as quickly as she safely could. If she didn't announce her presence pretty soon, she might end up witnessing something just a little too private.

In her hurry, she missed her footing on the next-to-last branch. Her boots scraped against the wood, dislodging bark and making an absurd amount of noise as she scrambled to catch herself by straddling the final limb.

The two people on the riverbank looked up, clearly startled. The man held the woman even closer, instinctively protecting her from whatever might be lurching out of the trees.

Lara felt her cheeks flaming, but in spite of it all she began to laugh. It was really too ridiculous.

"Hi," she said, trying to control her chuckling. "I didn't mean to scare you. I just—well, I was up in the tree, and I saw you come by, and I thought I'd better announce myself before—well, before you—"

She grinned. "Oh, this is hopeless. If I can get down without killing myself, I promise to start over and introduce myself properly."

The two people were laughing now, too, obviously aware of what she'd been thinking. "Here, let me help you," the man said. He came over and held out his hand, which had a small gold band on the fourth finger.

Up close he was even better-looking than she'd realized. No wonder his wife had melted into him like that. Lara gratefully accepted his help. She gripped his strong, warm hand, swung free and landed on the ground with a plop.

Dusting off her bottom, she smiled. "Thanks. I'm Lara. Lara Gilbert. I'm renting Lazy Gables Ranch."

As always, she watched carefully, wondering if she'd see any recognition flickering behind his eyes. She wasn't particularly anxious this time. She was dressed like a lumberjack, in corduroy slacks, a flannel shirt and a denim jacket. Her hair was jammed under her cap, and she was scraped, wind-tossed and dirty. She didn't even have any lipstick on.

But he recognized her, anyhow. She saw his eyes narrow, dart to his wife, and then come back to her. He gave her a small smile.

"Gilbert?" he queried lightly, his head on one side.

He knew. She could tell by the light in his eyes that he knew she had another name, a more familiar name. He knew she was Lara Lynmore.

It was the moment she'd been dreading. But something in his gentle tone gave her courage. Sooner or later this had been destined to happen. She should be glad it was here, in relative privacy, with such clearly pleasant people.

"Yes, Gilbert. That's—that's my real name." She pulled her cap off and let her hair tumble free. "I came to Heyday to go to college. I actually was hoping no one would recognize me." She shrugged. "Up to now, I've been pretty lucky."

The man smiled. "I'm sorry. But I had an advantage. I followed your career pretty closely for a while there. I'm Kieran McClintock. Bryce's brother. And technically, you're renting Lazy Gables from me—though you've been dealing with my property manager."

"Oh," she said, trying to hide her shock. This gorgeous hunk of manhood was Bryce's saintly little brother? She could hardly believe it. From Bryce's description, she would have pictured someone much less potent. Far less charming. Bryce had always referred to Kieran as the goody-two-shoes, the rule-follower, and the implication had been that he was a bit of a bore.

"And this is my wife, Claire, who shouldn't be out here at all. She's a full week overdue, and the doctor said she—"

Claire stepped forward and gave Lara a welcoming smile. "The doctor said I should get plenty of exercise," she said. "Hi, Lara. Sorry about that. Obviously we thought we were alone."

"You mean you didn't imagine anyone would be lurking in the treetops?"

Claire shook her head. "Not really. But we'll be sure to check next time."

Kieran put his arm around his wife, as if he could go only so many minutes without touching her. He smiled over at Lara. "So how have you been finding the ranch? Is Oscar taking care of everything for you?"

"He's a treasure," Lara said. "I honestly don't know what I'd do without him. I rented the ranch because I wanted to be alone, but to tell you the truth, without Oscar I think it might feel a little *too* solitary."

Claire shook her head. "You mustn't let yourself be alone too much. Brooding always makes things worse. Believe me, I know all about it." Suddenly she straightened, eyes wide. "Why don't you come over for dinner some night soon? We could invite Bryce, and—"

"Oh, no," Lara said. "I don't really think that would be a very good idea."

Claire paused, taking a minute to look at Lara quietly. Lara could tell she was processing the nuances of that statement. "No?"

"No." Lara tried to smile, as if this were all rather amusing. "I think Bryce may have had about all of me he can stand for right now. Remember, while he was my bodyguard, we were pretty much joined at the hip night and day."

She hated the way her face flushed when she said that. God only knows what Kieran and Claire were reading into those red cheeks. "Nothing personal, of course. It's just that it—it was a very stressful time. And it didn't really end—all that well."

"No," Kieran said in an understanding voice. "No, I can see why neither one of you would be eager to revisit that just yet."

"Still, you shouldn't be alone," Claire said. "Kieran, what about Roddy? He's—"

"Please," Lara said. "I'm not looking for dates right now. Men— I mean…after Kenny…after Bryce…"

With a low sound of dismay, Claire put her hands out and touched Lara's arms. "Oh, of course not. I don't know why I'm being so stupid. I'm like a reformed alcoholic. I finally allowed myself to fall in love, and so suddenly I think everyone in the world ought to pair up and live happily ever after."

Happily ever after. Lara fought back the wistful longing that had been threatening to sweep over her like a winter wind ever since she first saw Kieran and Claire standing together. She hadn't realized, until that moment, just how lonely she really was. How lonely she had been for a very long time.

"I'm in favor of happily-ever-afters, too," Lara said. She shivered suddenly, as an echo of Bryce's cold voice presented itself in her mind, telling her how ridiculous he found the idea that she might care for him.

"I've just learned the hard way that sometimes it's not that simple."

KARLA LIKED FLYING. You were never lonely in an airplane. She enjoyed the sense of camaraderie with the other passengers, as if they were, for a couple of hours, one big family sharing the same problems, the same goals, the same experiences. A few years ago, when one of her flights had been stranded on the tarmac for an hour, the passengers had spontaneously launched into a silly sing-along of Beatles tunes. Though it seemed a bit pathetic to admit it, that laughing hour had been among the happiest of Karla's life.

Plus, the flight attendants were so solicitous, especially today, when she had this cast on her arm. The nice woman next to her had offered to change seats, so that Karla's good wrist would be on the aisle side. After that, the two of them had struck up a very pleasant conversation. It turned out the woman had seen *The Highwayman* three times, and was absolutely thrilled to meet Lara Lynmore's mother.

They had spent almost the whole flight discussing Lara's beauty and talent, and the outrage of Kenny Boggs. The conversation had finally turned to the inevitable…what was next for Lara?

"To tell you the truth, I'm on my way to see her now," Karla said proudly.

The woman's mouth opened. "Really? Lara Lynmore is in Virginia?"

"Yes. Of course she doesn't want everyone to know that. She needs some peace and quiet. She's taking a sabbatical—you can imagine how undone she was by the whole ordeal with that horrible man. But when she heard I had broken my wrist, she insisted that I come down and let her take care of me."

The woman beamed, shaking her head in amazement. "Imagine! What a wonderful daughter! You know, you hear such terrible things about movie stars. But I could tell she wasn't like that. She's a nice person. You can feel it, don't you think? When you see her on the screen?"

Karla nodded, pleased. This woman wasn't just a

mindless movie nut—her comments about *The Highwayman* had been quite intelligent. "Absolutely," she agreed. "And that sweetness you see in her up there—that's really how she is. She always has been, ever since she was a baby."

It sounded like hype, but for once Karla wasn't merely spinning the legend of Lara for her adoring public. It was all true. A warmth spread through her, just remembering Lara as a baby.

It had been so easy then, so peaceful to snuggle together, letting Lara's little body warm the cold places deep inside Karla's breast. So easy to be honest, to whisper the secrets of her heart to those delicate, unjudging ears.

No one but another mother would ever know how painful the loss of that easy intimacy could be. How hard it was to accept that the adored little girl had become an adult who had the power—and occasionally the desire—to withhold the love, to recoil from the touch, to judge and condemn.

Hard to believe that her little hand, which had always reached for you first, could ever push you away.

Karla felt her throat tightening, and she instructed herself sternly to stop indulging in such stupid self-pity. Lara didn't *condemn* her. Not always.

Certainly not right now. Lara had invited her to visit, though she could easily have refused to. When Lara first broke the news of her move to Heyday, Karla had said some hateful things.

But that was in the past, and now Karla was going to have the chance to take them back. And oh, how comforting it would be, finally to see Lara again, to hug her, to talk to her. For the past month, Karla had felt like a disconnected fixture, a cold bulb unable to chase its own darkness away. She needed her beautiful little girl. It felt as if plugging into Lara's vibrant energy would turn back on the power of her own life.

The plane banked to the left, and suddenly she felt the pressure building in her ears. They must have begun their descent. She looked at her watch. They'd be at the terminal in fifteen minutes. So soon... Her pulse picked up its pace. She could almost see Lara's smiling face now.

Impulsively, Karla turned to her companion. "Would you like to meet her?"

"Lara Lynmore?" The woman gasped, just a little. "Could I?"

Karla smiled, her happy anticipation spilling over onto anyone she touched.

"Of course. She's a little shy right now, but if I ask her, I'm sure she'll give you an autograph."

She tried not to sound smug, but she was so proud of her daughter, her beautiful, successful daughter. No one could say her life had been wasted when she had a daughter like that.

"Follow me when we get off, and I'll introduce you. She'll be waiting for me at the terminal."

CHAPTER SEVEN

THE MINUTE HE WALKED into the classroom that Wednesday afternoon, two weeks after his encounter with Lara, Bryce knew that something dramatic had happened.

Ordinarily when he arrived the desks were only half full, and most of the kids were sending one final text message on their cell phones, or rooting around in their fast food bags for the last stray French fry.

But today the room was packed, and the air was humming with excited conversation. Even his most dedicated slackers had managed to show up on time. When they saw him open the door, all thirty-eight pairs of eyes turned in his direction.

"Mr. McClintock! Is it true? Did you know?"

"Man, why didn't you tell us?"

"Oh, my God. I can't believe it."

There was no making sense of the chaos of voices. But, even without names or details, his internal sensors began to send off alarm signals. He knew his students— and he knew the list of things that could get them this stirred up was very short.

Video games, drugs, money, sex and celebrities— that was about it. And it was pretty clear that there was only one intersection between that list and Mr. McClintock's Deadly Dull Criminology class.

Celebrities. Or rather *celebrity,* singular.

Lara Lynmore.

Ignoring the buzz of questions, he put his briefcase beside the podium and propped himself against the edge of the desk. He never lectured from the chair. He never lectured, period. His goal was to force them to debate and discuss. If he couldn't get them to argue, he couldn't get them to think. These kids, he'd discovered, had lots of opinions, but very few thoughts.

He gazed calmly at them until they subsided.

"Okay," he said. "Let's see if you can formulate coherent questions. So far all I have is, why didn't I tell you something about something that you can't believe is true."

Rob Overton, who always sat in the back of the room, hoping Bryce wouldn't call on him, spoke first. "We just heard that Lara Lynmore is here. Like, *here.*" He jabbed his forefingers down toward the carpet to emphasize his point. "Like, at this *school.*"

Bryce scanned the rows of heads, all nodding in agreement. "And where did you hear that?"

"My little brother Cullen told *me,*" Rob said. He waved toward the other students. "I told *them.*"

Bryce raised one eyebrow. "And your little brother Cullen would know this because…"

"Because he *knows.* I hear you, you're thinking Cullen's just a kid, he's still in high school. But he's, like, got a thing for Lara Lynmore, so he knows everything about her. He says he's seen her."

"Seen her where?"

"Around. On campus. At the bookstore. He says she dresses down, just jeans and stuff, like a regular college kid, and she's using some other name. But he says he'd know her anywhere. I believe him. He's hooked on this chick. He talks about her in his sleep."

Everybody laughed at that. "She'd better watch out," the boy next to Rob said. "Sounds like another stalker."

It was obviously a joke, but Rob scowled darkly. "Don't be an asshole, Santiago. Cullen's no psycho. What, you never had a crush on a movie star?"

Bryce, who hadn't ever much liked Rob Overton, developed a new respect for the young man. At least he had the loyalty to stick up for his little brother. After what had happened to Lara's first stalker, no one wanted to be labeled Stalker Number Two.

But damn it, the students really did know. Clearly it was only a matter of time now before Lara's secret was out everywhere. Even so, Bryce was oddly reluctant to be the one to confirm it.

"Okay, enough," he said, casting a quelling glance Rob's way to stop the quarrel from getting out of hand. "Seems to me that if the lady really is here, it's pretty clear she doesn't want to be hassled. We all know what she's been through lately. Let's cut her some slack. You don't want her to think that people in Heyday are all a bunch of drooling rubes and autograph hounds, do you?"

"Of course we do not," Ilsa said earnestly. He could have predicted her support. Ilsa, who sat in the front row, had been campaigning since the first day for the position of Teacher's Pet. He could have told her Saturn was made of sauerkraut, and she would have eagerly agreed.

If she hadn't been so gorgeous, the other kids would have hated her, would have turned her heavy accent and her "yes, Master" attitude into the class joke. But as it was, even the most cynical males in the room lay down and began to purr when she walked by.

"Yeah, but come on, Mr. McClintock," Rob insisted. "Give us some details. You had to know she was here."

Bryce stifled a sigh. This kid's persistence might serve him well one day, if he could learn to channel it into more productive areas.

"You gotta tell us. Is she here because of you?" Rob grinned. "It's a helluva coincidence. You like save her life in Hollywood, and suddenly she shows up here, right where you're teaching?"

Bryce eyed the boy coolly. "I think you have a fallacy in your argument, Mr. Overton," he said.

Rob flushed, his cocky grin quickly turning to a frown. He liked to poke fun at other people, but he didn't much enjoy being the poke-ee. "You mean the part about the coincidence? That's not a fallacy. You already taught us that coincidences are suspicious and should always be given a second look."

"No," Bryce said. "I mean the part about how I 'gotta' tell you anything."

Ilsa giggled, as she dutifully did at all Bryce's jokes. For once, though, he was glad. Because rather than risk looking foolish in front of the Swedish centerfold, Rob Overton finally shut up.

Class that day was a failure. He kept them quiet, but nothing could keep them focused. He was glad when the clock on the wall finally crawled its way to three o'clock.

As they noisily shuffled out, he shoved their papers into his briefcase without bothering to arrange them in any logical order. They would all be junk, anyhow. He might as well toss them in the trash on the way out.

"Mr. McClintock?"

He looked up to find Harry Wooten standing by the desk. "Hey, Harry," he said. "What's up?"

"I—" The young man cleared his throat. "It's about Lara Lynmore."

Bryce waited. He was surprised. He wouldn't have thought that the already overburdened Harry would have time to indulge in celebrity fantasies. He worked hard in class, and for the past two weeks he'd been working hard at the frat house, too.

Harry shuffled from one foot to the other, obviously miserable. "I really hate to do this, Mr. McClintock. But I need to ask you another favor."

As she ambled down Hippodrome Circle after her Friday-morning class, Lara caught a glimpse of the clock in front of the bank. Was it really almost noon? She ought to get back to the ranch.

But saying that didn't make her walk any faster. She was uncomfortably aware that her mother was probably still up in her bedroom pouting. They'd had a nasty row last night, and Karla in a snit was something to be avoided at all costs.

It was their third serious quarrel since her mother had arrived only two weeks ago. The first had started the minute Karla set foot in the ranch house. It seemed she was mortally offended that Lara had sent Oscar to pick her up at the airport instead of skipping class to do it herself.

It had taken all Lara's patience to smooth that episode over. But that had been just the beginning. Nothing in Heyday, it seemed, pleased her mother. Karla hated Lazy Gables because it was remote and rundown. She disliked Oscar because he was intrusive and impertinent. She complained about the damp, chilly weather, the homemade food, the rinky-dink stores and, of course, the ridiculous zebras everywhere.

She had brought a briefcase full of scripts with her, and when Lara refused to read them, they'd had their second quarrel. Even two days of the silent treatment hadn't changed Lara's mind, and eventually Karla gave up. Instead of badgering Lara outright, she sat around reading the scripts herself, laughing out loud heartily, or gasping with emotion to try to pique Lara's curiosity.

But the worst quarrel of all had started last night, when Lara had overheard her mother talking long-distance to Lara's agent, assuring the woman that Lara would be back in Hollywood very soon. "She's stubborn, but believe me, no one could stay in this absurd place very long," Karla had said. "It's like being buried alive."

Lara had lost her temper then, and the ensuing argument had been ugly. At the end, Karla had, as usual, retreated in huffy indignation to her bedroom and shut the door, refusing even to come down for dinner.

She was still up there when Lara left for class this morning, though Lara could tell that she had been downstairs in the night. The plate of spaghetti Lara had left in the refrigerator was gone. So she had left another plate of fruit and muffins, along with a note explaining that she'd probably be back in time for a late lunch.

She glanced at the big black-and-white striped clock again. If she planned to make good on that promise, she ought to get going pretty soon. But still she dawdled, window-shopping and appreciating the crisp, clear morning.

Postponing the inevitable.

Besides, she liked downtown Heyday. It wasn't big, but it was charmingly eccentric, with elegant antique stores rubbing shoulders with the tackiest souvenir stands she'd ever seen. An authentic French bistro mingled its delicious aromas with the Circus Corn Dog Stand two doors down. Breathtaking handmade quilts decorated the window of Heyday Heirlooms, while the next window exhibited twenty-seven different zebra T-shirts.

She paused in front of Valley Treasures, an antique store she'd discovered the first time she allowed herself to come into town. They had the most beautifully crafted furniture, glittering chandeliers, fine porcelain figurines and silver candelabra. She had spent many happy hours in there, fantasizing about how she might decorate Lazy Gables if it actually belonged to her.

Not that she'd dare admit that to her mother. Karla

would probably go into cardiac arrest if she knew such thoughts ever entered Lara's mind.

Suddenly, just as she was falling in love with an inlaid-rosewood music chest, she heard, right behind her, the two-toned, high-pitched bleat of a car alarm. She tensed, turning around to see what on earth had happened—did tranquil little Heyday actually have crime?

But she should have known better. It was only a young mother standing in front of a gleaming white, brand-new minivan, struggling with her many packages, which were falling everywhere, her baby stroller, which teetered at the edge of the curb, and a set of car keys that were apparently completely unfamiliar to her.

"Damn, damn, damn," the woman said, aiming the keys at the minivan and pressing buttons wildly. Suddenly the keys dropped onto the sidewalk, and, though she tried to reach them, she couldn't do so without letting go of the precariously perched stroller.

Lara smiled. She recognized that voice, even though she hadn't at first glance recognized the trim outline. The last time Lara had seen this woman, she'd been nine and a half months pregnant.

"Claire," Lara called loudly, hurrying over. "Let me help!"

Claire turned around, her pretty face scrunched up against the blasting noise. "I have no idea what I did wrong," she yelled.

Lara knew. She retrieved the keys, pressed the panic button, and suddenly peace was restored to the bright blue morning. Only the slight reverberation in Lara's ears remained.

"Oh, my God, you are a lifesaver." Claire put her hand over her heart, as if to quiet its beating. "Just for future reference, Lara, a person should never, ever get a new baby and a new car at the same time."

Lara peeked down at the rumpled bundle of knitted blankets in the stroller. "Is there really a baby hiding in there?"

Claire smiled. "Yep. And when she wakes up and starts screaming, you'll think that car alarm was pure Mozart."

She bent down and gently brushed one of the blankets aside. To Lara's delight, a sweet, miniature face appeared, half swallowed by the pink flowered cap on her head. The baby was soundly asleep, her impossibly tiny rosebud lips moving softly in and out.

"Meet Stephanie McClintock, who was born sixteen days ago. Remember the day we met you out by the river? I went into labor on the way home. I told Kieran you must be good luck."

Lara doubted that, unless she had startled Claire into labor by tumbling out of the tree and falling at her feet.

"Oh, she's beautiful!" She gave Claire a grin. "But how on earth did she manage to sleep through the car alarm?"

Claire tucked the blanket back in place, protecting the fragile infant from the cold. "Oh, she'll sleep through anything as long as she's in the stroller. It's when I try to put her into that car seat—or into her crib—that all hell breaks loose."

Lara laughed softly. "That sounds problematic."

"It is." Claire looked down at her slumbering daughter, then eyed the minivan without enthusiasm and sighed. "To tell you the truth, I'm just not ready to face it yet. Are you busy? Want to go into the Big Top and get a cup of hot tea? I'd love to talk for a while."

Lara thought of her mother at home, sulking. She really should go back soon and do some damage control. But the idea of spending a little time with Claire, hearing about the baby, was just too tempting. She hadn't allowed herself to interact with very many people since she got here, for fear of being recognized.

And, though this wasn't Lara's main reason for wanting to say yes, she hadn't forgotten that Claire was Bryce's sister-in-law. It was just possible that the subject of Bryce might come up....

"I'd like that," she said.

The Big Top Diner, which had a roof shaped like a circus tent, with fat, bright orange-and-yellow stripes, was only half a block down from the antique store. Inside, it was warm and comfortable and very cute. The booths were covered in animal-patterned vinyl, and the little jukeboxes at each table twirled like merry-go-rounds.

It was fairly crowded, as they were hitting the lunch hour, but obviously Claire McClintock got red-carpet treatment. Probably, Lara thought, her husband owned this place. Lara had been in Heyday long enough now to know that the McClintock brothers had inherited darn near everything.

The waitress showed them to a quiet corner booth, roomy enough for Claire to pull the stroller right up beside her. Claire gingerly unwrapped and eased away

Stephanie's extra blanket and the flowered cap without disturbing a single hair on the baby's head.

She smiled up at the waitress. "You haven't met Stephanie, have you, Betty? This is our first outing—an exciting trip to the pediatrician—so I'm introducing her around town."

"No, but we've sure heard a lot about her." The waitress bent down to admire the oblivious infant. "Look how good she's sleeping! Bet she's a little angel, isn't she, just like her father?"

Claire opened her menu with a soft chuckle. "Sorry, Betty. Apparently sainthood skips a generation. This one's a tyrant with a will of iron and lungs like bellows. Aurora says she already reminds her of old Anderson."

"Oh, yeah?" The waitress laughed out loud. "Well, God help you, then, Claire, honey. You've got your hands full."

Claire and Lara both ordered tea, and for several minutes conversation flowed easily, with comfortable laughter about trivial topics. Though their lives and circumstances were obviously quite different, the two of them hit it off well. Lara felt she might have found her first real friend in Heyday.

Even if Claire had been no relation to Bryce whatsoever, Lara would have liked her. She was intelligent, modest and gentle…but Lara sensed a core of inner steel. Perhaps, she thought, not all of little Stephanie's gumption was a result of her McClintock genes.

But, even though she'd promised herself she wouldn't exploit Claire's friendly invitation, she couldn't stop herself from wishing Claire would mention Bryce. Lara hadn't seen him since the night they went to Absolutely Nowhere.

It was ridiculously difficult to know he was right here, in the same town, and not seek him out. For a couple of days she had driven a much longer route from the ranch to the campus, just because it went by the fraternity house where she'd heard he was living. But she never saw him. Once, a young man had been dragging a roll of old carpet down the front porch steps, and her heart had nearly stopped. But the man had red hair, ten extra pounds, and a soft, freckled face. It definitely hadn't been Bryce.

After that, she had taken the direct route. She was a grown woman with a life to live, not a teenager with an unrequited crush. Driving by his house…God, what would be next? Asking his friends…or his sister-in-law…about him? *Did he mention my name? Do you think he likes me?*

Never. She had too much self-respect. So every time she felt herself about to bring up his name, she lifted her cup and swallowed the words along with some tea.

Eventually, though, it became clear that Claire had something on her mind, too. It was obviously time to go, but Claire was stalling. Their cups of tea were nearly empty, and yet Claire stirred the dregs around, a thoughtful look on her face.

The baby wriggled and made a restive mew. Claire put her hand down and stroked the feathery curls, cupping her palm over the little round head. Stephanie subsided immediately.

"You know, I'm actually very glad I ran into you,"

Claire said, looking over at Lara with a serious gaze. "I wanted to let you know what I've been hearing."

Lara took a sip of lukewarm tea. "About what?"

"About you. I don't know if you realize this, but I don't think your identity is much of a secret anymore. Lots of people seem to know, and word is spreading fast." She bit her lower lip. "I'm not sure how they found out. Please believe me—Kieran and I haven't said a word to anyone."

"No, of course you haven't," Lara said. "I wouldn't have imagined that for a moment."

But she knew who probably had. Her stomach tightened, partly from nerves, partly from pure annoyance. Surely it wasn't a coincidence that, just about the time her mother arrived in Heyday, the secret started leaking out.

She tried to force her muscles to relax. As she'd told herself the day she met Claire and Kieran, this had been inevitable. She couldn't remain anonymous forever. She didn't even really want to. She wasn't ashamed of her past—she was just determined to leave it behind and move on.

"Kieran and I have been urging everyone to avoid pestering you. Heyday is a pretty laid-back town, and I don't think you'll have too much trouble. But of course, there will be some people who can't resist."

"That's okay," Lara said. "Giving a few autographs, having a few pictures taken with somebody's uncle…well, that's actually kind of fun, in moderation. Thanks for the warning, but I'll be fine."

"Good." Claire smiled and sat up straighter. "Now…

I probably don't have any business bringing this up, but I'm going to stick my neck out anyhow. It's about Bryce—"

Lara opened her purse and rummaged for her wallet, avoiding Claire's gaze. "What about him?"

"Well, you're here. And he's here. And after what happened in California…" She folded her hands on the table in front of her. "I can't help wondering if there's something—if you might be—" She stopped. "Oh, blast. This really *isn't* any of my business, is it?"

Lara took a breath and put her purse on the booth next to her. "Are you asking me if I am in love with Bryce?"

For the first time Claire looked truly uncomfortable, and Lara could see that she hadn't expected her to be so blunt.

"No," she said finally, her cheeks tinged with pink. "I don't know you well enough to ask anything so personal. And, even if I did, I still wouldn't ask. I just noticed how you reacted to the idea of coming to dinner with him and—"

"Honestly, that didn't mean any—"

"I understand," Claire said. "I just wondered if you might have heard about his past. People love to talk about what happened to Bryce the last time he was in Heyday. But about ninety percent of what you hear about the McClintocks is pure myth."

"So I've gathered."

"I thought maybe, if I told you the whole story, the true story, it might help you to—understand him."

Lara, who had been ready to brush it off, looked into

the other woman's worried face, and found that she could not. Claire was such a kind person, and somehow Lara felt closer to her than she would have imagined possible in such a short time.

Somewhere in the past, Claire had known pain—it could be read in the shadows that lay at the corners of her present happiness. Perhaps, Lara thought, the road Claire had taken to this new bliss as Mrs. McClintock had been a difficult one. Perhaps she merely hoped to spare Lara the same fate.

"I already know that he's complex," Lara said quietly. "I know he's not going to be an easy man for any woman to love. Although I suspect that many women have, and still do."

"Right on all counts." Claire smiled a little. "There's nothing easy about Bryce. Around here they call him The Sinner. Partly because he has that sardonic manner and that…incredible sex appeal. But mostly because…well, you see, when he was only eighteen, he—"

"Don't." Lara reached across the table and touched Claire's hand. "I know you mean well. I know you want to keep me from getting hurt. But whatever is—or isn't—going on between Bryce and me, we're going to have to sort it out ourselves."

"Of course. It's just that this thing that happened, it was so unfair, and he—"

"Please. Don't tell me," Lara said. "It's not that I don't want to know, Claire. It's just that… It may be stupidly idealistic, especially given how things stand between us, but I would like very much for Bryce to be the one to tell me."

BRYCE HADN'T SEEN Lazy Gables Ranch since he was a teenager. Determined that his sons would become perfect Virginia gentlemen, Anderson used to make them take riding lessons here every summer. Bryce, who had lived in Chicago with his mother since he was four, had no intention of training to be any kind of Virginian, so he'd usually ditched the lessons and wandered the nearby trails alone on foot.

He had forgotten—or maybe, in his adolescent snit, never even recognized—what an unaffected charm the old house had. The front looked a little like a friendly face. The long white porch sagged in the middle, creating a goofy smile effect, above which two tilted gables sat like eyes.

He parked his car off to the side, under the maple tree, which in summer, he remembered, was tall and broad enough to spread shade over the entire house. He heard horses whinnying from the stables, and for a minute he was seventeen again, wishing like hell he could escape from this place.

The errand that had brought him here today was even more disagreeable than those dreaded long-ago riding lessons.

He had come to ask Lara Gilbert for a favor.

Just his luck, when the door swung open in response to his knock, the person standing on the other side was Oscar Allred, the man who had been Lazy Gables' caretaker and riding instructor for the past thirty years.

"Hi, Oscar," Bryce said in his most polite voice. "You probably don't remember me. Bryce McClintock."

"Oh, yeah," Oscar said without expression. "I remember you."

Bryce managed not to sigh. That didn't sound good. Was this another overdue apology? Had Oscar perhaps taken it personally when the teenage Bryce had played hooky from riding lessons?

Oh, hell—it was more than that. Bryce suddenly remembered the whole, ridiculous story. The summer he was seventeen, he had coaxed pretty Mary Shimmler into meeting him by the river to go skinny-dipping. Oscar, who had been expecting Bryce for his riding lesson, had come looking for him in the woods. And found him.

Oscar had been toting a pellet gun at the time. He'd pointed it at Bryce just as he was about to shed his jeans.

"Think carefully, son," he'd said. "Whatever I see, I shoot."

Mary, who was only sixteen at the time, had fled in tears. Oscar had just stood there silently, pellet gun in hand, while Bryce put back on his shirt and shoes.

Bryce had been furious. Mary Shimmler had been his number-one choice that summer. She had a body like Barbie and a mind like Jell-O—the perfect combination, Bryce had believed at the time. After that day, he had simply refused to go to the ranch for lessons at all.

"So." Oscar gave him a cool once-over. "You here to see Lara?"

"Yes." Bryce smiled. "That is, unless you've still got that pellet gun."

Oscar's eyes tilted a little, and his lips twitched, but overall he was great at maintaining that rugged poker face. "Lara is a grown woman with the sense to kick your ass if she has to. Mary Shimmler was fifteen, and a fool."

"Sixteen," Bryce corrected automatically. He could hardly believe that Oscar remembered Mary's name.

"Whatever. She was dumber than a gnat. Her daddy was a friend of mine." He opened the door. "I'll get Lara."

Bryce stepped inside, into a front foyer that was as gleaming white as the exterior of the house. Someone had bought cut flowers from a greenhouse and put them in a big milk-glass pitcher on a wooden table, bringing a touch of spring to this winter morning. On the coat rack he noticed the brown woolen coat Lara had worn the other night, and a green scarf he'd never seen before.

And on one of the hall chairs, a pile of what clearly were movie scripts.

Suddenly he heard light footsteps on the staircase, which dominated the entryway. He looked up, and there she was.

He wondered if she knew how beautiful she looked, with her hair falling free like this. Without makeup, her face was a pure, pale oval in which her dark eyes were like sparkling gemstones. She wore an oversize blue sweater that drooped over one bare shoulder, and a long, full, flowered skirt. Her feet peeked out as she hurried down the stairs, and he found it absurdly endearing to see that she wore wildly mismatched socks.

She didn't look surprised to see him. Naturally Oscar would have told her who was waiting. Instead, she looked wary, as if she couldn't imagine what he wanted, but didn't dare speculate, for fear she might get it wrong.

"Bryce." That was all she said. She stood on the bottom step, her hand on the newel post, and waited.

"Hi, Lara." He didn't waste any words, either. He was determined to get straight to the point. "I'm sorry to show up unannounced like this, but I need to ask a favor."

"All right," she said without hesitation. "Whatever you need."

"Don't you think you ought to hear what the favor is first?"

"No." She shook her head, and a long curl slid over the bare skin of her shoulder. "You saved my life, remember? If there's anything I can do for you, *anything,* I'll do it."

"The favor isn't for me." But as soon as he said it, he wished he hadn't been so curt. A shadow passed over her pale face, as if his words had been a rejection of her offer. To be honest, she hadn't imagined that. He hated the idea that she considered herself in his debt. He'd just been doing his job, that was all. He hated even more the implication that he might ever collect on that debt.

"All right, then." She straightened her shoulders. "Who is it for?"

"A student of mine. Harry Wooten. He's a good guy, but he's having a tough time. His ten-year-old daughter was badly burned in a car crash last year. She's having skin grafts, and she's in a lot of pain. It's tearing Harry up."

"I'm so sorry," she said, and he could tell that she was. Or he thought he could tell…he had to keep reminding himself that she was an actress.

"What can I do to help? Does he need money? Or—" Her eyes suddenly brightened. "Did you think music therapy might be a good idea? It is an excellent pain management tool. I'd be glad to do whatever I could, or I could find someone from the school, someone with more training."

"No," he said. "Nothing like that. It's actually a lot simpler. Apparently Terri, that's his daughter, is a big fan of *The Highwayman*. She heard you're in town, and she's begging Harry to help her find a way to meet you."

She didn't respond for a few seconds. But then, slowly, she nodded. "I see. Of course. Well, I'd be glad to go visit her whenever you'd like. Maybe you wouldn't mind taking me there—to make the introductions a little less awkward?"

He would mind. He knew that the less time he spent with Lara, the better it would be for both of them. She might start getting ideas.

Or he might.

Hell, he already was getting ideas. He was having difficulty keeping his eyes off that bare, ivory shoulder. Good thing it was winter. If she'd come down those stairs in a bikini, he probably would have jumped her like a hungry wolf.

But how could he refuse such a reasonable request

without revealing just how susceptible he was to her charms?

"Sure. I'll drive you over. It's not far. Nothing's too far from anything else in Heyday." He put his hand on the doorknob. "Just let me know when it's convenient."

She smiled. "Well, I'd go right now, except I'm not really dressed to impress." She lifted her skirt and wiggled her toes, showing off her crazy socks. "She probably wouldn't even believe I *am* Lara Lynmore, if she saw me like this."

He kept his mouth shut. Lara knew she'd still look fantastic even if she dressed in sackcloth and ashes. In fact, there had been a moment toward the end of *The Highwayman,* just before her famous death scene, when Bess had been roughed up, then tied up, in her dirty, torn nightgown—and still she'd looked brave and beautiful and sexy as hell. The studio had chosen that shot for the poster.

Yeah, she knew. No need to feed her ego by telling her so one more time.

She seemed to think a moment, as if consulting some internal calendar. She ran her hand through her hair, and the gesture exposed her pale swan throat. He averted his eyes and clenched his jaw.

"Would tomorrow be okay? Maybe about three?"

"Three's fine. I'll see you then." He didn't wait for an answer. He pulled open the door and left quickly, like a man escaping from underwater. He breathed deeply. Cold air was good.

A cold shower would be even better.

CHAPTER EIGHT

WHEN LARA FIRST MET Terri Wooten, she was heart-broken at the sight of the little girl's bandaged feet and scarred legs. But after only fifteen minutes together, Lara had almost forgotten that the child had any problems at all, caught up in her lively mind and silly sense of humor. After an hour together, Lara was wishing she could stay all afternoon.

It had been great fun. First they'd had a soft drink and a piece of pizza with Bryce, and Terri's mom and dad. Then, because the afternoon was mild, Lara had rolled Terri's wheelchair out into the backyard, where they shared a lot of ridiculous girl talk. Eventually, Lara lifted Terri onto the swing set, where her painful feet didn't get in her way, and the two of them spent nearly half an hour just swinging and laughing and singing every song they both knew, from "Twist and Shout" to "100 Bottles of Beer on the Wall."

After a little while, Bryce and Harry wandered out, finally finished with the plans they'd been reviewing for the fraternity house renovations.

When Bryce offered to take a picture of the two of them, Terri was ecstatic. She fluffed her hair and rubbed some dirt from her cheek, and insisted that they pose as they were, side by side on the swing set. She didn't want her wheelchair anywhere in sight.

Finally, though, their time ran out. Terri's mom came out—and apparently the little girl knew what that meant. She had to go to physical therapy. Lara's heart tightened as she watched the light die in Terri's face, replaced by a grim and stoic dread.

The tragic expression haunted Lara as Bryce drove her home. On the way over to the Wootens' house, they had talked almost comfortably, with Bryce filling her in on what he knew about the little family. But now the car was thick with silence. If only there were something more she could do. A picture of herself with a former movie star wouldn't make Terri's pain go away.

"You know, you were great with her," Bryce said suddenly. "You really do have a way with kids."

She looked over at him, wondering why he sounded so surprised. Hadn't she told him that was one of the reasons she'd picked music therapy as a career? But of course…he hadn't believed a word she'd said that night.

"I've always liked children," she said. "They are very honest. Sometimes that's rare. Especially in Hollywood."

He laughed shortly. "Not just in Hollywood."

"No. Of course not."

They fell back into another silence. The drive hadn't been anywhere nearly long enough, she realized. They were already almost back to Lazy Gables. They had just passed through the gates at the low end of the pasture. Just a mile or so remained, uphill toward the house and stables, past low white fences and tall, frosty trees back-lit by a peach-colored sunset.

Their temporary alliance was at an end. She had given him what he needed. She wondered if, once he dropped her off today, he would ever voluntarily drive through these gates again.

"Well, I want to thank you for doing this," he said in a crisp voice, as if he, too, realized they were almost out of time and felt the need to tie up loose ends courteously. "It obviously meant a lot to her."

"No need to thank me," she said, equally polite. "I enjoyed it." In spite of her wistfulness, she smiled just a little, thinking back on the conversation she'd had with Terri. "Besides, it's good to be reminded now and then just how unimportant you really are in the grand scheme of things."

He flicked a glance her way. "In Terri Wooten's eyes, I'd say you're pretty high on the totem pole."

"Then you'd be wrong," she said, letting her smile deepen. "In Terri Wooten's eyes, I'm no big deal at all. In spite of what you all obviously thought, she didn't want to meet me because she worships the ground I walk on."

He turned to her with a quizzical smile. "No? Then why *did* she want to meet you? She made it sound important enough to have her father prepared to sell a kidney to make it happen."

Lara began to laugh. "It's simple. She wanted to meet me because she's crazy in love with Tony."

"Tony?" Bryce frowned, clearly drawing a blank. The ranch was in sight. He pulled off to the left, between the stables and the main house, and put the car in park. "Who's Tony?"

"My co-star? The dashing highwayman? Remember him?"

"Oh, hell. *That* foppish dweeb?"

She'd known he'd say something like that. To her knowledge, Bryce had seen *The Highwayman* only once, when he guarded Lara through the Hollywood premiere, but she suspected he'd always remember Tony and his ridiculous wig and mustache and his puny little musket.

In spite of the fact that pretty-boy Tony was clearly a bit short on testosterone, Lara had seen how it annoyed Bryce every time Tony/The Highwayman took Lara/Bess in his arms and kissed her. The sight of Bryce's stern face scowling at the screen had thrilled her that night, even more than the success of the film.

"That *foppish dweeb* is a very big deal," Lara said. "Especially with the ten-to-thirteen-year-old set. Terri has a scrapbook ten inches thick of his pictures. She made me tell her every single detail I could remember about him."

"Did you tell her about how he has his ass waxed?"

"Bryce," Lara said sternly. "I'm not even supposed to know that. You promised you'd never tell."

"And I haven't." He had begun to laugh now, too. "I just wondered how Terri took the news."

"I didn't tell her. Ten is a little young to have all your illusions shattered. I told her he was just as romantic and brave as The Highwayman himself. I promised to ask him to send her a picture."

The car faced the horse pasture, and in the distance, they could see Oscar exercising the Paso Fino. It was a scene that could have come straight from *The Highwayman*. The wind had kicked up, and the horse was racing into it, clearly loving every minute, his mane and tail streaming like trails of black smoke.

"That was very kind," Bryce said softly. Though Lara kept watching the horse, she could feel Bryce's gaze on her. He put his arm along the back of the seat. "So you honestly didn't mind that she just wanted to pump you for information about Tony?"

Finally she turned. "Of course not," she said. "I'm not completely addicted to fame, you know. Did you think that was why I agreed to see her? Because I needed an adoration fix, and I thought I could get it from a ten-year-old kid?"

He paused. Then he shook his head. "No, I didn't think that."

"Good." She bent over to gather up her scarf and gloves. It had been warm in the car, but now she was going to have to face the late-afternoon chill. "I guess I'd better go on in. My mother will be wondering what's keeping me."

"Lara…"

He had stretched his hand out, so that the tips of his fingers were only an inch away from her shoulder. One inch.

She didn't move a muscle. "What?"

He didn't answer right away. He remained motionless, too. His long fingers didn't close the distance between them, but they didn't retreat, either. It was like a freeze frame, the two of them suspended in time, only an inch apart.

She asked again, because the tension of that inch was unbearable.

"What?"

"Nothing," he said, his voice oddly vague. "It's just—"

She waited. She held her breath. She was acutely aware of her heartbeat, which seemed to be the only part of her still moving. One inch. If she leaned his way even the slightest bit, their bodies would connect.

But she couldn't. The distance between them, even if it was only an inch, was his distance. He had put it there, and only he could take it away.

"It's just that…hell, Lara, I don't know why it matters to you what I think about your decisions. But if you wanted my respect for what you did today—for what you're trying to do with your life… I thought I should tell you. You've got it."

Respect…

Numbly she thanked him, said goodbye and climbed out of the car. *Respect?* Well, it wasn't much, but at least it was *something,* she told herself as she walked through the thick orange twilight toward the ranch house.

But it wasn't true. Respect was nothing, worse than nothing. It was cold, completely without passion. You respected your congressman, your pastor, your fifth-grade teacher and your elders.

Respect had no power to do the only thing that mattered. It could never close that final, fatal inch.

"SURELY YOU DON'T *have* to go," Karla said as she watched Lara putting together her books and papers. She hated the whining note she heard in her voice, but she didn't seem to be able to stop herself. "Surely they'd understand if you said you can't go out to play just this once."

She saw the frustration tighten Lara's features, but Lara clearly had determined not to lose her temper, so when she spoke her voice was pleasant and well-modulated.

"I'm not going out to *play,* Mom," she said. "It's a study group, and I was lucky the ladies asked me to join them. I can't stand them up on my very first meeting. Besides, I really need their help."

"Need their help?" Karla drew herself up. "That's ridiculous. You've forgotten more about music than anyone in Heyday will ever know. Did any of those women in the study group ever star in *Phantom*? The *L.A. Times* review said you were—"

"Mom, that doesn't matter here."

Lara never liked it when Karla talked about her reviews. But Karla had a scrapbook of them, all the good ones, anyhow—some of those newspapers were so snobby about *The Highwayman*. They had called it a big-budget tearjerker, and museum-quality melodrama. She hadn't kept those, but still, the scrapbook had been growing gratifyingly thick, until Lara had gotten this insane idea about going to school.

And she showed no signs of changing her mind, either. If anything, Lara seemed to get more involved with the school, and this Podunk town, every day. She was volunteering at the seniors' home, and for the past two weeks she'd been working with some new little girl on pain management.

And now study groups, for God's sake. Didn't Lara even *want* to be with her mother? Karla had been here a month now, and she'd spent maybe one week of that with Lara.

She might as well have stayed in L.A.

She realized suddenly that Lara was still talking, still explaining.

"The classes I'm taking have an academic approach to music," Lara was saying. "Theoretical. It's different. My experience is just practical, performance-related stuff."

Karla frowned. She didn't like to hear Lara run down her accomplishments. They were Karla's accomplishments, too, damn it.

"And since when," she said, her voice rising, "was practical experience considered unimportant?"

Lara opened her mouth to respond, but Oscar chose that moment to come into the kitchen. Karla made a soft, irritated noise. The man was always right where you didn't want him.

He'd been working with the horses, and he looked filthy. Still, he seemed to dominate everything, even this huge, old-fashioned kitchen. He glanced at Karla, and then at Lara. "Everything okay here?"

Karla didn't answer him. She didn't understand why he thought he had the right to inject himself into things. He was the hired help, wasn't he? And why should he take such a protective, paternal tone with Lara? He'd known her all of about two months. What was that compared to a lifetime of a mother's love?

"Everything's fine," Lara said. "I was just heading out to my study group. I'll be back in a couple of hours, and then maybe we can all three go out to dinner."

"Good. I know that last test was hard for you. Maybe they can give you some tips."

Naturally Oscar would approve. Karla stared into her cup of coffee, hiding her annoyance.

Lara shrugged into her coat, then leaned over and pecked Karla on the cheek. "Bye, Mom," she said in a conciliatory voice. But Karla held her head motionless, too hurt to respond with a kiss of her own.

Couldn't Lara see? When Lara acted like this, Karla felt as if she were the outsider, not Oscar. She wouldn't go out to dinner with the two of them if Lara begged her on bended knee. Which she wouldn't.

When Lara was gone, Oscar walked over to the sink and pulled out a mug. He ran some tap water into it, drank it all down in one long, noisy gulp, then turned to face Karla, resting his dirty backside against the countertop.

"You know, if you're always sulking and complaining, that's not going to make her want to hang around," he said. "Might just drive her away."

For a moment of near-blind fury, Karla wanted to slap him. How could he say such a thing? Those were almost exactly the same words her husband had thrown at her, all those years ago, when she had dared to complain about his late hours and unexplained absences.

"If you're just going to bitch and cry all the time," he'd said, "why should I *ever* come home?"

Karla had known what that really was—just one of his typical passive-aggressive tactics. He didn't stay away all the time because she cried. She cried because he stayed away all the time.

And, of course, the real reason he was never home was that he'd fallen in lust with a twenty-one-year-old sexpot who had a supertight body and who told him daily that he was more exciting than God.

Still, it had hurt then, and it hurt now. Karla stood up, rinsed her coffee cup in the sink and said, "Excuse me. I have some scripts to read upstairs."

Not that she could concentrate on any of them. This particular batch of scripts was fairly dreadful, a bunch of slapstick comedies. She'd have to talk to Lara's agent about filtering out the garbage.

An hour later, she was sitting at her bedroom window, which looked out onto the western pasture, still brooding. She felt a little uncomfortable about the way she'd talked to Lara just now. After all, Lara had really only invited her for a couple of weeks, and when Karla had said she wanted to stay on a while, it had been with the understanding that Lara would be extremely busy, with little time to just "hang out," and Karla would have to fend for herself.

So she really didn't have a legitimate complaint. But that didn't keep her from being lonely, did it?

Suddenly, she saw movement below. It was Oscar, striding quickly across the field toward the house. His face seemed to be covered in…was that blood?

For a cowardly instant, she considered pulling her head in and pretending she hadn't noticed. But his movements were erratic. A few yards from the house, he stumbled over a rock in the ground, as if he hadn't been able to see it. He held the palm of his hand over one eye, and his hand was bloody, too.

She glanced at her watch. Lara wasn't due for another hour. Karla was the only one in the house. She had to go downstairs and see if he needed help.

When she got to the kitchen, he was bent over the sink, as if he were trying to keep from dripping blood all over the knotty pine floors.

"What happened?" She came as close as she dared. "What can I do to help?"

In typical Oscar fashion, he answered succinctly in spite of his obvious pain. "Barbed wire. A horse was stuck. I already called the vet." He hesitated. "Can you drive a stick shift with that cast on? Do you know *how* to drive stick?"

The open doubt in his voice annoyed her. Did he think she'd been born with a chauffeured Mercedes in the driveway? Hardly. She'd been born on a farm like this and had worked damn hard to get away from it. To make sure Lara could get away from it.

But now wasn't the time to rehash all that. "Yes," she said succinctly. "The hospital?"

"No, just the doctor." He took a deep breath, as if a jolt of pain had startled him. "Center of town. Hippodrome Circle. He can take stitches."

He turned, then, and for the first time she saw up close the damage to his handsome face. A deep, jagged

gouge split the left side from forehead to lip. She somehow kept from wincing. Instead she grabbed a dish
towel and a plastic bag from under the counter and
began to fill the bag with ice. She was a mother. She
knew how to handle cuts and scrapes and broken things.

Secretly she was relieved that she was already
dressed and had put on her makeup and styled her hair.
But she knew better than to mention it. Oscar would be
so disgusted at such vanity that he'd probably insist on
driving himself to the doctor, though he wouldn't even
be able to see the road.

"Put this against your cheek," she said, holding out
the ice. "The towel is to mop up the rest of you. Now
show me where the keys are. You're losing a lot of
blood, and we shouldn't waste any time."

He looked at her for a second before digging into his
pocket and handing over a ring of keys. It was hard to
be sure, because the blood covered so much of his face,
but she thought he looked surprised, and maybe a little
impressed.

Why on earth should that please her?

"Come on," she said. Holding his arm, she led the
way down the back steps to where his truck sat in the
driveway. She loaded him in and then climbed behind
the wheel herself. She jiggled the gearshift into reverse
and, twisting her head, smoothly eased the truck into a
three-point turn.

Out of the corner of her eye, she noticed he was still
looking at her. Well, let him. She put the car into drive and
accelerated with growing confidence. It was about time
some people around here stopped underestimating her.

THE NIGHT SKY WAS as shiny and cold as black marble. Against it, the stars looked like chips of cracked ice. Bryce, standing outside the front door of the neat little Wooten house, stamped his feet and blew into his hands, hoping Harry would open up quickly. It was freezing out here.

But when the door opened, it wasn't Harry. To Bryce's complete shock, it was Lara.

"Oh," she said, clearly flustered. "Hi."

She looked down at the spaniel, who had insisted on coming along with Bryce for this errand. The fool animal had bounced and panted, as if a ten-minute ride in the car was the one thing he'd been waiting for to make his life complete.

"How cute," she said, as if glad to find some distraction. "Is he yours?"

"No." But the dog sat smugly at Bryce's left leg and grinned up at Lara, as if to say, *don't listen to him.* "He's just a stray mutt who hangs out at the frat house. Why are you answering Harry's door?"

She seemed to be recovering her composure. She tilted her head and reached out to let the dog sniff her hand. "You rang the doorbell, remember?"

He didn't think that was funny, although the dog was thumping his tail in enthusiastic applause. "I mean why *you?* Why not Harry?"

"I'm baby-sitting," she said. "I stay with Terri twice a week now, so that Harry and Jan can spend a little time together."

He didn't answer right away. He couldn't think of anything rational to say. Lara was the Wootens' new baby-sitter? And he was standing at her door, with his pet dog at his side. It was like entering an upside-down universe. Did something in the Heyday water turn you immediately into Stepford people?

He remembered her at the *Highwayman* premiere party, with her beaded, backless tangerine gown, her eyes sultry and her skin sparkling with some spray-on crap he had told her was ridiculous, but which, under the dance floor lights had looked shockingly sexy.

Could this really be the same woman? The Lara at the door looked very young, very sweet, in her loose, cream-colored corduroy jeans and her tight, chocolate turtleneck sweater. She actually could have been a baby-sitter—if baby-sitters were made in heaven.

The dog certainly thought she was. He was lapping at her fingers now, as blissfully as if she'd dipped them in honey.

"They'll be back about midnight," she said. "If you really need to see Harry."

"No, no, that's okay. I was just going to drop off a key to the frat house. He's doing some work tomorrow while I'm in class." He put his hand in his pocket. "Maybe you could just give it to him."

"Of course. I'd be glad to." She was poised now, but extremely restrained. This was awkward. By being very careful, they had managed not to encounter one another for almost two weeks, since the day he introduced her to Terri Wooten.

She must have made quite a hit that day, and not just with Terri. With Jan, too. Harry had told Bryce that since Terri's accident, Jan hadn't been willing to trust any baby-sitter to take care of her. It was making a mess of their marriage.

Not that Bryce had wanted to know those personal details. But it was amazing how much students revealed to their teachers. And with Harry working around the frat house these days, things just naturally got said.

"Lara?" A little voice from somewhere inside the house called out pitifully. "Lara, who are you talking to? It sounds like Mr. McClintock."

Lara tossed him an apologetic smile. "It is," she called back. "But you're supposed to be asleep."

"Can't he come in and tell me a story? I can't sleep yet. The aspirin isn't working."

Lara looked at Bryce. "She talks about your stories all the time," she said. "Apparently they're very exciting, all that FBI blood and danger. She tried to get me to tell her one tonight, but apparently mine are too girly."

Bryce chuckled. "What a little manipulator. I've told her exactly two stories, a couple of times when her dad brought her over while he worked. It's not exactly a regular routine."

Lara shrugged. "Want me to say you don't have time tonight?"

But Bryce knew when he was cornered. Fortunately, he liked Terri a lot. She had an amazing amount of spunk—even if she was spoiled rotten.

"No," he said. "I don't mind, if it's okay with you." He hesitated. "Unless...did her parents say you couldn't have any boys over while they were gone?"

"No," she said, biting back a smile as she moved

aside to open the door wider. "They just said I shouldn't talk on the phone too much. Come on in."

SHE LEFT HIM in Terri's little bedroom, which was the wildest mix of Jan's pink-lace efforts to create the perfect little-girl's room and Terri's own taste, which ran to female superheroes and Japanimation.

Terri lay in bed, deceptively demure under her pink-eyelet covers, smiling at him sweetly, pretending to be a saint. Bryce had pulled up a chair, carefully avoiding all the paraphernalia of sickness strewn around the room. "Okay, hotshot, one story," he'd said. "And then you sleep."

Lara went back into the living room to straighten up her books and papers, which she'd been studying when Bryce arrived. She hoped it was a very long story. She needed time to straighten up her own psyche, too. Seeing him like that had rattled her more than it should have.

She was putting away Terri's toys when the dog started growling. Bryce had insisted that the poor thing sit on the porch and wait for him to return. The dog had obeyed without balking, simply lying down with disappointed resignation. Lara had smiled inwardly. Bryce might say the dog didn't belong to him, but the animal obviously saw things differently.

He'd been perfectly quiet this whole time. She peeked through the curtains, though she suspected she was overreacting. Still, she felt a prickle of anxiety, wondering what could be making the friendly dog sound so hostile.

The dog was standing now, and he'd ducked his head

low between his forelegs, shoving his muzzle forward. The growl was loud, low in his throat, and the message was clear. *Keep away.*

Lara knew she had locked the door behind Bryce, but she checked it again, anyway. It was nothing, she assured herself, nothing but the memory of Kenny Boggs haunting her, making her start at her own shadow. Dogs barked at innocent things all the time. Squirrels, rabbits, the neighbors' dogs...

Here in Heyday, nothing terrible ever happened. Wasn't that the main reason she'd picked this quaint little town? Still, she looked through the slit in the drapes and wondered when she'd ever stop being afraid.

Suddenly the dog erupted into a machine-gun barking. Lara instinctively backed away from the window, her heart pounding.

In an instant, Bryce was there. He went straight for the door. "Stay here," he said, his voice curt, professional. She remembered that voice. "Lock the door behind me."

When the dog saw Bryce, he stopped barking instantly. Bryce clicked his fingers, and together the two of them climbed down the porch steps and disappeared into the side yard.

Then there was only silence. Lara went to Terri's room, thinking the little girl might need reassuring. But Terri really was asleep this time, and Bryce had turned off the bedside lamp. So Lara went back into the living room and perched on the edge of the sofa, waiting.

Bryce was gone almost five minutes. A very long five minutes.

But finally she heard his knock on the door—the

code knock they'd developed back when he worked for her. The code that meant everything was fine.

She unlocked the door and let him in. She watched his muscular virility take over the modest little room and thought how comforting it was just to be near him. He radiated strength and power. She had known, from the moment she met him, that he wouldn't let Kenny Boggs—or anyone else—hurt her.

"Did you see anything?" She realized that the dog had come in with him this time. He nudged Bryce's hand with his nose, and Bryce automatically stroked his head and tugged one ear gently.

"Yes," Bryce said. "I saw a high school kid named Cullen Overton. I'd already heard about Cullen. His older brother is in my class. The word is that Cullen has a major crush on you."

She sat back down on the couch. "Oh, dear," she said. Once, she had thought these crushes were cute, even flattering. But that was before she knew how deadly they could be.

"I don't think this guy's a problem," Bryce said. "He's your typical seventeen-year-old small-town jock. Lots of talk, lots of strutting around, but basically he's just noise. His big worry was whether I was going to tell his mom and dad."

She wished that she'd seen the boy. She wished she knew what he looked like. Right now, in her mind, every fan wore Kenny Boggs's avid, hungry face.

"Are you going to tell them?"

"Hell, yes." Bryce looked grim. "They need to rein

that kid in. He's old enough to know better than to come skulking around in the dark, trying to sneak a peek through the curtains."

She looked over at the window. The drapes were still open an inch, from when she had been standing there, trying to see through the darkness. In spite of her best efforts, she shivered.

He must have noticed. He went first to the window and straightened the fabric so that the ends of the drapes met and overlapped. Then he came to the sofa and put his hands on her shoulders.

"It's okay," he said. "I'll stay until Harry and Jan get home."

She looked up at him. "You don't have to do that," she said. "I can—"

But then she shook her head. "Thank you," she said softly. "I'd appreciate that."

He took his hands away then and sat on the adjoining chair, ignoring the fact that the rest of the sofa was available. The dog saw his chance and jumped up beside her and laid his head in her lap. The warmth of his body felt comforting, and she reached down to kiss the dome of his head.

When she sat back up, her eyes were filled with tears. She blinked, trying to make them go away. She did not want to look weak in front of Bryce.

More than that. She didn't want to *be* weak.

Bryce was watching her, though, and obviously she wasn't fooling him.

"This isn't another Kenny Boggs, Lara," he said roughly. "Believe me. I can tell the difference."

She took a shaking breath. "But I can't," she said. Her voice sounded strange and thin. "That's the terrifying part. I can't."

CHAPTER NINE

WHEN BRYCE ENTERED the front office of Valley Pride Property Management Inc., Elton Fletcher jumped up like a private who has just spotted a five-star general.

"Mr. McClintock!" He checked his tie, then his hair, neither of which needed any attention. The man was always as spiffy as a plastic G.I. Joe action figure. "I didn't expect to see you here!"

Of course he didn't. Bryce had made it clear that he had no intention of opening an office and holding court, side by side with Kieran, like twin feudal overlords. He had inherited the properties, he couldn't help that. But he damn sure wasn't going to sit here and grant audiences to petitioners who wanted their rents forgiven or their sewers cleaned.

In fact, he'd stayed so far away from it that he'd been surprised when he saw the large, beautifully renovated building, which used to be called simply McClintock Incorporated. Apparently Kieran, who as favorite son had inherited the business, had changed the name. Maybe he, too, was a little squeamish at the antiquated notion of "owning" a town.

Old Anderson, of course, had relished it.

"I'm just here to see my brother," Bryce said. "Is he in?"

"Oh, yes, of course," Elton said. He hesitated, clearly unsure what to do. He must have heard that the relationship between the two McClintock boys wasn't exactly overflowing with fraternal camaraderie. A brother should be able to walk in unannounced. But an estranged brother…a brother like Bryce…

Bryce took pity on him. "Why don't you buzz in and let him know I'm here?"

"Yes. I'll do that." Elton picked up a telephone, murmured something and then smiled up at Bryce with undisguised relief. "His secretary will be out to show you the way."

Within seconds, the reigning Miss America opened the door to the back offices and gave Bryce a stunning smile. "Mr. McClintock? Mr. McClintock is waiting for you. I'm Darlene. If you'll follow me?"

In spite of her amazing looks, Darlene was the perfect professional. She hadn't even stumbled on the double McClintocks. Bryce was happy to follow her, enjoying the view and chuckling inwardly. First Ilsa, now Darlene. His baby brother practically had a harem. Bryce wondered what Claire thought of all these busty, subservient beauties waiting on her husband hand and foot.

They went down three thickly carpeted corridors, with Darlene making pleasant noises about the weather, which they both agreed was not too bad, for winter. Finally they reached the inner sanctum, the corner office. The office that had once belonged to Anderson.

Kieran was already standing at the door, with a cautious smile on his face. Bryce wasn't surprised by the caution. The past four invitations to dinner with St. and Mrs. Kieran had been politely declined. Bryce hadn't even been by to see the baby, though, because he did like Claire, he had sent pink roses and something the baby store had suggested over the phone, he forgot exactly what. *Fine, whatever,* he'd said. *Just send it.*

"Hi, Bryce," Kieran said evenly. "It's good to see you." He turned to Darlene. "If you could just take care of the Richardson documents, Darlene, then that should be it for today."

Nodding, Darlene withdrew smoothly, making almost no noise even when she closed her door, and leaving only the faint scent of very expensive perfume in the warm corridor. She was like a cross between a secretary and a geisha, Bryce thought cynically. Ilsa, on the other hand, was a cross between a housekeeper and a sex toy.

He wondered if he might have to rethink the whole "St. Kieran" thing.

Kieran brought him into the office and shut the door. Bryce took a chair, but Kieran propped his hip against the edge of his desk, a habit Bryce recognized as one of his own.

"It's good to see you," Kieran said again, "but frankly it's something of a surprise. What's up?"

"I need some information. I've been asking around about a boy in town. I hear he's on the football team. Since you're his coach, I hoped you might be able to tell me what kind of kid he is."

"What's his name?"

"Cullen Overton."

"Cullen?" Kieran looked surprised. "He's a good quarterback, kind of cocky, not brilliant but basically okay. Why do you want to know?"

"It's Lara." No reason to be cagey. Everyone knew about Lara now. They talked about her openly at the diner, at the bar, at the grocery store. "Cullen's pretty damn obsessed with her. I wondered whether, in your estimation, the kid could be dangerous."

Kieran frowned. "Dangerous? You mean like a stalker? Physically dangerous?"

"Yes."

"I don't think so." Kieran shook his head slowly. "I'm no psychiatrist, but I've never seen anything…like that. He's a teenager, so he can be difficult. He's spoiled—his mom dotes on him, which gives him a bad attitude. And he can be rough on the weaker kids. But I've coached him for three years now, and I've never seen anything creepy."

"Okay." Bryce felt better. Kieran wasn't stupid. If Cullen were twisted, Kieran would have picked up on it. "Thanks. That meshes with what I've seen. I just wanted another opinion."

Kieran tilted his head. "So what's the deal? Why is this your lookout? I thought your bodyguard days were over."

Bryce shrugged. "They are. I'm just checking into it as—a friend." Damn it. He heard how stilted his voice was, as if he had something to hide. But he didn't. It was just that word. The word sounded ridiculous. He wasn't Lara Gilbert's *friend*. But he wasn't her body-guard anymore, either.

He didn't know what the hell he was. Maybe he was just a fool.

"So…" Kieran hesitated. "You haven't seen Stephanie yet, have you?"

Bryce realized that Kieran was holding out a small silver-framed picture. It would have been impossibly rude not to take it, so he did. A squishy little face with a button nose stared out at him. It could have been someone's Cabbage Patch Kid.

"Stephanie? That's her name?" Bryce was embarrassed to realize he'd even forgotten that the baby was a girl. "She's cute."

Kieran grinned. "She's gorgeous. She looks just like Claire. But she's got a temper like Dad's."

"Great." Bryce handed the picture back. "That should be fun when she hits adolescence."

"You should come see her," Kieran said, looking at the photo instead of at Bryce, as if he wanted the comment to sound completely casual. "Claire would love it if you'd come to dinner sometime."

God, Kieran really was a saint, wasn't he? How many times did Bryce have to shove this invitation down his throat before he stopped offering it? Maybe it was time to lay the truth on the table.

"Look, Kieran," he said bluntly. "I think you know I'm not coming to dinner."

"Yes." Kieran finally met his gaze. "What I don't know is why."

Bryce made an impatient gesture with his hand.

"And what *I* don't know is why you feel the need to put up some kind of happy family facade. Surely you don't have to save face in Heyday. People around here are used to feuding McClintocks. No one expects us to be friends."

"Maybe not. But that's all in the past, isn't it? Dad's gone. Both our mothers are gone, too. Surely their sins can die out with them."

"I'm not sure my mother committed any sins," Bryce said coldly. He hadn't intended to get into this, but now that Kieran had started it, perhaps it was better to finish it. "She was Anderson's *wife*. His first wife. She wasn't the one who had an affair."

Kieran looked for a moment as if he might lose his temper. He probably thought it was a low blow to accuse *his* mother, who had died giving birth to him, of anything. But facts were facts. Colleen Donnelly had carried on an affair with a married man, and Kieran was the product of that affair. When Anderson found out his new mistress was pregnant, he had ditched Bryce's mother…and Bryce in the bargain.

But somehow Kieran seemed to get himself under control. That's what saints did, Bryce supposed. They suffered silently. Bryce might have respected him more if he'd landed one right on Bryce's nose.

"You're right," Kieran said. "Your mother was wronged. But the things that happened in the past weren't our doing. Can't you and I just…start over?"

"I don't think so. Look, Kieran, our roles were handed to us years ago. You're the saint. I'm the sinner. There's not a lot of overlap in those two job descriptions."

"God, Bryce." Kieran moved abruptly away from the desk and went over to the window, which looked out on the central downtown park. "I'm no saint. If you only knew—" He broke off. "And you're no sinner, either. Ancient history isn't—"

"Not so ancient, little brother. Everyone still believes it, including you. Yes, you. From what I hear, you couldn't even trust your bad big brother not to make a pass at your pregnant wife."

Damned if Kieran didn't flush, his cheeks turning a dark, uncomfortable red. Looking at him, Bryce suddenly remembered Kieran as a boy...twelve, maybe, or thirteen? He had asked Bryce to teach him to drive, and Bryce had responded with something he thought was brilliantly rude. Kieran had flushed just like that, and for the first time in their relationship Bryce had been a little ashamed. It was too easy. Kieran was too nice, too needy, too eager to be Bryce's friend.

To his credit, Kieran didn't try to play dumb.

"You mean New Year's Eve," he said. "I'm sorry about that. But Aurora made it sound..." He shook his head. "There's no excuse. It was ridiculous. It's just that Claire—we haven't been married long, and I think in some ways I still can't believe she said yes. And you've always been—"

"I've always been the oversexed bastard with a reputation for stealing other men's wives."

Kieran's flush was fading, replaced by a maturity, an equilibrium that surprised Bryce—and reminded him that it really had been fourteen long years since he'd seen his little brother. Apparently a lot could happen in fourteen years.

"That wasn't what I was going to say." Kieran looked at him with a straightforward gaze that might have made Bryce flush, too—except that Bryce never would allow himself to do anything so vulnerable, anything so exposed.

"Well, what, then?" He made his voice deliberately harsh. "I've always been what?"

"More exciting." Kieran smiled. "To tell you the truth, I guess I'm still scared to death that, if it's a choice between me and you, the great girls will always pick you."

IT WAS A GOOD THING, Lara decided as she struggled through the new arrangement of "The White Cliffs of Dover," that the retirement home's spring concert was still a few weeks away.

Vivian, who at ninety-two still had the loveliest soprano Lara had ever heard, couldn't remember the lyrics to "White Cliffs." And Joy, her eighty-nine-year-old best friend, still hadn't decided whether she wanted to sing "Begin the Beguine" or "Livin' La Vida Loca."

Just as Lara thought they might make it through, Vivian did it again. "The white diffs of clover," she warbled. As soon as Vivian realized her mistake, she dissolved into helpless laughter, which made the other residents, who were sitting in the common room watching, begin to laugh, too.

Lara tried to keep playing, hoping Vivian would catch up, but eventually she couldn't resist. She started laughing, too, and missed so many notes she finally slipped into a two-fingered version of "Chopsticks."

She finished with a silly flourish, swiveled on the piano stool and faced the audience. "Okay, guys, that's it for today. We'll have another rehearsal next Friday. Nelson, you still have a hundred stars to cut out, so get busy!"

Nelson gave her a thumbs-up. He couldn't sing a note, but he was a dashing dancer, and he had a lot of style, so she'd put him in charge of choreography and set design.

The others milled around with a ton of questions, which Lara did her best to answer. She loved being here. It was exciting to see the good her music therapy could do. When she was here, she had no doubts at all about her career choice. Ordinarily, she hung around far beyond her official two-hour schedule.

But today her mother had borrowed the car to do some shopping while Lara worked. Karla would undoubtedly be waiting in the retirement home parking lot impatiently, eager to get back to the ranch and fix lunch for Oscar.

Lara could hardly believe the change in her mother since Oscar got scissored up by the barbed wire. It had left him with thirty-six stitches, and two weeks later he was still in a good bit of pain. Karla had appointed herself his unofficial nurse. He fussed and complained that she treated him like an invalid, but Lara could tell he liked it. Even Karla seemed to have mellowed, now that she felt needed again.

Just to get down off the stage, Lara had to sign an autograph for a nurse's daughter-in-law, listen to Joy try one of her songs in two different keys and practice a quick waltz with Nelson. Finally, though, she made it to the table where she'd left her purse. Hooking it over her shoulder, she glanced at her watch. Thirty minutes late…

She sighed. Her mother was going to be furious.

"Lara, honey, can I talk to you privately a minute?" Vivian, who had suddenly appeared at Lara's side, put her white-parchment fingers against Lara's wrist. She spoke in a near-whisper.

"Sure," Lara said with an encouraging smile, hoping to set the old lady at ease. Vivian was a tiny woman with a personality as sweet as her singing voice, but she was a little paranoid. She often confided to Lara that she suspected one conspiracy or another. "What's up?"

"I just wondered if you knew about this." Vivian held out a piece of paper, some kind of advertising flyer. "It worries me, dear. It truly does."

Lara took the flyer, but didn't really look very carefully. She'd seen a very similar one earlier in the week. It was a radio promotion to help raise money for a renovation of the downtown parklands. Local merchants were donating items, and residents were being invited to bid on them, with all proceeds going to the park.

The list she'd seen before had included some very nice things. A two-day cruise from the local travel agency. Free dinner for five from the Italian restaurant. A decoupage class worth seventy dollars from the art studio. She'd even thought about bidding on one herself—a white oak sideboard from her favorite antique store, Valley Treasures.

"Why does it worry you?" She couldn't imagine what conspiracy Vivian might have found in this innocent piece of civic do-gooding. But Vivian had quite an imagination. She had once suspected Nelson of having an affair with one of the nurses. He had been ridiculously flattered when he heard of it. "It seems like a good thing to me. The park is getting a little shabby, don't you think?"

Vivian worked at her lower lip. "But do you really think it's wise, dear?" She lowered her voice even further and glanced around furtively. "I mean, after what happened? You know what men are like."

"What *men* are like?" Lara must be missing something. "What men?"

Vivian's eyes widened. "All of them," she said. "But I don't have to tell you about that, do I, you poor dear?"

Something was definitely wrong here. Had someone added something racy, like a shopping spree at the local adult novelty store? Did Heyday even *have* an adult novelty store?

Lara looked down at the paper. And then she saw it.

A romantic picnic for two with Lara Lynmore, star of *The Highwayman*.

"Oh, no," she said. She read it again, hoping that somehow she'd misunderstood. But the big, red, forty-eight-point type was unmistakable. "*No*. This can *not* be true."

"That was exactly what I said." Vivian was nodding rhythmically, like a dog on a dashboard. "And yet, there it is, big as day. I don't like to intrude, dear, but surely you can see that this might be inviting trouble."

"Oh, there's going to be trouble, all right," Lara said, glaring in the direction of the parking lot, where her mother was waiting, unaware that Lara had discovered her treachery and was on her way out to strangle her. "There is *definitely* going to be trouble."

YOU COULD ALMOST SMELL spring in the air, Bryce thought as he sat on the patio of the Student Union building, drinking surprisingly good black coffee and grading surprisingly bad exam papers.

The weather was an illusion, of course. It was only the beginning of March, and spring didn't come to the Shenandoah Valley for another couple of weeks at least. But, if just for today, the midafternoon sun was warm on his shoulders. It had melted almost all the snow, leaving the campus grounds and buildings wet and freshly glistening.

As he grabbed his red pen to mark another incorrect answer, a shadow fell over the paper. He looked up and saw Dilday Merle standing beside the table.

"Looks as if you're running through a lot of red ink there," Dilday said, smiling. "Are you tough, or are they terrible?"

"A little of each." Bryce waved Dilday into the adjoining chair. The two of them had developed quite a comfortable friendship over the past weeks. The professor Bryce had once found deadly dull turned out to have a wicked sense of humor. "Some of them have potential. A few of them ought to drop out now and save us all some grief."

He put down his pen and took a sip of coffee. He

looked at Dilday over his cup. "I hope you aren't expecting me to go easy on them just to keep enrollment up."

Dilday laughed. "Of course not. We have a fairly good reputation, and we want to keep it that way. We have no intention of becoming a diploma mill. Your brother Tyler hasn't brought us that low, thank God."

His brother Tyler. Bryce thought about once again correcting Dilday. His *half brother* Tyler.

But even that much relationship seemed ridiculous. Bryce had never met Tyler Balfour, and he probably never would. Apparently Tyler was even more allergic to the idea of Heyday than Bryce had ever been. Tyler had provided Valley Pride Properties with an account number for depositing any checks pursuant to his inheritance and an attorney's address for sending urgent documents requiring signatures or decisions. He had made it clear that nothing else would be forthcoming.

"So…I guess if you're wrestling with the staggering incompetence of the average college freshman," Dilday said, leaning back and staring out over the campus, "this might not be the very best time to ask you if you'd like to stay on and teach another class next semester?"

Bryce waited, refusing to answer until finally Dilday turned back toward him again.

"This would be as good a time as any," Bryce said, meeting the older man's quizzical smile evenly. "No matter when you ask, the answer is going to be the same."

"Oh, well." Dilday sighed and shrugged good-naturedly. He put his palms on the arms of his chair and hoisted himself up. "That's okay. I can always ask again next week."

"Dilday." Bryce said firmly as the professor began to walk away. "My answer won't change next week."

Dilday didn't even look back. "Then the week after," he called over his shoulder. "Or the week after that. Or the week after…"

His voice dwindled off as he melded into the crowd of students hurrying to class. Bryce chuckled and picked up his pen again. The old guy was one of a kind.

"Mr. McClintock? Can I talk to you for one minute?"

Bryce put his pen down, recognizing Ilsa's accented, throaty tones even before he looked up and saw her standing there, looking like a goddess, her blond hair blown by the wind. A couple of strands had caught in her thick pink lipstick.

"Sure," he said, because what else could he say? Ilsa knew he didn't have to go to class. Their class had ended an hour ago, and she had stayed after, which she did all too often these days, to talk to him about her exam.

These after-the-bell sessions always began with pertinent discussions of the class materials, but somehow they always ended with Ilsa telling him some tidbit about the Kieran McClintock household. What color Claire had painted the nursery, for instance. Or that the baby had caught a cold.

He had tried to make it clear that he wasn't interested, but Ilsa's English had a way of getting very bad when she didn't care to understand something. She continued to think—or to pretend to think—that he wanted regular updates on his brother's family.

This was the first time she'd cornered him outside the classroom, though. He felt a little annoyed. This was going to have to stop.

But when she moved closer, he could see there were tears in her big blue eyes. Oh, hell. What now?

"Mr. McClintock, I know I did not do a good job on my exam. I am sorry. I have many sad things on my mind."

He refused to ask the obvious question—what sad things? He wasn't the guidance counselor, thank God. He stacked the exams and laid them facedown so that no one's grade was exposed. "I haven't looked at yours yet, Ilsa. But if you did poorly you can always work on some extra credit."

"Oh, Mr. McClintock. May I sit down?" She didn't wait for his answer. She angled herself into the chair Dilday had just vacated and put her elbows on the table, with her pretty face between her hands. "I am sorry to not do a good job for you. I work hard. But my heart—" she pressed one hand over her left breast "—my heart is very much hurting."

Under normal circumstances, if a beautiful woman had sat down and started crying into his coffee, he would have had two courses available to him. If he wanted to go to bed with her, he would grab her and kiss her out of it. If he didn't, and he usually didn't find crying women one bit appealing, actually, he would have chased her away with a few well-aimed darts of sarcasm.

But teachers had to be so bloody circumspect. He had to pretend to be concerned without actually getting involved at all. Good thing he didn't intend to be a career teacher. Restraint didn't suit his personality.

"I'm sorry to hear that," he said, tucking his pen into his jacket pocket and preparing to rise. "But, as I said, you can always do some extra—"

"It's Kieran," she blurted out. She gulped, sobbed, leaned even closer, and then the tears began to flood. "I am so much in love, Mr. McClintock. I do not know what to do."

Bryce slowly lowered himself back into the chair. He was so shocked he could hardly form a thought, much less an intelligent sentence. "Did you say you're in *love* with my brother?"

She nodded, pressing her forefingers horizontally under her eyes, obviously trying to deal with the moisture without messing up the mascara. It was hopeless. The tears just ran over her lovely fingers.

"Since I first worked for him. He is so—" She inhaled with sound effects. "He is so very…"

While she searched for the perfect superlative, Bryce tried to untangle his thoughts. Okay, maybe she "loved" Kieran. Kieran was handsome, he was rich, and he had that steady-Eddie, lean-on-me upright character that, amazingly, seemed to play well with a lot of women. But just because Ilsa had the hots for Kieran, well, that didn't mean Kieran had actually…

He ran his hands through his hair. *Oh, man.* Surely not.

"Ilsa." He chose his next words carefully. "Does Kieran—does he know how you feel?"

That just made her blubber more. People at nearby

tables were starting to look curiously in their direction. Setting his jaw, he took out his handkerchief and handed it to her. "Does he?"

"Yes," she said wetly. "Yes, I have told him. And he...he cares for me, too. But he is such a man. He is a saint, which they say of him. He knows he may not hurt his wife, so he says we must not be together."

Okay. So far so good. Bryce felt something tight inside ease up a little. At least Kieran hadn't been *that* big a fool. Damn, the guy had an infant at home, a beautiful, intelligent wife. He couldn't. He wouldn't...

Suddenly Bryce realized that he had rather liked the idea that at least one of them had been able to break the family curse.

But who was he kidding? A baby, a wife—what difference did any of that make? Look at old Anderson. When Bryce, the first-born son, had been only four years old, Anderson had found himself with not just one but *two* pregnant mistresses—Kieran's mother, and Tyler's mother. Neither of those women had been more beautiful, or one bit smarter than Bryce's own mother, Anderson's legitimate first wife. They had just been the newer, fresher flavors.

Subtly annoyed with Ilsa for bringing him into the sordid mess, he watched her sob prettily into her graceful hands and wondered what she really hoped would happen here. Did she want to marry Kieran? Was she that stupid? Didn't she know that, even if she could force a divorce and insist on a wedding ring of her own, she wouldn't last any longer than Claire had? She'd just be Number Two in a line of…well, Anderson had ended up with five.

He knew better than to laugh while she was still crying, but in a certain twisted light, it was actually kind of funny. Bryce and Kieran had spent their whole lives living up to—or, in his case, down to—the labels assigned to them in childhood. *Sinner. Saint.*

But apparently the only label that mattered was the one old Anderson had written in their blood.

The selfish, reckless label of *McClintock.*

CHAPTER TEN

ON THE NIGHT OF the downtown park auction, Lara, her mother and Oscar all sat around the kitchen table, staring at the radio they'd placed in the center. Lara felt as if she were in a World War II movie, playing the daughter of an anxious family all tuned to Winston Churchill's voice, waiting to learn the future of the free world.

Instead, they were just waiting to hear the results of the auction of Lara's special dinner. When she first heard about it, Lara's immediate reaction had been to march her mother down to the radio station and force her to confess that she'd volunteered her daughter's time without permission. But Lara had finally realized how cruel that would be. Karla would have been made to look like an annoying meddler, and even though Lara privately thought that the label fit just fine, she couldn't bring herself to humiliate her mom in public.

Oscar, who still wore a patch over his eye and wouldn't get his stitches out for another week, had somehow managed to think more clearly than either of them. He had come up with an intelligent compromise.

Obviously Lara couldn't sell a secluded, "romantic" tête-à-tête with a total stranger—even *before* Kenny

Boggs that would have been foolish. But why couldn't she offer a wholesome group picnic instead? Say five lucky winners who could share fried chicken on checkered blankets somewhere on Lazy Gables property, with Oscar waiting table and playing chaperone.

The park supporters couldn't complain. Five winners would be even more valuable than one.

So that's what they had done. And at seven o'clock tonight, with the soundtrack from *The Highwayman* playing in the background, the bidding had begun.

About twenty-five people were locked in heavy competition…the price was already up to five hundred dollars each. But the radio host kept pushing the callers to go higher, and, amazingly, they did.

"I don't recognize any of the voices," Lara said, chewing on her fingernail. Her mother noticed and seemed about to pull Lara's hand away but clearly thought better of it. Karla was learning, Lara thought. Slowly but surely, she might someday come to realize that her daughter was a grown woman and must be allowed to make her own decisions about important issues, like whether to bite her nails.

"Why would you recognize them? Did you think Bryce McClintock was going to bid for you?" Karla sounded waspish. She was still annoyed that her idea had been nixed by Oscar. The episode had completely blown their truce. "He probably assumes he already owns you, along with the rest of this town."

"Of course I wasn't expecting Bryce to bid," Lara said. She hadn't considered that possibility for a single moment. The very idea of Bryce paying to spend an afternoon with any woman was laughable. "I'm just surprised anyone's bidding at all. I'm around Heyday all the time. At the retirement home, at the school. It's not that hard to get a chance to talk to me."

"That's why it's only up to five hundred." Karla tapped the table irritably with the tip of her fingernail. "If you'd stayed in Hollywood, you would have been able to auction yourself off for five *thousand!*"

Lara and Oscar stared at each other for a minute, and then Oscar burst out laughing. Karla briefly tried to look huffy, but even she realized how ridiculous it sounded, and finally she began to laugh, too.

"Go ahead and laugh, you old pirate, but it's true. Every day she stays buried away in this town, her value falls lower and lower."

Lara didn't bother to argue, and neither did Oscar. This discussion was circular, and they'd already worn a groove in the track.

A last flurry of bidding sent the total up to six hundred dollars each. When the host knocked the gavel down at a total of three thousand dollars, Lara and Oscar slapped hands in a triumphant high-five.

Karla sighed. "Now I'll have to start thinking of what to serve them," she said, but her plaintive tone wasn't quite convincing. She loved to cook, and Lara knew she would have a ball planning this picnic. She went over to the cupboard to see what ingredients they had on hand.

Oscar was just reaching out to turn off the radio when the host began to introduce the next item for auction.

"And those of you who read the gossip pages will know why this item was listed right after Miss Lynmore," the host said in a sly voice, the audible equivalent of a wink. "Mr. Bryce McClintock, who is renovating the old Omega Alpha house, has offered a Decorate and Destroy Party. Mr. McClintock, you may remember, is the handsome hero who saved Miss Lara Lynmore's life."

"Wait," Lara said, holding out her hand to stop Oscar. "I want to hear this."

Oscar nodded. "Surprises the hell out of me. He's not exactly civic-minded. Did you know about it?"

"Terri Wooten told me her dad was trying to talk Bryce into something like this, but last I heard Bryce was adamantly refusing to play."

Karla spoke from the pantry, her voice muffled. "What on earth is a 'decorate and destroy' party?"

"Shhh…" Lara said. The radio host was describing the donation.

"Not only is Mr. McClintock one of Heyday's premier citizens, owning, with his brothers, more than seventy-five percent of the publicly held properties in town…. Not only is he the dashing bodyguard who shot a stalker dead to save the lovely lady's life…"

Lara closed her eyes, trying not to imagine Kenny Boggs lying on the stage. She simply couldn't understand why people thought the tragedy had been glamorous. If they had seen the blood, the terrible emptiness left behind when a man dies…

"But he's also the owner of one of our most fascinating civic landmarks, The Omega Alpha Fraternity

House. This beautiful old mansion, which used to be a private home, has a wild and crazy history, ladies and gentlemen. From a resident ghost to...well, you all remember the college-girl call-girl scandals of a few years ago, right? Now, we don't really know that Omega Alpha boys were involved in that, but we do know that the school banned fraternities from campus right about then, and the Omega Alpha house was abandoned."

"Oh, get to the point." Karla came over with her hands full of spices and glared at the radio. "What is a 'decorate and destroy' party?"

"So here's how it's going to work," the radio host went on, almost as if he'd been able to hear Karla. "Mr. McClintock is planning to restore the house to its former glory as a private home. He intends to tear down the walls that were added to create bedrooms for the fraternity brothers, but before he does, ten lucky Heyday-ans are going to get to have some fun."

Oscar smiled at Lara, his one good eye glimmering. He obviously saw where this was going. She smiled back. It really did sound like fun, didn't it?

"Next Friday, our ten lucky winners will put on their overalls, and they'll drive to this great old spooky house with spray cans and paintbrushes and Magic Markers. And when they get there, they're going to make an old-fashioned, fun-house mess of the place!"

"What?" Karla looked horrified. "They're going to trash that classic old mansion? Well, if that isn't typical of a backwoods town like this—"

"So if you're a ghost-hunter, a local history buff, an artist, or a frustrated graffiti poet...or if you just love the idea of smashing your hammer into drywall, pick up your telephone now!" In the background they could hear the sound of ringing phones. "The ghost of Omega Alpha House is waiting for your call!"

Still smiling, Lara began to walk out of the kitchen.

Karla frowned and pointed the cinnamon sticks at her. "Where do you think you're going, young lady?"

Lara tossed a grin over her shoulder as she headed for the hall telephone. "Didn't you hear the man, Mom? I've got to call now. I can't keep the ghost of Omega Alpha house waiting."

LUCKY FOR HARRY, a bunch of senior citizens won Bryce's "Decorate and Destroy" party…for the whopping price of fifteen hundred dollars. If their nearest competition, a group of loud, coarse teenagers, had won it, Bryce would have strangled Harry, who had talked him into this insanity.

The kids would undoubtedly have come storming through the house, destroying load-bearing walls instead of the add-ons.

Listening to the kids screaming out their bids, Bryce had belatedly realized that, though he didn't give a damn about the future of the downtown park, he had actually grown rather fond of the old frat house.

Or, even worse, what if that other group had won— that bevy of mindless middle-aged women? The radio host had tried to whip the ladies into a frenzy, reminding them how big and strong and rich and cute Bryce was.

Hell, if they had won, Bryce would simply have had to leave town.

Luckily, though, the seniors had been politely persistent, and apparently well-heeled enough to outlast all other bidders. Bryce was so relieved he even arranged for the local caterer to bring in snacks and hot tea while the nice old folks were on site.

The caravan of cars arrived in front of the frat house at ten o'clock sharp that Friday morning. Bryce stood on the porch to greet them, but when the doors opened and the "nice old folks" began to spill out, he realized that his idea of senior citizens might have been somewhat out of date.

These weren't blue-haired, prissy old prunes and wizened, courtly old codgers with green rayon slacks belted just under their armpits. These seniors were sharp-eyed, laughing, irreverent men and women in jeans and T-shirts that said things like Don't Ask Me My Age, I Won't Ask You Your IQ. Yes, they had white hair, if they had any hair at all, and one or two of them even had their paint cans hooked around their walkers. But they also had a gleam in their eyes that told Bryce he might have been better off with the teenagers.

He greeted the first nine of them and sent them in to Harry, who was going to set the ground rules and show them which walls were earmarked for destruction. Just nine? Maybe Number Ten had decided to stay home?

No such luck. He was just turning to go back inside when the last car drove up.

It was Lara Gilbert's car.

She gave him a devilish grin as she climbed out, her arms full of paint cans. "Sorry I'm late," she said. "Looks as if my guys are here already, huh?"

She looked about sixteen in her blue jeans, her tie-dyed T-shirt and her bouncing ponytail. "That depends," he said. "Are *your guys* a bunch of eighty-year-old commandos?"

She swung up the walk with that trademark Lara Lynmore sashay. "Well, Vivian's actually ninety-two, but otherwise that sounds about right. We're your lucky winners."

She hurried toward the door, but he moved subtly and blocked her way. "Come on, Lara. You and nine octogenarians? How exactly did you get elected president of this particular club?"

"I do volunteer work at the retirement home. When I heard your party announced on the radio, I thought of them right away. I knew they'd love it."

"And the fifteen hundred dollars. That was all your money?"

"Heck, no." She laughed. "I'm not a movie star anymore, you know. I can't afford that kind of money. I paid a hundred and fifty, just like the rest of them."

"A hundred and fifty dollars…for what? Why?"

"It's a good cause." She shrugged and grinned again. "And besides, how else was I going to get a look at how you live? You've made it pretty clear I won't be getting an invitation the normal way."

He took one of the paint cans, to lighten her burden. "The *normal* way?" Shaking his head, he pushed open the door. "Let's be honest, Lara Gilbert. There isn't a single normal thing about you, as far as I can tell."

THREE HOURS LATER, when the octogenarians were finally tuckered out from painting, Bryce sent them downstairs for a sandwich and tea break. Next came the demolition part of the adventure, and they needed to recharge their batteries.

Deciding Harry could handle the refreshments, Bryce stayed upstairs, wandering through the rooms, checking out the artwork.

He chuckled as he went, enjoying their pictures and their graffiti, which stopped short of outright vulgarity but had, in places, brought tacky innuendo to a new low. Anyone who believed old people didn't think about sex should get a look at these walls.

But they also thought about poetry and love and nature, and they understood harmony of color and form. One of them, a dapper little guy named Nelson, was a bona fide artist. He had chosen to paint a picture of Lara Lynmore on his wall, so large it was almost a mural. It was a scene straight out of *The Highwayman*.

While the others had been up here, Bryce had allowed himself only occasional, casual glances. But now that he stood, alone, in front of Nelson's painting, he saw that it was inspired. The old guy must have a photographic memory, or else he carried a promotional photo from *The Highwayman* in his pocket.

He had chosen to paint one of the scenes at the inn, with Bess standing in the courtyard twilight, waiting for her lover. On one Tudor-timbered inn wall, the dying sun cast a golden glow, and on the other lush red roses climbed and twined, so real Bryce could almost smell them. Bess stood just to the right of center, leaning over the side of a stony well, staring into it as if she sought answers in its murky depths.

Nelson had captured the essence of Lara so completely it almost took Bryce's breath away. He had caught the longing in her posture, and the graceful, sensual lines of her body. He had found the living ripples in her magnificent hair, and the hidden strength in her sweet, vulnerable profile.

All this in just three hours. The man was a genius. Bryce didn't see how he could let them smash this wall with hammers. But what could he do? Chain himself to the door and refuse to let them in?

"He's great, isn't he?"

Bryce turned at the sound of Lara's voice. He had thought she was safely downstairs with the others. But suddenly she was standing beside him, munching on a cookie and studying the picture.

"It's exactly like the movie," she said. "Only somehow more…poetic."

Bryce looked at her, at the reality standing alongside the dream. She couldn't have resembled Bess any less right now, with her rough-and-tumble clothes, her hair poking wildly in all directions, her face dotted with blue and green paint. She even smelled of fresh paint, and Bryce wondered why he'd never noticed before what an erotic scent that was, so sharp and thick and wet.

"That's the artist in him." She tilted her head to get another angle on the painting. "He takes things and makes them more wonderful."

"I'm not sure he could," Bryce said, though he knew it was madness.

"Could what?" She frowned a little. And then she got

it. "Oh." She flushed, adding red to the flecks of green and blue. "Oh, for heaven's sake. I never really looked like that."

"Yes. You did."

He heard voices coming back up the stairs, and he knew their time alone was almost over. The old people loved her, and they'd clamor for her attention, her admiration, her laughter. And she'd give it to them. He'd never seen anyone give themselves more freely. She held nothing back. These three uninhibited hours had allowed him to know things about her that six weeks of policing the starlet, twenty-four hours a day, seven days a week, had never revealed.

"You did, and you do." He turned back to the picture. It was somehow safer to stare at the elegant, tragic Bess than it was to look at the mussed, dirty, temptingly real woman who stood beside him, close enough to touch.

"You have something, Lara. Something that makes people want you so much they go a little crazy."

"Like Kenny," she said softly.

"Yes," he said as the voices on the stairs grew louder. The commandos were almost upon them. "Like Kenny. And like any poor fool who isn't very, very careful."

CHAPTER ELEVEN

THE NEXT AFTERNOON, as soon as the professional demolition team had come in and finished up the job the seniors had playfully begun, Bryce drove downtown. He had seen some attractive furniture in the window of one of the antique stores, and, though he had absolutely no decorating skills himself, he thought he might see if the store's owner would take on the job of redoing the interior of the house.

He wasn't sure why he had this sudden interest in freeing the mansion from its years of frat-boy abuse. He was probably just going to sell it as soon as the term was over, and he could leave Heyday. But still, the urge to at least restore some dignity to the handsome old place was compelling. And it would bring more, he knew, if he kept the décor consistent with the age of the structure.

Luckily, the antique-store owner was thrilled to get the commission. Bryce ended up leaving an extremely large check and extremely minimal instructions—really just two words: *fix it*.

As he walked back down Hippodrome Circle toward his car, past Rackham Books, he stopped cold. In one of the bookstore windows, a huge, smiling poster of Tony "The Highwayman" Barnett looked out at him.

Bryce stifled a rude sound. Good lord, that was one damn irritating face. For the life of him, Bryce could not understand how this guy managed to make a career in romantic movies. One glimpse of that dimpled, toothy smile, and anyone could tell the only person Tony Barnett loved was himself.

In fact, the only flaw in *The Highwayman* was that it was completely incredible that the beautiful Bess would sacrifice herself in order to save this dweeb. Much more likely that she'd just say "good riddance" and let him ride blithely into the Redcoats' trap.

So what was Tony up to now? *The Highwayman* was yesterday's news. It wasn't hot enough to warrant this kind of advertising.

Bryce scanned the window. Oh, that's right—Terri Wooten had told him about this. The dweeb had put out a CD. Tony and Lara had actually sung their own duet for *The Highwayman*'s theme song, and the song had received a good bit of radio play.

Of the two, Lara had by far the better voice, but it was Tony who had cashed in on it. *Typical.*

Bryce was ambivalent. He didn't want to increase the dweeb's sales even by the count of one, but he knew Terri would love to have this CD. The advertising said it came with its own four-by-seven-foot, life-size poster of Tony Barnett.

What a horrible thought.

In the end, though, he couldn't resist the thought of how thrilled Terri would be. Harry's budget was so tight he rarely allowed frivolous purchases, so she probably didn't have it yet. Bryce gritted his teeth, twisted the doorknob and entered the store.

"Bryce! How nice to see you!"

He'd been prepared to deal with the pierced and punky Wally, but today Mallory Rackham seemed to be running her own store. She looked up from a box of books she'd been unpacking and gave him a charming smile.

As she climbed to her feet and held out her hand, he felt a pinch of regret that he had never followed up on their New Year's Eve dinner. Clearly Kieran and Claire had hoped he and Mallory might hit it off. And he did like her. What was not to like? She was blond and beautiful, bright and fun and completely unaffected.

But what would be the point in starting any kind of relationship here in Heyday? Talk about inviting someone for a short walk down a dead-end street! Besides, when he closed his eyes at night, he didn't see Mallory's perky smile and breezy, short blond curls. He saw someone else, someone with darkly sparkling eyes, like candles at midnight. Someone with fistfuls of soft hair that moved like water, and a mouth as sweet and red and full as a half-blown rose.

He caught himself, and shuddered inwardly at the sound of his own nonsense. Ruthlessly, he forced himself to remember that Kenny Boggs's letters had been full of similarly sappy phrases, at least the early ones, before his adoration had turned sour.

"Hi, Mallory," Bryce said, giving her his best smile. What was wrong with perky? What was wrong with breezy? A woman like this would certainly be a hell of a lot less stressful than a complicated, unpredictable siren who made every man she met start babbling bad metaphors.

"How have things been?" He glanced around the store, which was warm and unassuming, like Mallory herself. "Your place is great."

"Thanks. I heard you came in the other day. I was sorry I wasn't here. I was with Claire. Have you seen the baby yet?"

Again that uncomfortable pinch. God, he needed to get out of Heyday. Why should he feel guilty for not visiting his brother? Until a few months ago, he hadn't seen Kieran for fourteen years, and neither one of them had lost any sleep over it.

"No, not yet," he said. He didn't elaborate. "Sorry to interrupt your unpacking. I just stopped in to pick up a copy of Tony Barnett's new CD."

"You did?" She widened her eyes. "Now there's one I wouldn't have predicted. Do you secretly have a pre-teen daughter hidden away somewhere?"

"No." He smiled. "Believe it or not."

She put her hand over her forehead and groaned. "Oh, brother. When will I ever learn to think before I speak?"

"Never, I hope," he said with a laugh. "It's actually kind of refreshing to talk to someone who doesn't tiptoe around my reputation."

"Okay, then, well, let me get you that CD." She moved toward a central display case, where "The Hot Forty" CDs were arranged in order. Tony was pretty close to the top. She pulled a disc out, and then she looked back at Bryce with a small frown. "You do know his duet with Lara isn't on here, right? There's nothing from *The Highwayman* on the whole CD."

"I know." He gave her another grin. "Tell me, do you usually work this hard to keep your customers from buying things?"

"Sorry. Of course not." She laughed, then, too, and handed the CD over with a bow. "What I meant to say was, is one enough? Are you sure you wouldn't like two, sir?"

"One is *plenty*," he said with a grimace. "But don't forget my poster. That's the most important part." Before she could put words to her obvious skepticism, he gave up the joke. "You were right about the preteen daughter. It's just not *my* daughter. She belongs to a friend of mine. I'm getting it as a surprise for her."

Mallory nodded, her curiosity apparently satisfied. She walked over to the counter where the cash register stood and took the CD from Bryce so that she could scan it.

She turned the case over. The bar code label was right under Tony's dimpling smile. "He's much easier on the eyes than he is on the ears," she said with a wistful sigh. "Have you actually heard any of this?"

"No," he said, deciding not to openly express his surprise that a smart woman like Mallory would be attracted to Tony Barnett. Lara wasn't—or at least she had always said she wasn't.

"Well, turn on your car radio on the way home, and you will. That's all they play." She took his money and handed him the change with a grin. "When they aren't talking about the park auction, that is. I hear your 'decorate and destroy' party was a big hit."

"Yeah. I think everyone had fun."

"I sure hope Lara's picnic goes as well," she said. "It's this afternoon, you know. Probably going on right now. Although, with that group…"

Bryce knew about the picnic, of course, but he hadn't heard who won it. "What group? Did it go to her favorite senior citizens from the retirement home?"

"No, that would have been fine. It went to five separate bidders, all single men around here who obviously are downright delusional. They probably think they can be so scintillating that they can take one picnic and turn it into a full-blown relationship. Heck, one of them isn't even a man! He's just a high school kid." She shook her head. "Pathetic, really. I don't envy her."

Bryce began to wish he had bid on it himself. At least then he could have helped Oscar keep all those libidos in check. And the high school kid…

"Who's the kid? What's his name, do you know?"

She frowned, thinking. "I'm pretty sure it was Cullen Overton, but maybe it was Eddie. One of the football players, I'm almost positive." She looked over her shoulder. "Wally?"

Wally's red-and-green head slowly emerged from behind a display case of magazines. Obviously he'd been there the whole time, listening. "Yeah?"

"You bid on Lara Lynmore's picnic, didn't you?"

Wally scowled. "Yeah. But just because I thought she might have some industry tips." He turned the scowl toward Bryce. "I'm not one of those idiot fan club types. I'm going to be a film student. I'm going to be a director someday."

"Super," Bryce said, though he couldn't care less about Wally's career plans. "I take it you didn't win."

"No, it went way too high for me. That's why it was all grown-ups at the end. They're the ones with the flow."

"He means cash flow," Mallory explained helpfully, as if she had hired a foreign exchange student who didn't speak English.

"Yeah." Wally shrugged. "The only kid from our school with enough cash to play in those leagues is Cullen. Not 'cause he earns it, though. Cause his old man just rains it on him."

Damn it. Bryce had been afraid of this. "You definitely are talking about Cullen Overton?"

Wally tugged on one of his ear studs. "Yeah. He's being a total *tool* about it, too." He glanced at Mallory. "Sorry, Ms. Rackham. But he is. He goes around saying he's definitely going to, you know, get lucky. He thinks she'll want him to stay after the middle-aged dorks go home, so that he can show her, you know, what it can be like when a guy is young and can still—"

Wally tried again. "You know."

Mallory rolled her eyes. "Well, gross," she said succinctly. "I hope Oscar carves the charming Cullen up and serves him for hors d'oeuvres."

BRYCE KNEW that Oscar was perfectly capable of dealing with a snotty eighteen-year-old kid. He wouldn't bother with Mallory's hors-d'oeuvres idea. If Cullen got out of line, Oscar would drop-kick his arrogant ass all the way back to downtown Heyday.

So there was nothing to worry about. Oscar would have everything under control.

But somehow, by the end of the afternoon, Bryce found himself driving up the long dirt road toward Lazy Gables. The picnic was probably over, but just in case it wasn't...

He'd like to be nearby. Just in case Oscar—or Lara—needed help.

He didn't have to go all the way to the house. He cruised along outside the white paddock fence until he saw the picnic table out on the southern edge of the property. And then he parked his car.

The group was packing up—and it was about time, too, Bryce thought, glancing at his watch. They'd begun, according to Mallory, at one this afternoon. It was almost five o'clock now, and though the sun was still out it must be getting cold. How much of Lara's time did they think they had bought with their lousy six hundred dollars?

Some of the winners must already have left. Bryce identified Oscar, Lara, Lara's mother...and Cullen.

Little punk. He really was trying to be the last. He was bustling around picking up things, as if he wanted to show how useful he was. More of that youthful energy and stamina, no doubt.

Bryce got out of his car and stood there, leaning against the side casually, watching them. They could see him, too, though they didn't notice him right away.

Oscar spotted him first. He squinted with his unpatched eye and then just shook his head, grinning. Seeing that, Lara's mother stared irritably, her hands on her hips. Lara smiled and waved. But when Cullen realized what was going on, he dropped the picnic basket he was holding, spilling knives and forks and napkins everywhere.

And then, within seconds, Cullen was stiltedly shaking hands and saying goodbye. He didn't run away from the picnic area exactly, but he didn't dawdle, either. Three minutes later, a bright-red BMW came speeding by, revving its engine aggressively just as it passed Bryce.

Good try, Cullen, Bryce thought. But the display of horsepower would have been more impressive if the kid hadn't been using it to beat a cowardly retreat.

When the BMW had disappeared into the horizon, Bryce looked once again toward the picnic table, and realized it was dark and empty now, the spot deserted. But as his vision adjusted, his gaze was caught by movement to his left. A woman was walking toward him, silhouetted against the lowering, deep gold sun.

It was Lara, and when she got close enough, he could see that she was smiling. He moved toward her, almost without thinking.

She stopped at the paddock, so that only the white wood was between them. "Hi, Bryce," she said. Her eyes were twinkling. "I guess it's true what they say... once a bodyguard, always a bodyguard?"

"Apparently." He chuckled. "Sorry if I broke up your party."

"You didn't." She leaned against the fence, her long green skirt swirling in the breeze, licking through the gaps in the boards. "Cullen was the only one left. But then he was the one you were worried about, wasn't he?"

"I wouldn't exactly say *worried*."

"Well, I was," she said. "When I heard he had won a spot, I almost called the whole thing off. If Oscar hadn't been there…"

He could imagine how she'd felt. The night they'd found him sneaking around the Wootens' yard, she'd been nearly undone. "So did he behave himself?"

She laughed, a charming sound that carried on the cool, early-evening air. It was a golden sound, like the sun that gilded her shoulder and her hair.

"I'll say he did. He was obviously intimidated, poor kid. By me, by Oscar, by the other auction winners, even by my mother. He just sat there and tried to look invisible."

She leaned down with her elbows on the top rail of the fence, which brought her very close to him, and subtly shifted the way the sunlight struck her. She looked even more beautiful now, with her cheeks bronzed, and her lips shining.

"Once he said, 'This chicken is great.'" She shook her head. "That was his longest sentence all day."

Oh, brother. So Kieran had been right. Cullen was just another spoiled-rotten package of hot air.

"I guess he did all his talking ahead of time." Bryce was still incredulous that anybody could be such a fool. Had Cullen really thought he stood a chance with Lara

Lynmore, who had turned down millionaire celebrities routinely found on the "50 Most Beautiful People" list?

"What do you mean—ahead of time?" She knitted her brows together. "What has he been saying?"

"He's been telling everyone at his school that he didn't plan to sleep in his own bed tonight. *Jackass.* I thought I might come over and help him think of a *new* plan."

"Oh, Bryce, the poor kid," she said, shaking her head again. "He'll be so embarrassed. He won't be able to hold his head up when he has to admit all he got was some fried chicken."

"Are you kidding? This jerk? You'll be lucky if he doesn't tell everyone you had an orgy for dessert."

She laughed. "It's too cold for an orgy."

He suddenly realized she wasn't wearing a sweater. Her yellow shirt was soft, thick velour, and it had long sleeves, but still… "Are you cold now?" He looked back at the car. "I might have a jacket you could—"

"I'm fine." She hesitated for a second, then reached out and gently touched him on the arm.

"Thank you," she said. "Even if Cullen didn't really pose a threat, it was comforting to look up and see you there, watching over me. It felt right, somehow."

The light pressure of her fingertips sent goose bumps racing up his arm and into his chest. It was cold. He shuddered slightly, but the ripples seemed to move inward, not out, and couldn't safely dissipate into the air. They just kept washing through him, doubling over themselves, like a tide caught in a bottle.

He wanted to say something. Words would be at

least a kind of release. But what was there to say? *I want you. I want you. I want you.*

"Bryce," she said. She tightened her fingers on his arm. "Bryce, look at me."

And because he was weak, he did. He looked at her face, which was made of golden shadows, and suddenly his self-control, which had been fiction from the start, simply melted away.

He took her shoulders, and he pulled her toward him, ignoring the bite of the fence that separated them. He kissed her.

She made a small, shocked sound, but before the sound was complete it had melted into pleasure. She opened her lips, and as he touched the vulnerable spaces between them, she shivered softly, too. She reached up and threaded her hands into his hair.

Had they thought it was cold? It was warm, she was warm, so blissfully warm that suddenly all around them it was summer.

He ran his hands down her back, and felt her firm, high breasts press against his chest. *Yes.* Her heartbeat spoke the word to his. *Yes.*

Somewhere he knew how strange this was, this soft bliss. He had been so sure that, if he ever gave in to his desire, it would be wild and mad, like a hurricane, like a natural disaster. He had kissed her once before, and it had been like that. So hard and needy it was almost painful.

But right now it was so easy. So right. It was a sweet relief, like drinking when he was thirsty. Like putting down something very heavy that he'd been forced to carry for too long.

"Lara?" The voice calling from the front porch of the ranch was familiar, and yet completely strange. He didn't want to hear it. "Lara? Where are you?"

Lara's lips stilled. She pulled back, just a little. "It's my mother," she said. She looked at him, her eyes holding a question. "I can tell her—I'll tell her we need to be alone."

There was something he should be saying. He knew that. But what was it? His body was, without his conscious directive, leaning toward her, reaching for her. He had to fight to keep from kissing her again.

"Lara! The phone is for you, Lara. It's your agent."

The golden summer began to recede, like a stage set being rolled away. Once again they were surrounded by the dank, fading twilight, the last ugly patches of snow on hard, brown ground.

"Don't look like that," Lara said suddenly. She took his hand. "Bryce, don't. I don't want to talk to my agent. I haven't talked to her in months. It's my mother—"

"You'd better go take the call," he said.

"She has nothing to offer that I want, Bryce. Nothing to say that I want to hear."

But he had seen the piles of scripts on the hall chair, and he knew the truth. He knew, maybe even better than she did, that the fingers of her past were still reaching forward, had never let go, would never let go. He knew they waged a silent battle against the fragile grip of this new life.

And he knew that, someday, they would win.

ON MONDAY, after the students were dismissed, Bryce stayed in the classroom going through his predecessor's notes. They had another exam Wednesday, and he wanted to be sure he'd covered everything.

When he heard a light rap on the door, he felt a ripple of irritation. He got up and headed toward the door, which he had closed ten minutes ago, in hopes of preventing just this kind of interruption.

If this was Ilsa again, he was going to have to get tough and tell her—

But it wasn't Ilsa. He looked through the small square window, and saw the woman standing there, looking nervous and determined at the same time.

It was Karla Gilbert.

He opened the door. "Hi," he said. "This is a surprise. I hope everything is all right."

With Lara, he meant. He hoped Lara was all right.

"I hope it is, too," Karla said. "May I come in? I think we need to talk."

"Of course." He threw the door wide open and watched her walk in. Karla was always a little over-dressed, he remembered, but this was ridiculous. She wore an ice-blue, very expensive suit and high-heeled dress shoes. At her neck, an ornately tied scarf was pinned with a large diamond stud. Her hair was slicked into a twisted knot so complicated she couldn't possibly have done it herself, not with that cast on. And her makeup was as thick as war paint.

She was probably a beautiful woman—Lara actually looked a good bit like her mother. But it was hard to find anything attractive, anything even particularly human, under such a mountain of artifice.

She stopped at the front, near his desk, and scanned

the room slowly. He wondered if she was imagining Lara in one of these rooms, listening to a teacher not unlike Bryce. With its institutional beige walls, its dusty chalkboard, its antiquated overhead projector rolled awkwardly into a corner, it was no better or worse than a million classrooms all over the country. But he knew enough about Karla to know what she was thinking. It wasn't good enough for Lara.

More to the point, *he* wasn't good enough for Lara. Lara had always jokingly said that Karla dreamed nightly about being Brad Pitt's mother-in-law. It probably had something to do with the failure of her own marriage, he thought. When she lost her husband, she had sewn her hopes and dreams into her daughter, the way an exiled queen might sew rubies and diamonds into her cloak before she flees in the night.

Bryce had seen all that the first time, back when he was Lara's bodyguard. Karla had watched him suspiciously, obviously sensing the chemistry and recognizing potential danger. She had gone out of her way to put him "in his place," so that the footman would never get ideas about the princess he served.

But things were different now. He wondered, looking at her, if she had any idea just how different they were.

"Well, I suppose you know why I'm here," she said finally, when it became awkwardly clear that he wasn't going to speak first.

He shrugged. "Why don't you tell me?"

She put her purse down on his desk, its cool, soft blue leather incongruous against the cheap Formica. "It's about Lara."

He waited.

"I know that she thinks she—has feelings for you. It's ridiculous, but there it is."

"She's told you that?"

"No." Karla stood as straight as a soldier. "But I know my daughter, Bryce. I know what's in her heart."

"You didn't know she hated acting," he said. He didn't mean to be cruel, but if they were going to have this conversation, they needed to tell the truth, and tell it straight.

"That's because she *doesn't* hate it. She is frightened right now, that's all. That man frightened her. She'll get over it. She'll heal. And then she'll want to go back."

He had said those things himself. He wondered why, now that Karla Gilbert was the one saying them, they sounded oddly hollow.

"Will she? Are you so sure of that, Karla?"

"Yes." Her face tightened under its mask. "But I'm also sure that, if she waits too long, if anything keeps her buried here in Heyday, she will miss her chance. She'll try to go back. Maybe she'll even get a few parts here and there. But it will be too late."

Karla's hands—even the one in the cast—were closed tightly. Tension vibrated off her in humming waves. Bryce realized that this wasn't just a control freak trying to assert her will. She desperately believed what she was saying.

"This is Lara's moment, Bryce. Right now. She can have it all. The golden ring is hanging just above her head. All she has to do is reach up and grab it."

He felt a muscle in his jaw twitch. "What if she doesn't want it?"

"Doesn't want what? Success? Money? Freedom? Respect?" Karla lifted her chin. "Don't kid yourself that this is all about ego and signing autographs. It's about security. It's about independence and power and control over your own destiny."

He tried to smile. "Are you sure that's her list, Karla? Or is it *yours?*"

"It's the *world's* list," she said harshly. "It's what *matters*. It's why most people get up every day and drag themselves to jobs they despise. It's why women marry men they don't love, and vice versa. It's why every one of your students is enrolled in this college. It's why fifty thousand girls would cut off their right arms to be in Lara Lynmore's shoes."

Was that true? He looked out the window, to the campus's central square, where charming young boys and girls were talking, reading textbooks, spooning yogurt, laughing, kissing…

They all had different dreams. They dreamed of being cops, or judges, or veterinarians, or teachers. They dreamed of big houses and little kids, of making Dad proud, or making a hundred grand. Some of their dreams were so private they had never uttered the words aloud to anyone.

What were Lara's dreams?

He turned away from the window and drew the blinds shut. "Why are you really here, Karla? Why are you telling me this?"

"Because I want you to make her leave Heyday."

He raised one eyebrow. "How on earth would I do that?"

"You'd tell her the truth. You don't really want her. Or maybe you do want her, but you wish you didn't. Either way, it isn't going to work, and yet you never quite cut her loose. You never quite convince her that it's hopeless."

"Damn it, Karla—"

"It's true. And that makes you the problem, Bryce. Because as long as she's reaching out for you, she'll never reach up for the ring."

CHAPTER TWELVE

LARA LOOKED at her term paper one last time before she tucked it away into her notebook—just for the pleasure of seeing that big, red A.

Nice work, her professor had written beside it. *Much better.*

If she kept going like this, she was going to get an A in Psychology of Music. She bit her lower lip, trying not to grin. But she couldn't help it—an A would be more exciting than an Academy Award.

And she'd worked for it, too. She'd spent more hours in the library these past two months than she had in the entire rest of her life.

"Hey, good going," one of her study group partners said as she passed Lara's desk. "This guy is tough. He's damn stingy with his A's."

Lara smiled. "Thanks," she said. "You guys helped a lot."

The other young woman smiled and patted her shoulder. "It's not just the study group, I promise you. I got a C." She waved her own paper in the air to illustrate her point. "Oh, well, that's life, huh? See you next week."

Lara was the last one in the classroom. She put the paper away, aware that she couldn't just sit here all afternoon and rest on her laurels. She had another paper due in English on Tuesday, so it was right back to the library for her. She sighed, thinking how annoyed her mother would be when she found out Lara wasn't coming straight home after class.

She gathered her things, leaving her cell phone free. As she walked through the double doors that led to the courtyard, she hooked her backpack over one shoulder and began punching buttons. She decided to send a text message. It would be much easier than arguing voice-to-voice.

G.o.i.n.g...t.o...l.i.b.r.a—

That was as far as she had gotten when, because she wasn't looking at anything but the keypad, she ran straight into Bryce McClintock. Hard. The impact knocked the cell phone out of her hand.

"Bryce!" She felt flustered. She had never, ever seen him on campus before. She'd sometimes wondered whether it was all a fiction that he taught here. But, of course, she knew it was just that he was determined to avoid her.

So what was he suddenly doing over here by the music building now?

He bent down, retrieved her cell phone and handed it to her. "Sorry," he said. He looked strangely serious, with less of his usual sardonic detachment. The expression made her insides twist nervously. Was something wrong?

"I was looking for you." He hesitated. "Do you have a few minutes? We need to talk."

"Okay." She tried not to let her mind race through the possibilities, guessing, second-guessing, trying to prepare herself. "Where?"

"It doesn't matter," he said. "How about over there?"

He pointed toward the central fountain, which had just been restarted the other day, when the weather forecasters predicted that the threat of frost had passed. It was animal-themed, naturally. Everything in Heyday was. Three elephants stood on their hind legs, back to back, spouting water through their trunks.

It was a silly thing, but everyone loved it, anyhow. On a warm day like this, it was swarming with students killing time after class. So Bryce must not need total privacy. Was that good or bad?

Maybe he was deliberately avoiding being alone with her.

But there she was, trying to guess again.

She took a deep breath and smiled. "That's fine."

They settled themselves on one of the few clear segments, right by the elephant's trunk. She felt a light mist touch her cheek—which was probably why this spot was empty.

"So," she said, folding her hands in her lap. "What's up?"

He hadn't sat down. He stood in front of her, very close, with one foot up on the fountain's low cement rim, and his elbow resting on his thigh. He looked at her for a long minute before he spoke.

"I guess you already know I'm not the marrying kind."

She must have let her mouth fall open. Tiny tingles

of fountain mist began to touch her tongue. She closed it and swallowed hard.

"I—" What was the appropriate response to that? It felt like a trick question. "I suppose I did know that. I honestly hadn't thought about it like that."

"You *should* think about it. It's not a temporary glitch in my emotional development. It's not a cute flaw that the *right woman* can mend. It's who I am. I have no interest in being mended."

"All right." She still felt as if she were trying to find her way in this conversation blindfolded. "I believe you."

"I come from bad stock, as I'm sure you've heard. My father had five wives, dozens of mistresses, and at least one illegitimate son that we know of. I'm a lot like him, I think, though it isn't something I'm proud of. I've had more lovers than I can count. More than I should. I began early, and I like to change frequently. I dislike being tied down."

"Yes," she said. "I heard about that. You're quite a legend in Heyday."

"And have they told you yet about Cindy?"

She shook her head. "No. They've tried, once or twice. But I wouldn't let them. I hoped that someday you might tell me yourself."

The hand that dangled next to his knee tightened into a fist, the knuckles going ever so slightly white. "God, you really are an idealist, aren't you?"

She shook her head again. "I don't know what the right label is, Bryce. Maybe, like you, I just am what I am."

He nodded. "Fair enough."

The other students were gradually leaving. Classes were over for the day, and the campus was slowly shutting down. They had more privacy now, and she thought about moving out of the spray, but decided against it. She didn't want to do anything that might interrupt him.

"All right then," he said, "here's the dirty little story everyone has been dying to tell you. My parents were divorced when I was only four, and my mother and I lived in Chicago. I came to Heyday only in the summers. I was miserable here, and I pretty much made everyone around me miserable, too. I hated my father. I hated finding a new stepmother every few years, and new live-in lovers the rest of the time. I would never have come back at all, but the custody arrangements required it. That summer was definitely my last, because I was eighteen that year."

His voice was so matter-of-fact he might have been reading from a book. But those white knuckles told her this was a very important story.

"My mother hated Anderson, too, so they were hardly ever in touch. We didn't even know he had married yet another woman that past Christmas, not that it would have surprised us. He was a fool where women were concerned."

He moved his foot a little and plucked at the fabric of his expensive slacks, as if he needed something to do while he gathered his thoughts.

"Anyhow, that summer I was particularly pissed off. I thought I was too old to be packed off to spend the summer at my father's personal brothel. As I came into town, I stopped at Absolutely Nowhere and got myself falling-down drunk." He squinted a little, looking into the middle distance. "There was a woman there. Older than I was, but not by much, not that I cared. Blond, gorgeous, great body. She was nearly as drunk as I was and kept buying me drinks. I didn't think twice. We took one of the rooms and spent the night together."

Lara looked at her hands, which were still folded in her lap. Her knuckles were white now, too. She found herself praying this story would not end the way she had begun to guess it would. *Oh, Bryce...*

"She left before I did in the morning, which was a relief, considering I spent the first hour puking my guts up in the bathroom. I cleaned up, although my head was splitting and I still could hardly see straight, and I drove on into Heyday to present myself at my father's by noon, as legally mandated in the custody papers. Imagine my surprise when he introduced me to his new, beautiful, blond, seriously hungover wife."

She felt slightly dizzy. "Oh, Bryce."

"I must still have been a little drunk, because when she reached over to shake my hand, I laughed out loud. And then I proceeded to tell my father exactly what was so funny."

"Oh, my God."

"Yeah." He laughed shortly. "It wasn't a pretty scene. Things were said. Hideous things, on all sides. Needless to say, that was the end of the summer visits, the end of my father's five-month-long marriage to the delightful Cindy, and the last time I ever laid eyes on Heyday, until I came back after his death."

For a moment neither of them spoke. Words seemed inadequate, with these ugly pictures still hanging in the air between them.

"I'm so sorry," she said quietly.

"Don't be," he said. "It was the thing that finally set me free from this place. And who knows, maybe I was to blame. I've always thought that maybe, deep inside, I suspected who she was. We were careful not to give each other our names. But I definitely knew she was Anderson's type. She even looked a little bit like wife number four. Maybe I thought, on some subconscious level, that it might be a good way to announce my adult-hood, to assert my independence."

Or to take something from the father who had, in his time, taken so much from the unwanted, abandoned son? Lara didn't begin to know about the workings of the subconscious. All she knew was that Bryce had carried a crushing load of anger and guilt for far too long.

She looked around. They were the only ones left in this sun-dappled courtyard, where the bare-limbed trees cast jigsaw shadows on the brick paths.

"All right," she said, trying to make her voice as level and self-possessed as his. "Now I know what happened all those years ago. But what does that have to do with *today?* What does it have to do with *us?*"

He frowned. "Lara, there is no *us.*"

"Is that why you wanted to talk to me? Is that what you really wanted to tell me?"

He closed his eyes for a minute, and his hand made another fist, even tighter than before. For five long seconds, she was aware that a battle raged inside him.

Finally he opened his eyes.

"No," he said. "I wanted to tell you that I've run out of willpower. I can't resist you anymore."

Instinctively, she leaned forward, but he subtly tilted away from her. She read the message clearly. *Not yet.* There was still more to say.

"I know that, whatever you think at the moment, you won't stay in Heyday very long," he said. "Neither will I. But we're both here now, and this physical thing between us…it's real, and it's not going anywhere."

"No," she said. "It's not."

"I want you, Lara. And I think you want me. So as long as you understand exactly who I am, and what I'm capable of offering, I think we should be together."

Her stomach was so tight that breathing had ceased to be a natural, involuntary activity. She had to fight for every tablespoon of air she inhaled.

"Let me be sure, then, that I do understand," she said. "You think we should be lovers?"

"Yes. For whatever time we have left to us. I'll be here until the end of the term, that's all I'm sure of. I don't make promises, Lara, and I don't do forever. The only thing I can offer you is a few really nice weeks. In fact, I'd be willing to bet it will be the most amazing sex of our lives."

She had to laugh a little at that, though it also brought foolish moisture to her eyes. She hoped he'd chalk it down to the misting fountain.

"And for you," she said, "that's really saying something."

"Yes." His eyes were somber. "It is."

She looked at her hands, which now lay limp and pale in her lap. She fought for one more deep breath. This wasn't what she had imagined. She had dreamed of him coming to her, but the script had never read quite like this.

Was it enough?

"I need time to think," she said.

"Of course." He took his foot down, and straightened, clearly ready to leave. "If you decide I'm right, come to the fraternity house tomorrow night. I'll be waiting. If you don't show up, I'll know what that means. I won't bother you again."

A BIG, ROUND BLUE MOON shone from the sky like a spotlight on an empty black stage. It seemed to be waiting for Lara's grand entrance.

Bryce was waiting, too. He stood on the front porch and thought of all the things that could so easily keep her from coming. Her mother might weep. Her agent might call. Her own common sense might rebel, might tell her that this was one role she should turn down. The role of Bryce McClintock's newest plaything.

Her heart might simply say *no*. It might tell her she deserved more. She deserved better.

She *did* deserve better. Bryce knew that. But this was all he had to offer.

For her sake, he almost hoped she didn't come. For his sake...

Every time he heard a car approaching, his hands tightened on the balustrade. Even the dog's ears perked up. Every time the sound dwindled away, the night grew a little darker. And the dog lay back down, his head resting dejectedly on his paws.

Bryce checked his watch. He should have given her a deadline. He would have, except it might have sounded too much like an ultimatum. But at least if he'd said, *be there by nine,* it would be over by now. As it was, he told himself at nine that he'd keep watching until nine-thirty. At nine-thirty, ten sounded more realistic. At ten, he moved the line to ten-thirty.

At eleven, when he was half-frozen and almost ready to give up, she came.

She parked right in front of the frat house. He was halfway down the steps before she had even opened the door, with the dog loping along behind. As she got out of the car, Bryce caught her in his arms.

He took her head between his hands and kissed her cheek, her chin, her mouth. "I thought you weren't coming," he said.

She was laughing, a little breathless. "You liar." She leaned her head back so that he could kiss her throat. "You knew I would. Has any woman ever had the strength to resist you?"

"You're not any woman."

She pulled back then, and looked at him, her dark eyes catching the light from the moon. "Thank you for that," she said softly.

For answer, he kissed her again. The air was cold, and her lips were warm. Her body was soft, and his was as hard as a steel blade. He wondered if the back seat of her car was big enough....

But no, it wasn't going to be like this. With effort,

he regained control. *Patience*. She was here, she was his. There was plenty of time. He would treat her like the treasure she really was.

"Come." He tugged her hand.

"No, wait. My purse…"

"Leave it," he said, forgetting to be patient already. "It'll be fine. This is Heyday."

"It's not that." He could have sworn she was blushing. "It's that, well, I brought…I mean, I bought some—"

He grinned. "Me, too," he said. "But get yours, too. You never know."

Laughing, she grabbed a shapeless, knitted purse from the front seat and then, when he tugged her again, she flew along beside him up the stairs and into the house. She frowned when he insisted the dog stay on the porch, but she didn't argue. She just patted its head and tugged gently on one ear. "Sorry, buddy," she said. "Maybe next time."

He almost relented, but at the last minute he got tough. Since Bryce had started letting him sleep indoors, the damn dog had taken to crawling up on Bryce's bed in the night. The pooch could make all the sad eyes he wanted. That was *not* going to happen tonight.

As soon as they got into the house, Bryce kissed her in the foyer, because he couldn't help himself. She smelled like flowers, and she tasted like mint and sugar.

Finally, when he let go of her, she held on to his hand. She looked around the foyer, as if she were suddenly shy.

"You've been busy," she said, as she noticed the new furniture and light fixtures. "It's beautiful."

When she noticed the oak hall stand, with its ornate carving and beveled glass, she gave a little cry of pleasure. "Oh, I wondered who had bought this! I used to look at it in the window of Valley Treasures and wish I could have it for the ranch house."

He was suddenly sorry that he hadn't taken a more active role in the redecoration. "I didn't pick it out," he admitted. "I just wrote the man a check, and he did everything else."

But she was determined to think the best of him. "Well, you had the wisdom to pick the best antique dealer in town." She pulled a little on his hand. "Show me what else he's done."

Only a couple of the downstairs rooms were finished, the front parlor and the kitchen—and one more—but they were everything he'd hoped for. In those rooms, the Animal House ambiance was gone, and the dignity of the old Brennan estate had returned. She was, of course, delighted with everything, and he was delighted with her.

"There's one more room I've done over," he said when they had thoroughly admired the parlor and the kitchen. "But it's kind of a surprise."

Her eyes lit up. "Let me guess. Your bedroom?"

"No," he said. "That wouldn't be much of a surprise, would it? But we're not going up there just yet. First we're going to have some fun."

She wrinkled her nose mischievously. "I was kind of counting on having fun up there, too."

He kissed that silly nose. And then he kissed those tempting lips. "First," he said firmly. "The surprise."

He took her to the far side of the kitchen, where a door opened onto a room that had probably, in the Brennan's days, been a large sunporch or mudroom. But the frat boys had closed it in, turning it into a small movie theater.

"Oh!" She gasped with happy surprise. "It's darling!"

He was glad she hadn't seen it two weeks ago. The antique dealer had worked miracles here. He'd been surprised that this was one of the rooms Bryce wanted fixed up first, but once he got going he seemed to enjoy the challenge. He had left the high-tech viewing screen and projection box, but he had taken out all the ratty chairs and nasty shag rugs. He'd replaced them with a plush navy carpet and about six red-velvet seats, modern replicas of those used in the grand old movie houses.

Then he'd brought in an old-fashioned popcorn cart that looked a little like a circus wagon. Hours ago, Bryce had stocked it up, hoping that this moment would come. Now all he had to do was flip a switch, and the large silver bin of popcorn began to heat and spin.

"In the Omega Alpha days, they probably used this place to watch *Crazed Cheerleaders* or *Steamy Stewardesses*," he said with a wicked grin. "But for tonight I chose something a little more romantic."

She put her hand over her eyes and groaned. "Tell me it's not *The Highwayman*. I'd rather watch *Crazed Cheerleaders* any day."

"Well, we can have a double feature, if you like," he said. "First, though, I have *Roman Holiday*."

"Oh," she cried. "How did you know? That's one of my favorite movies in the world."

"You told me. A long time ago, when I first came on as your bodyguard. You told me that being *in* movies had almost killed your fun in watching them. You said it was the only movie you still loved, no matter what."

She dropped her purse on one of the chairs and came over to him. "You're a very special man, Bryce McClintock," she said.

He smiled down at her, his whole body, from heart to groin, throbbing with an exquisite awareness. She was amazing. Her joys were as clear and uninhibited as a child, and yet he knew she had the courage and heart and passion of ten women.

She reached up, as if she might stroke her fingers along his cheek.

"I think I'd better warn you," he said, his muscles already tightening in anticipation. "If you so much as touch me right now, we may not see much of this movie."

THEY ALMOST MADE IT. Lara was very careful to stay lighthearted and silly for the first half of the movie, and she knew he, too, worked at avoiding anything overtly sexual. He did make it fun, just as he had promised. They laughed out loud at jokes they'd heard a hundred times, jokes that somehow seemed brand-new to her tonight.

He was as playful as a teenager, doing foolish things

like holding out the bag of popcorn, then snatching it away the minute she put her fingers in. He even pretended to yawn and stretch, and then, oh-so-casually rest his arm along the back of her seat, the way her most insecure teenage boyfriend used to do.

When his fingers began to creep down, in a parody of the awkward date sneakily trying to get hold of her breast, she batted them away, just as she might have done at fifteen. He tried again and was rejected again.

It wasn't his fault that the game turned out to be an amazing turn-on. When he leaned over and nuzzled her neck, as if to distract her from what his hand was doing, she felt an electric shock go through her, and she murmured in astonished pleasure.

She forgot that her part in this game was to shoo his fingers away. They continued their downward quest, and suddenly she felt them close, hard and sure, over her breast.

She shut her eyes, melting. His hand stroked, and his lips sucked lightly at her earlobe, and she couldn't ever remember being so close to climax with so little physical contact. But his fingers were so knowing. They moved in slow circles, and then somehow, without her even being aware of it, he had unbuttoned her top button and was sliding his hand inside her shirt.

Oh, he must have been a terror, even at fifteen. His hands were like a magician's, creating warmth and color and blooming flowers out of nothing. She arched her back, pressing her breast against his hand.

Somehow, because the movie was still rolling, and the room was dark and filled with the sweet-salty scent of popcorn, they remained completely silent throughout it all. Their actions carried the titillation of the forbidden, and she never wanted it to stop.

The bag of popcorn he had been holding spilled on the floor as he tilted toward her, putting his other hand on her knee. She let her head drop against the seat back and waited, watching the images flicker on the screen. She felt as if she had been suspended very high, on something very precarious, and at any minute she might fall.

Slowly, he slid his hand up her thigh, deftly folding her skirt into tiny accordion pleats as he went, so that soon her leg was bare, and his fingers were sliding under the silk of her panties.

She breathed shallowly, as her legs began to shake and ease apart to give him room. "Bryce," she whispered helplessly.

"Shhh," he said, as if, unless they were very, very careful, the nonexistent usher could hear them. "Just watch the movie."

Somehow she kept her eyes open, though she had stopped seeing anything, really. His fingers were moving, were filling her with heat, a heat like thick honey and sweetest pain. At the same time, his other hand mapped her breast with fire.

Music played, and on the screen Audrey Hepburn and Gregory Peck talked and smiled. But here in the velvet seats the world was coming apart. She called his name, and her own name echoed back to her, as if from a great distance.

And then suddenly, although she gripped the armrests for balance, she was falling. Falling from that high, precarious place, tumbling helpless and headlong into the black and empty spaces.

WHEN SHE WAS READY, when she could walk, she let him lead her upstairs to his bedroom.

And there they made love, over and over again.

She could hardly believe how wonderful it was. From the innocence of their movie game to the dark, painful fire of their first real joining, he found every emotion she had ever tried to hide. She moaned, she begged, she writhed with sweat. Sometimes she laughed, and so did he. Once, when he stretched the tension out so far she felt as if she were made of hot, melting strings of glimmering glass, she even wept.

It took the whole night, but finally, because he had done all the work, he was spent. He lay beside her, his damp, beautiful body glowing in the silver dawn light. His breath slowed, and his rugged features softened, revealing an inner sweetness that might have surprised her yesterday, but not today. And then, slowly, he sank into sleep.

She was tired, too, limp with satisfaction, but she didn't shut her eyes. She didn't know how many nights like this they would have before he grew bored and wanted to move on.

And so, just this once, she watched over him, the way he had always watched over her.

CHAPTER THIRTEEN

KARLA FOLDED HER favorite lemon-colored satin shirt carefully, wondering why she had bothered to bring it to Heyday in the first place. If she'd realized what a hick town this was, she would have packed only stone-washed denim and plaid flannel yee-haw clothes.

And if she'd realized Lara wasn't going to spend any time with her, wasn't going to listen to a word she said about anything, including Bryce McClintock, she wouldn't have come at all.

She pulled her creamy linen skirt from the hanger, snapping the jaws that had held it in place. She'd be finished packing in half an hour or so. If Lara hadn't come home by then, well, too bad. Karla would just leave a note, call a cab and get herself to the Richmond airport.

In her jerky anger, though, she was clumsy. She flipped open the lid to her second suitcase, and it came down hard on the nightstand, knocking last night's mug of tea to the floor. It crashed into a dozen pieces.

And if that weren't bad enough, clearly the noise carried all the way down to the first floor. The next thing she heard was Oscar climbing the staircase.

He seemed to stop halfway up. "Everything okay?"

"Fine," she called back, her teeth clenched. "Everything's fine."

But her voice didn't sound fine—even she could hear the fraying edge of stress. And of course Oscar wasn't the type to mind his own business, so he came slowly loping the rest of the way up the stairs.

He paused in her doorway, his gaze taking in the two suitcases open on the bed, the half-empty closet, the gaping drawers.

He looked at her, then, with that wounded-pirate face he'd had ever since the accident. The black patch over one eye, the red, jagged scar on forehead and cheek—it should have been hideous, but on him it wasn't. He just looked even more rakish, powerful, inscrutable. He could pin you down with that one good eye more completely than most men could do with two.

She set the pieces of broken pottery on the table. "What?"

He chewed the inside of his cheek. "This is a mistake," he said, as usual reducing the conversational equation to its simplest terms.

It was a particularly annoying gimmick. She happened to know he had a doctorate in farm management—Lara had told her—so the wise old rustic primitive routine was just an act.

"I'm sorry you think so," she said, returning to folding her linen skirt. "But perhaps you'll consider the possibility that I might know better what to do with my own life."

"No," he said. "I doubt it. Not when you're all riled up and hurting."

She wheeled on him. "I'm not *hurting*," she said icily. "If you must know, I'm damn angry."

He shrugged. "Maybe. In my experience, there's not a whole lot of difference."

For a minute she thought about throwing something at him, but the only things within reach were her clothes, and that would have been ridiculous. A silk shirt, even one launched with real conviction, didn't make much of a missile.

"I really don't care to talk to you about it." She glared at him, wondering why she suddenly felt tearful. "Why don't you just get out?"

"You know, that's not a bad idea. Why don't we both get out for a while? Take a walk, maybe. A little fresh air never hurts."

"You go." She folded that same skirt a third time. It just would not lie flat, damn it. "I'm busy right now."

He came into the room then, as if she'd invited him. "No, you're not," he said. "You've dug yourself into an emotional rut, and you're just spinning your wheels, kicking up mud all over everything."

She squeezed the skirt, crumpling it. "Damn it, Oscar, I will *not* talk to you about this—"

To her surprise, he reached out and took hold of her wrist. He shook it lightly, urging her to drop the creamy linen. Then he wrapped her hand inside his large, callused fingers.

"Come on, Karla," he said gently. "Let's take a walk by the river."

She wasn't quite sure why she said yes. The view from the window was hardly inspiring—it had snowed a little in the night, and now that the sun was up everything was runny and slushy.

Maybe it was just because she could see he wasn't going to take no for an answer. Or maybe it was because she knew her mood was dangerously overwrought, and she needed to get some perspective before she gave herself a stroke.

Still, she almost changed her mind three times before they finally got outside. The worst moment was when she insisted on stopping by the downstairs half-bath to freshen up her lipstick and brush her hair.

"Well, sure, obviously you can't go for a walk without lipstick," he said, laughing. "Imagine what the squirrels would say."

But somehow she held on to her temper and finally they made it out of the house. The sky was blue, and the air was crisp. The river was a ten-minute stroll away, and Oscar didn't say a word the entire trip. Maybe that was smart, she thought. The rhythm of walking was soothing, and the cool air on her cheeks was invigorating, chasing off some of the confusion and resentment.

By the time they got to the river path, which ran along the edge of a wooded copse, she felt a good bit more relaxed.

So relaxed, in fact, that when they saw a squirrel, and it froze in place, its forepaws raised, staring at them in total horror, she was able to laugh out loud.

"See?" She grinned over at Oscar. "Squirrels are more judgmental than you think."

He chuckled. They walked in silence a few more

yards, and finally, as she'd known he would, he asked her about the suitcases.

"So why exactly did you want to leave?" The shade here had kept the snow from melting, and their boots made crunching sounds as they walked. "You couldn't have been that upset just because Lara spent the night with Bryce."

Karla took a minute before answering. He sounded as if he really wanted to understand, and it made her realize that she didn't fully comprehend the intensity of her anger herself.

"No," she said. "Probably not. I'm not a prude, and she is an adult. It's just that…she seems completely indifferent to my advice. They both are. Just a few days ago I specifically asked Bryce to—"

She stopped, realizing that she had intended to keep her visit to Bryce a secret.

Oscar was looking at her. "God, Karla, do you have to play into every stage-mother stereotype there is? You went to Bryce behind her back?"

"Yes, I did," she said defiantly. "I don't care what names you call me. Lara is my daughter, and she is standing at a fork in the road. She has decisions to make that will affect the rest of her life. Getting involved with Bryce McClintock is the worst possible thing that could happen to her right now." She kicked a small stone out of her path. "Or ever."

Oscar slowed down. "Ever's a mighty long time. Why do you think that?"

She felt herself getting wound up all over again. "How can you ask such a question? You know what kind of man he is. He doesn't care about Lara, except as a notch on his bedpost. He's going to use her as long as it amuses him, and then he's going to toss her out like stale bread."

She folded her arms across her chest. It was colder out here than she'd realized. "Losing her chance to make it big in Hollywood is bad enough. But the real tragedy is that she *does* care about *him*. She may not tell me all her secrets anymore, but any fool can read that one on her face. She's in love with the bastard, and he's going to break her heart."

Oscar kept walking, but he didn't speak. The only sound was the gossipy chittering of squirrels and the sluggish trickle of the winter-shallow river beside them.

She waited as long as she could, and then she looked over at him. "Well? You know I'm right. You know it's all true."

"No, I don't," he said evenly. "I don't have a clue what's going on between those two, and frankly I don't care. They're going to do whatever they want to. Young people always do. What I'm really curious about is why you care more about her life than you do about your own."

"Damn it, Oscar." Tears stung at her eyelids. "She *is* my life!"

"Yeah, but she doesn't have to be. She doesn't even want to be." He dug his hands in his pockets. "You're still a young woman yourself, you know. You're good-looking, or could be if you'd leave off some of the paint. And you've still got a lot of fire."

She was so angry she could hardly keep from sputtering. "How dare you tell me, tell me how to—"

He chuckled. "See? It happens whenever I tick you off. You're not dead yet, not by a long shot. So why don't you forget about Lara? Why don't you get out there and get passionate about something?"

He turned and looked at her with that pirate's eye. "Or, better yet…some*body?*"

ABOUT TWO WEEKS INTO their affair, Bryce realized that Lara was one woman he might never get tired of. As far as he could tell, she wasn't ever going to give him the chance to.

He'd never met a busier woman. She had classes, she had study groups, she had research at the library. She had dinners and shopping trips with her mother, and evenings of baby-sitting for Terri Wooten. And she had two full volunteer afternoons a week at the retirement home.

None of which she was willing to cancel just so that she could be with him. That was the real difference. His other lovers had always been eager to put their own lives on hold, in order to fit into his. For Lara, work commitments always came first. Then family and the friends who counted on her. Personal playtime—which apparently included even earth-moving, star-shaking, mind-boggling sex—finished a distant third.

By the second week, when she told him she'd have to put in extra hours at the retirement home because their spring concert was coming up, he found himself desperate enough to offer to help out. At least if they were in the same building, maybe he could steal a kiss or two behind the stage curtain.

So far, though, he hadn't had any luck. She was always either conferring with Nelson, who was in charge of the choreography and decorations, or playing the piano for Vivian, who apparently was going to sing "The White Diffs of Clover" as the concert finale.

He had been put to work cutting out silver stars with two adorable but extremely senile old ladies who probably shouldn't have been allowed to touch anything as sharp as scissors in the first place.

They'd each completed about one star so far. They were too busy whispering about him behind their pieces of poster board. Unfortunately, because they were both deaf, their whispers were as loud as foghorns, and everyone within three tables heard every word.

The one in the perky platinum-blond wig started it. "He's a major stud," she "whispered" to her friend. "Who did they say he was?"

The other, who had fake diamonds the size of dumplings hanging from her ears, smacked her bright red lips.

"He's a McClintock," she said. "He's the *bad* one. They say he's slept with everyone in Heyday."

The blonde rolled her eyes in his direction, jiggling with excitement. "Did he sleep with me?"

Her friend slapped her with the poster board. "Of course not, you dirty old woman. You're too old for him. Although they do say he slept with his mother."

Bryce hadn't thought that story could ever make him laugh again, but at the look on Blondie's face, he almost lost it. Covering the sputter with a cough, he stood up and wandered over to the vending machine. Too bad they didn't sell straight Scotch in aluminum cans. He could have used a drink right about now.

Actually, what he really needed was Lara. Abandoning the colas and juices, he climbed up to the stage, grabbed her hand and pulled her out of sight behind the curtain.

"Bryce," she scolded him after he'd kissed her thoroughly. "You promised me that if you came you'd really, truly help."

"I'm trying," he said. "But I can't think about anything but getting you in bed. If you don't come home with me now, I don't know what I'll do. There's a hundred-year-old blond woman at my table who is hitting on me pretty hard."

She sighed dramatically. "Well, you did warn me it would happen. I hope you both are very happy. Now may I please get back to work?"

Grudgingly, he relinquished her. He stayed in the wings, safe from his antiquated admirers, and watched as Lara and Nelson got ready to rehearse their number, "I Could Have Danced All Night" from *My Fair Lady*.

At first it was all jumbled skip-steps and laughter, with Nelson barking new choreography orders every few seconds and Lara struggling to keep up with his changes. But somehow, as if by magic, it all came together. Someone started the tape, and they began to run through the number in earnest.

Everyone in the room fell silent as the beautiful young woman and her courtly, elderly partner began to twirl across the stage. Bryce's hand dropped from the curtain and fell numbly at his side.

She was magnificent. Even here, with no spotlight, no makeup, no costume, no camera, she was a star. Her voice was clear and sweet, and her dancing was pure joy made visible. Within seconds, she wasn't Lara Gilbert anymore. She was the love-struck Eliza Doolittle, a smudged and hungry flower girl who had spent an evening masquerading as a princess and never wanted it to end.

When it was over, the hushed room seemed almost too mesmerized to react. But slowly, as the spell wore off, the clapping started. And it didn't end until all the people in the room, even the oldest residents who used walkers to stand, were on their feet calling her name.

Lara was blushing, and shaking her head, pulling Nelson out for his share of the recognition. When he refused, merely bowing humbly before her talent, she curtseyed and blew him an embarrassed kiss. Then she faced her audience again, laughing and waving her hand, begging them to stop.

But they didn't. They couldn't. They were all in love with her.

And from his quiet corner of the stage, Bryce watched like a frozen man, stunned by the warring emotions of swelling pride and aching fear.

He suddenly realized that, in spite of all his tough words, he had let himself start to hope. To hope that the exotic, sparkling starlet was gone forever—and that the simple girl-next-door might be here to stay.

But the cheers still ringing through this humble hall showed just how desperately wrong he'd been.

This woman didn't belong in Heyday.

And she didn't belong to him.

CHAPTER FOURTEEN

"YOU'RE EARLY, LARA." Karla glanced over at the handsome grandfather clock in the corner of the antique store, which said 12:05. "Oh, no, you aren't—I'm running late. Sorry. Be right there."

Lara had to smile. Just a couple of weeks ago, Karla would have been sitting around counting the minutes until Lara showed up to take her to lunch. She would have been chilly and offended if Lara had been even five minutes late, as she was this morning.

But now that Karla had something of her own to do, everything was different. Wonderfully different.

Karla, who had spent a lot of time browsing around Valley Treasures, which she considered the only decent store in Heyday, had become friendly with the owner, Dan. When Dan landed the commission to redecorate the frat house, he had needed to hire temporary part-time help. He'd offered the job to Karla. Lara had been shocked to hear that Karla had said yes.

"That's okay," Lara said. "Take your time. I can amuse myself in this place forever."

Karla was wrapping a bisque shepherdess for mailing. "Hey, check out that bronze stallion in the far corner," she called as Lara wandered off. "Do you think Oscar might like it?"

Lara cast a curious glance back at her mother, but Karla was busy filling a box with popcorn packing material. Would *Oscar* like it? *Hmmm...* Lara had not been at Lazy Gables much lately. She wondered if she might have missed some interesting developments.

"It's lovely," she said as casually as possible. "I'm sure he would." She suddenly couldn't wait for lunch. It seemed they were going to have plenty to talk about.

While Karla finished up, Lara wandered the crowded aisles contentedly, running her fingers over the glossy old wood and tickling tiny musical notes out of the dangling crystals of Victorian candelabra.

She saw a gorgeous oil, an English country landscape, that would look perfect over the mantel in the frat house, but she forced herself to move past it without even checking the price. She had to fight all urges to begin "nesting." She could only imagine how spooked Bryce would be if she started rearranging furniture and hanging pictures. She'd be his newest ex-lover before the sun went down.

She wouldn't do anything to risk that. She was too happy the way things were. In truth, it almost frightened her to be this happy—as if surely disaster must be waiting around the corner.

But for now everything was practically perfect. Amazingly, even Karla seemed to have accepted Lara's relationship with Bryce. They'd had one hot argument, that first evening, when she'd told her mother she was going to Bryce's house, and she did not expect to be back until the next day.

Karla had been furious, accusing Bryce of exploit-
ing Lara, toying with her, planning to break her heart.
Accusing him of deliberately trying to derail any
chance Lara might have of salvaging her career.

But Lara had stood her ground. "I'm sorry you don't
approve," she'd said. "But this is my decision, and nothing you can say will change my mind."

By the time Lara returned the next afternoon, Karla
seemed to have come to terms with the idea, more or
less. She still didn't like it, that was obvious. She still
made the occasional snide comment about how she
hoped Bryce was worth it, always adding a fatalistic
sigh that said she knew full well he wasn't.

"Okay, let's go!"

Karla flipped the sign to Closed...Back At 1:00, and
they walked the half block down to the Big Top Diner.
Karla still grumbled about the tacky carny décor, but
she'd had to admit that the Southern Fried Circus
Chicken Salad was delicious.

"These people just need to get over it," Karla said as
they sat down in one of the window booths. "What on
earth is a 'circus chicken,' anyhow?"

It was her favorite joke. She said it every time they
came here, which was about twice a week. Lara rolled
her eyes. "Mom, give it up," she said. That was her standard line, too. It had become part of the fun.

They were halfway through lunch when Karla's cell
phone rang. She looked at the caller ID and made a happy
sound. "Oh, it's L.A.!" She always acted as if she'd been
banished to one of the solar system's outer planets, and
a call from L.A. was a message from Mother Earth.

Lara sighed and went on eating. Karla talked cryptically for a couple of minutes, then handed the telephone to Lara with a triumphant smile. "It's for you! They've got a buyer for your condo. Looks as if you'll be going back to L.A., after all!"

"IT'S ONLY FOR A COUPLE of days," Lara said, giving Bryce's hand a squeeze. "I just have to sign some papers, supervise the movers and grab a few things I left behind at the condo."

The two of them were standing on the porch at Lazy Gables, saying an early good-night. Ever since she'd told him about her upcoming trip to L.A., their evening had been tense. She found herself babbling awkwardly here at the end, wishing she could say something to take that skeptical look from his face.

It didn't help that Karla had come to the door twice already, asking Lara whether she'd remembered to pack this blouse or that skirt. Just as Bryce was about to answer, Karla popped open the door again, and peeked out with an apologetic smile. "What about the dark green Armani? You will want to look your best," she said. "L.A. isn't exactly Heyday."

"Mom, I'll do the packing myself when I come in," Lara said, trying to keep her exasperation out of her voice. "And why would I need the Armani to go to a real estate closing? Did the King of England buy my condo?"

Karla laughed, clearly too excited to take offense. "Well, you just never know what might come up while you're there. Sylvia will want to see you, of course, and…well, it's just better to be prepared."

When she finally shut the door again, Lara turned to Bryce with an apologetic smile. "Sorry about that. I guess I'd better go in before she implodes."

He nodded, and then he leaned in to give her a quick kiss. She wrapped her arms around his neck impulsively, urging him to make it a real one. He held back for a split second, but then he put his arms around her and did it properly. So properly, in fact, that her knees went a little weak, and she began to wonder if there weren't some way to go back to the frat house, at least for an hour or so.

But there wasn't, of course. The best thing was just to get this done, get it over with. The condo was her last real tie to L.A., and once she'd sold it she was completely free.

"I'll miss you," she said.

"I'll miss you, too." He kept his arms around her. "I don't like to think about how much."

She grinned and pressed herself even closer. "Oh, really?" She nipped at his lower lip. "Like…how much, exactly? Can you show me?"

"Not here, I can't, you witch." He put his hands on her bottom and tilted her into him. "Your mother would have me arrested."

Just then a courier truck came lumbering up the driveway. Lara groaned and watched as the driver got out of the cab and walked up to the front porch, the suspiciously familiar thick envelope in his arms.

"Hi," he said. "Looks like you got another care package. Sign here?"

As Lara was signing, she could feel Bryce's eyes on

her. He knew what it was, of course. She had told him about the mounds of scripts piling up in the front foyer. He'd even seen them for himself.

"Thanks," she said as the driver took back his hand-held electronic tracker, where she'd just scrawled her name.

He was pulling away when her mother opened the door yet again.

"Oh, it did come!" She patted the top of the package happily. "Sylvia said she'd get it here in time. She thinks this one is really special, Lara. She wants you to read it on the plane so you two can talk about it when you get to L.A."

Lara held out the package, stiff-armed and furious. Was Karla just trying to stir up trouble? Surely she knew how hard Lara was struggling to make Bryce believe she really was through with Hollywood.

"Put it with the rest of the scripts that are moldering in the hall, Mother. I'm not going to read it. And I'm not going to be seeing Sylvia, either. I'm flying to L.A. for the real estate signing. Nothing else."

Her mother took the package, her cheeks pink and her eyes flashing. "Well, that's some way to treat Sylvia, a woman who slaved night and day for you, every day for ten long years."

"For a fee, Mother. She was well compensated for her efforts."

"Yes, and just when they were really beginning to pay off, you decide to throw it all away. Well, just because you've decided you're having fun playing house here in Heyday doesn't mean you should treat your old friends without respect. Surely even Bryce McClintock doesn't mind if you have lunch with your agent just one time."

She swiveled and glared at Bryce. "Does he?"

"Mom!" Lara held her hand up between them.

But she needn't have bothered. Bryce seemed unfazed by Lara's mother's antics.

He looked down at Karla coolly. "Lara and I have put absolutely no restrictions on one another. She knows that, as far as I'm concerned, she's free to do whatever she wants." He paused. "I've offered her freedom. Perhaps you should ask yourself if she can say the same about you?"

BRAVE WORDS, but over the next two days he nearly went insane. He couldn't sleep. He found himself talking to the dog, whom Lara had named Lucky. The two of them watched idiotic television shows until even Lucky couldn't take any more and wandered out to sleep in the hall.

Bryce snapped at his students, growling at Ilsa, who got tears in her eyes, and nearly biting Rob Overton's head off just for making a dumb comment. As if Rob Overton could make any other kind.

What the hell was the matter with him? He'd always found girlfriends to be completely interchangeable, like lightbulbs or air-conditioner filters. You had a certain size, style and wattage you preferred, but after that what difference did it make whether you were out with Sally or Becky or Kim?

And it wasn't as if he was some kind of sex-crazed

teenager. He was thirty-two years old, for God's sake, and perfectly capable of keeping his pants on. During his FBI years, he had been known to get so involved in a case that he might go a month or two without dating anyone.

So why did two days of celibacy suddenly feel like torture?

When the telephone rang, he jumped. It wasn't until the second day that he realized why. Yes, he was eager to hear her voice—it took the sting out of the loneliness, just a little, when they had a chance to talk. But that wasn't what made him so edgy. Deep inside, he was always afraid that the next time the phone rang it would be Lara calling to say she had decided to stay in L.A.

When they talked, he didn't mention her mother, or the script, or whether she'd met with Sylvia. If she had, she'd tell him. This wasn't a relationship where anyone had to lie, because there were no strings attached, ground rules they'd set from the beginning.

And did it really matter, anyhow? Even if the bigwigs didn't talk her into staying this time, they would talk her into it eventually.

In fact, on some level he understood that it might be better if she just never came back at all. If he was this dependent on her already, how bad would he get if their relationship went on much longer?

"Tell me a story, Bryce." Terri Wooten had rolled her wheelchair into the kitchen, where Bryce was installing new pantry shelves. "Dad's no fun."

"Dad's working on electricity, and he has to concentrate," Harry said crossly from the other side of the door, "or he'll zap us all to kingdom come."

Terri rolled her eyes. "See?"

Lucky had followed her in and came over to give Bryce's hand a hello lick. Bryce patted the dog on the head, then got down on his knees to check the hinges on these old-fashioned shelves. They had Phillips-head screws. He shooed the dog away and felt around behind him for the other screwdriver.

"What kind of story?" He glanced over his shoulder at the little girl. "I've told you all my good FBI superhero stories already. Last time you complained that I was repeating myself."

"Yeah, I'm tired of superhero stuff," Terri said. She had rolled herself across to the kitchen table, where the remnants of a plate of peanut butter cookies still sat. She fed one to Lucky, and then stuffed one into her own mouth and talked around it. "Tell me about Tony Barnett. You knew him, right?"

Uh-oh. This was dangerous ground. Bryce didn't like Tony on a good day, and today, when Lara was in L.A., and Bryce was cranky, sleepless and horny… today was definitely *not* a good day.

"I didn't know him very well. I met him a couple of times."

"Were he and Lara like, in love?"

Bryce dropped the screwdriver. "Hell, no!"

"Hey," Harry warned. "Keep it clean."

"Sorry," Bryce mumbled. "But no, they were not in love."

"Are you sure?" Terri sounded doubtful. "When you

see them kissing in *The Highwayman,* they sure look like they are."

"Believe me, squirt, they're not," Bryce said grumpily, remembering those steamy kisses all too well. "It's called *acting.*"

From the other side of the door, Bryce could hear Harry chuckling. "And sometimes it's called the green-eyed monster."

"What is?" a light, smiling voice said from the doorway.

"Lara!" Terri squealed with excitement, and Lucky's paws went skittering across the floor in unabashed canine delight.

Bryce sat up so fast he bumped his head on the shelves. How could it be? Lara wasn't due in until late tonight.

But it was. She was standing in the kitchen, in a slanting ray of afternoon sun, wearing old blue jeans, sneakers and a Moresville College sweatshirt. Lucky was jumping all over her, trying to lick her face, and she was leaning down, giving Terri a high-five.

Bryce got quickly to his feet, crossed the room in half a second and swept her into his arms.

"Hey, gorgeous," he said, twirling her around. "You came back."

"Of course I did." She laughed. "In case you hadn't noticed, I even came home early."

He stopped spinning and looked into her eyes. "Because you missed me?"

She bit her lip, considering. "That depends. Did *you* miss *me*?"

"Maybe a little," he said. "Maybe every single second of every single day."

She smiled. "It was only one day," she said.

"And a half." He tucked a stray strand of hair behind her ear. "A whole day and a half. And don't forget the nights, too."

She shook her head. "No. I couldn't forget the nights."

He kissed her then, because he couldn't wait until they were alone. Just a quick one, he thought, but then one wasn't enough, and he had to keep going. He dug his hands into her hair, and he pulled her in as close as he could get.

"Terri, I think we'd better head on home now," Harry said, chuckling. "Your mom will be cooking dinner."

"I'm not hungry. I ate a million cookies."

"Still. She's expecting us. Besides, I think maybe Lara and Bryce would like to be alone."

Terri was silent a moment, and then she spoke in a speculative, thoughtful voice. "Hey, Dad," she said. "I'm pretty sure they're not just acting now, aren't you?"

Harry laughed. "I'd bet the bank on it, sweetie. *Nobody's* that good."

LARA KNEW she shouldn't keep secrets from Bryce, especially not secrets about such a sensitive subject. But it was so heavenly to be home. She just couldn't bring herself to spoil things by talking about Los Angeles.

Home. Funny, wasn't it? She'd already begun to think of Heyday that way….

She promised herself she'd tell him everything to-morrow. It might be cowardly, but she had missed him so much. She wanted at least this one unclouded night together.

At the park renovation auction, she had bought dinner for two at the Black-and-White Lounge. She didn't have any particular desire to eat there, but she'd felt sorry for the place, because no one was bidding. Apparently the lounge had just started offering meals, and most people in Heyday were fairly skeptical.

She'd tried to give the coupons to the Wootens, but they had declined with thanks—and a chuckle that made her wonder what they knew that she didn't.

Still, she felt a little guilty about not claiming her prize. The owner had called last week, excited to hear that the local celebrity had won and wondering when she'd be in to collect her dinner. After a good bit of begging, Bryce had agreed to go with her tonight.

Big mistake! The minute they walked in the door, she could tell they were in for it.

The owner recognized her instantly and insisted that she stand by the bar, surrounded by waiters and bartenders wearing tuxedos and zebra ears, while he snapped about two dozen pictures. Then he announced her arrival over the music system, and led the room in a round of applause.

The only good news was that the place was fairly crowded. Surely that was a good sign. The food couldn't be truly terrible, could it?

Yes, it could. Belatedly she realized that all those other guests were just eating pretzels, nachos and

chicken wings to help wash down their cocktails and
beer. Bryce got one whiff of the duck l'orange, and he
waved his hand for a round of drinks. "If you get drunk
enough, I hear your taste buds go numb," he whispered
as the waiter hurried off for refills.

Apparently he was right. By the second drink, she
didn't even think the duck was very disgusting at all,
although she noticed Bryce was still eating mostly lettuce and bread. She'd always been overly susceptible
to liquor, and by the third drink, when she told Bryce
it might be fun to use the undercooked asparagus spears
as tiny golf clubs, and the pearl onions as balls, he announced that, sadly, he was going to have to cut her off.

Neither one of them was drunk, exactly, but they
were unusually relaxed—something she was particularly glad of when the lounge door opened one more
time, and Claire and Kieran walked in with a couple of
friends.

Lara wasn't sure exactly where things stood in the
McClintock brotherhood, but it was common Heyday
knowledge that there was serious tension. She'd seen
it on Bryce's face whenever anyone mentioned Kieran
or Claire or the new baby. And she'd obviously noticed
that the two siblings never socialized—indeed, they
hardly even spoke.

Claire spotted Bryce and Lara, and, with only the ti-
niest hesitation, she began to walk in the direction of
their table. "Hi, Bryce," she called cheerfully. "Hi, Lara!"

Lara felt Bryce stiffen, but she put her hand on his
knee under the table. He glanced at her, and she gave
him a small smile that, she hoped, held a gentle plea.

"It's okay," she said softly. "It'll be fine."

He raised one brow, indicating his profound skepticism, but to her delight his posture relaxed, and he half stood, his napkin in his hand, and welcomed the others to the table.

"Hi, everyone," he said. He didn't actually suggest they pull up chairs, but he didn't say no when Claire asked if it would be all right if they joined him.

Besides Kieran and Claire, the newcomers included Mallory Rackham and her date, a man named Roddy, who apparently was a good friend of Kieran's. They all ordered beer and chicken wings, insisting with winks and grins that they wouldn't *dream* of depriving Lara and Bryce of even one bit of their gourmet dinner.

Maybe it was just that she'd had more drinks than usual, but Lara found the rest of the evening delightful. She'd met Mallory before, but this was her first chance to spend any social time with her. And Roddy was down-to-earth and funny and great-looking, too—though, in Lara's eyes, neither Roddy nor Kieran could hold a candle to Bryce.

She took off her shoe and ran her foot along his leg, meeting his rakish smile with one of her own. Bryce was the sexiest man alive.

He seemed to be enjoying himself, too—and not just the times when they played footsie under the table. She was relieved to see how well he got along with Kieran. Maybe beer, she thought, should be set out at every United Nations meeting instead of water.

At one point, when the hour got fairly late, and the bar got crowded, the three men went up to the bar to coax another round out of the busy bartender. They were gone a long time, and Lara looked over her shoulder to check on Bryce. To her surprise, they were standing comfortably together at the bar, looking at a large sheet of paper Kieran held and laughing.

Claire had followed her gaze. "I feel like one of those international diplomats, don't you?" She chewed on a pretzel happily. "I think we've just successfully brokered the first of the McClintock Brothers Peace Talks."

Lara smiled. "If only it doesn't all disappear with the hangover."

"Hey." Claire shrugged. "You've got to start somewhere."

Mallory leaned in. "Lara, I've just got to ask you something while the boys aren't here. I don't mean to be nosy, but—" She glanced nervously toward the bar. "I've just got to know."

Lara smiled. "About me and Bryce?"

"God, no. You and Bryce?" Mallory waved her hand dismissively. "Why would I waste a question on that? It's written all over your faces. No, what I need to know is, what's it like to kiss Tony Barnett?"

"Mallory," Claire scolded, laughing. "For heaven's sake!"

"Well?" Mallory looked defiant in a cute and tipsy way. "I'm sorry, Claire. Not all of us are so love-stunned that our hormones have stopped getting jiggy when we see a gorgeous guy. Come on, Lara. What was it like to kiss that man?"

"Well, let's see. How can I describe it?" Lara thought

for a moment, then she took her fork and speared the last soggy, overcooked mushroom on her plate. She held it up and raised her eyebrows.

Mallory gasped, her hand on her heart. "No," she said. *"No."*

Lara shook her fork, making the mushroom wiggle and droop. "Sorry," she said. "But yes."

The men came back then, drinks in hand. The paper they'd been looking at had disappeared, but they were still chuckling.

"What exactly is so darn funny?" Claire gave Kieran a mock-stern look. "How come we don't get to hear the joke?"

Kieran just shook his head as he sat down, and waved his hand, as if to say, *don't ask.* But Roddy and Bryce, apparently, couldn't wait to share the glee.

"You know how they're planning to put up a statue of Kieran in the park," Roddy said, "to honor him for donating so much land?"

"No." Lara really hadn't heard. News apparently didn't travel out to Lazy Gables very fast. "That's great, Kieran. It's quite an honor. But why is that funny?"

Mallory grinned. "Oh, yeah. The St. Kieran memorial. All the adoring women in town will leave flowers at the statue's feet daily."

Roddy raised his glass. "Starting with the sexy Swedish housekeeper, who already shines his boots daily, anyhow."

Claire grinned at Kieran and rolled her eyes. "She is pretty fawning, isn't she? But at least she hasn't erected a statue in his name."

Kieran groaned and polished off his beer. "Hell, now I wish I hadn't even mentioned it. I'm never going to live this down, am I?"

Bryce smiled. "Probably not." He turned to the others. "We were looking at the artist's rendering of the proposed design. And it's…well, it's…"

He nudged Kieran, laughing. "Words just won't do it justice. Come on, Kieran, show the ladies your statue."

Muttering under his breath, Kieran reached into his jacket pocket and brought back out the sheet of paper. He unfolded it, at least four times, until it practically took up the whole table.

The women all bent forward, eager to see what was so funny. At first, Lara thought she must be seeing things. She blinked, squeezed her eyes, and tried to clear her vision. Maybe she really had drunk too much.

"Is that—" She tilted her head, trying to see it from another angle. "Is that man riding a *zebra?*"

"Oh, my God." Mallory plopped back onto her chair, her mouth open. And then she began to laugh. "Oh, my God," she said again, as if there were no other words.

Bryce and Roddy were leaning back, laughing so hard their eyes watered. Claire, Lara saw, was trying not to laugh, but it wasn't working. She finally put her head in her hands and shook silently, unable to hold it in.

"If they put this thing up," Kieran said, his eyes, too, brimming with helpless mirth. "If they put it up, I swear to God, I'll move." He turned to his brother. "You're the lawyer, Bryce. Can't I sue them?"

"I don't know." Bryce was still laughing. "I think the law on excessive adoration may be a little murky."

Kieran glanced at the drawing one more time, then closed his eyes fatalistically. "God help me," he said.

"Tough luck, bro." Bryce patted his shoulder. "But hey, nobody ever said sainthood was easy."

THE BARTENDER CUT THEM OFF and served them coffee for at least an hour before he'd let them leave.

So technically, when they got home, Lara knew they were both sober. But something surreal and exciting remained from the evening, some sense of heightened awareness and the absence of barriers.

Bryce made love to Lara with a slow and dreamy precision. She drifted in a lovely haze of sensuality, where everything was pleasure, and everything was possible.

She wouldn't have thought they still had inhibitions, after the past couple of weeks, but tonight she saw what true honesty, true trust, could do.

They took their time, exploring every inch of each other, trying every idea that presented itself. The result was uncharted, unchoreographed, unfamiliar... and thrilling beyond words.

They couldn't get enough. But toward dawn they simply didn't have the stamina to go on. He wrapped her in his arms, touched a warm kiss to her shoulder, and, spooned together, they slept.

When she woke in the morning, he wasn't there. Stretching, yawning, feeling her head to be sure it wasn't pounding, she got out of bed.

He wasn't in the bathroom, either. She pulled on his shirt, buttoned a couple of buttons—why do them all, only to undo them again?—and walked barefoot down the lovely staircase to look for him.

He was standing at the front door, wearing only his blue jeans. His back was gorgeous, she thought. Long, sculpted lines of bronzed beauty tapering into a hint of tight, paler buttocks. Her palms tingled, remembering how the skin there felt, so cool and satiny smooth.

She tiptoed up behind him, wondering if she could slip her hands down inside his waistband without being seen by the person on the other side of the door.

Who was it, anyhow? Harry? She caught a glimpse of strange hair, red-and-green hair. Oh, yes—the kid from Mallory's book store. He was probably delivering the films Bryce had rented for their next movie date.

"Of course I'm sure. One hundred percent sure," the boy was insisting, and his voice sounded defensive, as if Bryce had challenged something he'd said.

Lara heard the sound of rustling paper, and then Wally spoke again.

"See? It's right here in black and white, on page four of *Variety*. Read the headline for yourself. 'Lara Lynmore Signs for New Film.'"

CHAPTER FIFTEEN

THE NEXT TEN SECONDS LASTED a lifetime.

She felt the winter morning air reach in through the open door, like an invisible hand. It touched her bare legs, and she broke out in goose bumps from ankle to neck. She felt the remnants of last night's liquor lying across her mind, a low gray fog preventing logical thought. She felt hammers of blood start pounding at her temples and twists of nausea waking in her stomach.

Snippets of last night played in her mind like a slide show. Her foot along Bryce's leg and the answering light in his eyes. Bryce patting Kieran's shoulder, true brothers for that one laughing moment. The silhouette of Bryce's lean, muscled arm against the dawn light, flexing with beautiful power as he moved over her.

She should file those memories away for safekeeping, she thought. Put them under glass. Because she had bought them, she finally understood, at a painful price.

By the time Wally said goodbye, she could tell by the subtle squaring of Bryce's bare shoulders that he realized she was standing behind him. How did he know? Did he smell her perfume, hear her steps on the stairs? Or did her half-frozen horror have a presence all its own?

She saw the pause before Bryce closed the door, saw him set his jaw. She knew, even before he turned around, what his face would look like.

"So." He shut the door and gazed at her. "When were you going to tell me?"

She held her shirt tightly closed at the throat, feeling exposed. She wished she'd taken another minute to get fully dressed.

"This morning," she said. "I was going to tell you as soon as we woke up."

"Why didn't you tell me when you first came home?"

"I wish I had. But I—I knew it would be a stressful discussion, and I—"

She stopped. She sounded like a guilty child caught trying to hide a bad report card. By refusing to be honest, she'd implied that her decision was shameful, something to be kept secret as long as possible.

But that wasn't how she really felt. She was proud of her new project. She would like it very much if Bryce were proud of it, too, but, if he couldn't be, she might as well know that now. She could take it. She was getting used to living without the approval of the people around her.

"I was stupid to try to hide it," she said. "I was afraid to upset you, which was not very mature. I wanted one happy night together first, but I can see that was selfish. I'm sorry. I'll be glad to tell you all about it now, if you'd like."

He smiled coolly. "I don't think that's really necessary, is it? Apparently *Variety* broke the story to the entire world this morning. And Wally broke it to me. Imagine my surprise when he wanted to discuss the exciting news about the woman sleeping in my bed—but I didn't know what the hell he was talking about."

She flushed, more in annoyance than in shame. Wasn't he overreacting just a little? He didn't give a damn how he looked in front of Wally. "Still, I'd like to tell you about it. I'm sure *Variety* didn't have the whole story."

"They had enough." He set the videos Wally had brought down on the hall stand. "Unless you're going to try to tell me it isn't true. That you haven't signed with your *Highwayman* director to do another film."

"No, it's true enough," she said, feeling a frost creep into her tone. She tried to stay open. If they both retreated into monosyllabic anger, this could really spiral out of control. "I have signed a new contract with him. But it isn't for a feature film. It's just a documentary—"

"And when exactly did this happen?"

"When I was in L.A. closing on the condo. I called my agent, to explain why I wasn't going to be able to do lunch, and she described the new project to me."

He laughed, a sound that was dripping with skepticism. "*Two days* ago? You expect me to believe you didn't know anything about any of this until two days ago?"

"No," she said. "I don't *expect* you to. Your tone makes it pretty clear you have already decided not to believe a word I say. However, that's exactly what happened."

Bryce turned his face away and stared through the etched sidelights toward the front yard, where remnants of snow still laced the edges of the brown, dry grass. His elegant profile and the rugged lines of his naked chest glowed in the sunlight. She thought, ironically, that he'd never looked so wonderful.

Lucky, who must have followed Wally out to the gate of the wrought-iron fence, suddenly noticed Bryce and came romping up to the porch. He parked himself in front of the sidelight and pawed the glass politely, his tongue hanging out in a goofy grin.

But Bryce seemed not to notice. He stood so still he might have been chiseled out of some beautiful, tawny marble. A hardness had settled over him that she couldn't quite understand.

She wasn't sure she wanted to understand it. She only knew it wasn't fair—and that she wasn't going to grovel to try to placate him.

"I think the part that bothers me the most," he said in a distant, contemplative voice, as if they were discussing something as abstract as Newton's laws of motion, "is that you didn't need to lie. We had agreed, I thought, to be perfectly honest. We're both planning to leave Heyday before long. The fact that you're leaving a little sooner than expected shouldn't be such a big deal. We both already knew this wasn't going to last forever."

The words fell over her like a trickle of cold water. "It sounds as if you're saying it's over already."

He shrugged. "If you're going back to L.A. to make a movie, that pretty much decides the issue, don't you think? Even if you come back this time, there will always be a next time."

She heard the emphasis on "if." Oh, he was so blind! He just would not see the truth. He saw only what he wanted to see. It would obviously take years to convince him that he was wrong. And she didn't have years.

In fact, it looked as if her time was already up.

She was angry, but the stronger emotion by far was an almost unbearable sadness. Because she could tell he still planned to leave at the end of the semester, and damn it, he belonged in Heyday. However he might fight to deny it, his roots were here. His family, what there was left of it, was here.

And *she* was here, ready to love him if he'd let her.

But he wouldn't. The truth was, that was exactly what he was running away from. Loving and being loved, needing and being needed. Being family. Those things were just too risky for him.

Damn Anderson McClintock! If she could meet him today, she'd tell him exactly what she thought of the way he'd treated his firstborn son. Of the cavalier way he'd condemned Bryce to a life without the comfort and satisfaction of real intimacy. Without the redemption of love.

And, at the same time, forcing Lara to live without it, too. Because *her* tragedy was that she loved this damaged man. And her love was strong enough to heal him, if he'd only give her the chance.

"Bryce," she said impulsively, "what about these weeks we've spent together? Don't they mean anything to you?"

"They've been wonderful," he said, still rigid, still taking refuge in detachment, as if he didn't dare be truly present in the moment. "We always knew how great the sex would be, Lara. But I did tell you right from the beginning—I warned you I don't do forever. I never lied to you."

She stared at him, disbelieving, an icy numbness taking over, banishing the sadness...for now.

Great sex. So he was back to that tired old line, was he? She stalked over and jerked open the door to let poor, whimpering Lucky into the house. Shutting her out was one thing. Shutting a dumb, cold animal out of its only home was another.

"No, you never lied to me, Bryce," she said. "You were always too busy lying to yourself."

BRYCE HAD LET HIS CLASS go early. They'd done pretty well on their last exam, so he was feeling fairly charitable. Plus, it was the first summerlike day of the year, and the kids had been completely unable to concentrate. Rob Overton had ridden his motorcycle to school, and he propped his helmet up beside his desk, with its blue lightning bolts on prominent display. A couple of the girls had even worn shorts, which probably wasn't all that comfortable, given that it was only about fifty in the shade, but which had met with universal approval from the boys.

It was hopeless to ask them to talk about torts. So,

twenty minutes early, Bryce walked out to his car, papers under his arm, and blinked open the remote locks to his car.

"Hey, Mr. McC!" It was Paul Santiago, one of his favorite students. Paul, who was cruising by in his rusted-out old Chevy, whistled at Bryce's XKE. "Nice ride! I'll trade ya!"

Bryce laughed. "In your dreams," he said. Paul grinned, beeped his horn cheerfully, then roared off.

He was going to miss the students, Bryce realized suddenly. They weren't bad kids, actually, and their energy and idealism were refreshing. Some of them were even learning to think. A couple of them might go on to make good cops or lawyers or FBI agents.

On the other hand, maybe it was just the softening weather making him temporarily weak-minded. The air smelled flowery and warm, and before he could stop himself he said the words in his mind: *It smells like Lara.*

Damn it. How was he ever going to get his head straight if he couldn't stop thinking about her all the time? Nearly a week had gone by since their breakup, which was about six days more than he ordinarily needed to forget a woman, but the pinch was as sharp as ever.

If only he weren't in Heyday. Every room in the frat house was alive with echoes of her. The bedroom, the movie room, the foyer where he'd seen her last. He couldn't even grab a bottled water out of the refrigerator without remembering her standing there, silhouetted in the appliance light, laughing at foolish men who subsisted on old apples and cold beer.

The college campus, too, was a minefield of memories. Half the female students looked like her from a distance, only to fade into strangers as they approached. The elephant fountain was haunted by the ghost of that day, that crazy, fatal day when he had asked her to be his lover.

The Black and White Lounge was obviously off limits, as were Valley Treasures, Big Top Diner, the bookstore and all points in between.

Now, if the very air he breathed was going to remind him of Lara, he was sunk for sure.

Still, he had to keep trying to get past it. He told himself frequently—he even sometimes told Lucky, who was slinking around the frat house, as dejected as if someone had died—that he was glad they'd ended it quickly. Bryce had known from the beginning that Lara had an addictive quality, and that a smart man would keep his distance. Hell, hadn't he watched crazy Kenny Boggs die for love of Lara?

Bryce did not intend to follow suit.

He turned the key to start the engine, but before he could pull away, the passenger door opened, and to his shock Ilsa climbed into the car and shut the door behind her.

"I'm sorry, Mr. McClintock," she said. She turned to him, and her beautiful face was running with tears. "I must talk to you. I must talk to *someone,* or I will not know what to do."

What the hell was going on? He ran through the short list of possibilities. She hadn't done badly on her exam, so it wasn't anything as simple as that. Which, God help him, only left one thing. *Kieran.*

But it was definitely not a good idea to have a weeping female student locked in his car alone with him. He had been a teacher only a couple of months, but common sense warned him this situation was tricky, to say the least.

"Ilsa, whatever's bothering you, this isn't the time or place to discuss it. We have counselors, and I'll be glad to—"

"I cannot tell the counselor these things," she said, putting her hands over her face. Her voice sounded so stressed it was backed with a high-pitched whine, like a bad audiotape. "*You,* you are the only one I can tell."

He turned off the motor. "Then let's go back into the classroom," he said, putting his hand on the door handle. "We can't do this here."

"No, I cannot talk in there where others may hear me." She brought her hands down and made fists with them on her lap. "If you will not listen to me, I will go to someone else." She stiffened. "I will go to Mrs. Mc-Clintock."

Bryce let his hand drop off the handle. *Oh, hell, hell, hell.*

"Okay," he said calmly, automatically adopting the same tone he might once have used with a lunatic holding a gun. In a way, that's exactly what she was. The *gun* was her incriminating information, and she was holding it to Claire's head. Bryce wasn't sure how, but he knew he had to stop her from pulling the trigger.

"Okay, talk to me. Tell me what's the matter."

"I have told you before, it is Kieran," she said. "He is breaking my heart to keep working for him, loving him so much. Knowing he loves me, too, but he must always act as if he loves her, because of the baby."

Her tears fell harder, and she twisted her hands in her lap. "Always the baby comes first."

Bryce decided to take it one small step at a time. He watched her carefully, trying to assess just what kind of threat her "love" really posed. Did she just want sympathy? Was she just a weeper? A talker? Or was she the kind of crazy that might take steps to eliminate the people who stood between her and the object of her fantasies?

"Okay," he said. "I can see how that would be very difficult. Have you considered finding another job? I could probably help you—"

"No, no," she interrupted, shaking her head vehemently, sending her blond hair bouncing, shining in the springlike sun. "I will still think of him all the time. I need to go home, Mr. McClintock. I need to be with my family, my people. I think there I could begin to forget."

He knew better than to look too enthusiastic about the idea, although his spirits leapt at the possibility. "Are you sure that would be a good decision? Sweden is a long way, and if you wanted to stay here…"

"No, I will not be able to forget here. Here everything reminds me of Kieran."

Bryce had to laugh inwardly. How ironic that he'd been thinking exactly the same things just now about Lara. It was a wry laugh, though. It didn't particularly please him to have anything in common with this overwrought obsessive.

"All right, then," he said. "If you're sure. Can that be arranged?"

She looked at him, sniffing and wiping her eyes with the back of her hand. "I do not have enough money." She inhaled with a sobbing hitch. "I went to him, and I said, please will he loan me money to go home? But he says he will not."

God, Kieran, you idiot. A lousy check would buy you out of this mess, and you're too dumb to write it? But that didn't make sense—Kieran wasn't dumb. Bryce felt his insides tighten. Could it be possible that Kieran didn't *want* Ilsa to leave? Was it possible he intended to hang on to a wife and mistress both?

"If he does not help me, I am desperate," Ilsa said when Bryce didn't answer immediately. She glanced at him out of the corner of her eye. "I do not want to, but I think I must ask Mrs. McClintock. She, I think, will give me the money for an airplane ticket."

The hell she would. Bryce, who had an extremely high estimation of Claire McClintock's spunk, thought it much more likely that she'd give Ilsa the boot, and probably Kieran, too.

And then what? Even assuming Kieran had it coming, and assuming Claire was tough enough to get on with her life, what about little Stephanie? Bryce knew all too well what would happen. She'd be caught in the same nasty domestic wars that Bryce and Kieran had endured all their lives. And instead of growing up protected and adored, with the confidence she deserved, she'd become, at best, a scarred, battle-weary scrapper. She'd have trust issues and intimacy screwups and—

She'd end up, in fact, as messed up as Bryce.

Which he suddenly knew he couldn't allow. Not if there were any way to prevent it.

He gave the weeping beauty next to him a reassuring smile.

"I don't think there's any need to involve Claire," he said, reaching in his jacket pocket for his checkbook and pen. "Tell me. How much does a first-class ticket to Sweden cost these days?"

CHAPTER SIXTEEN

WHEN KARLA HEARD the doorbell ring, the first thought that ran through her mind was that she hadn't put on her makeup yet today. The second thought was...*who cares?*

If Oscar had taught her anything, he had taught her how energizing freedom from physical vanity could be. He had helped her to see that fixating on the surface was a terrible waste of time. And fixating on the people who *cared* how you looked was even worse. Sooner or later everybody stopped looking good. They got old, got tired...got sliced up by barbed wire.

He had laughed when he said that, because he knew that nothing that happened to his face could ever make her find him less attractive. The things that drew her to him were his calm wisdom, his sense of humor, his sensitivity to all creatures and the world they lived in.

Thirty-six stitches hadn't changed any of that.

She wasn't sure, frankly, what about *her* appealed to *him*. Certainly not her makeup, or her five-hundred-dollar haircut. Two days ago, when he'd kissed her for the first time, he had told her he admired her courage, her passion, her warrior spirit.

But she secretly feared he was overestimating her. In fact, as she took stock of herself and her life in the days after Lara left to do the documentary, Karla had felt pretty grim about what she found.

She wasn't sure she had any particularly good qualities, but she was working hard every day to improve. The best she could say was that maybe she was making progress.

So when she heard the bell, she ignored her bare face and tousled hair, went to the door and opened it.

To her surprise, it was Bryce McClintock.

"Hello, Bryce," she said, her voice stilted. She didn't mean to be unfriendly, but she couldn't deny that the moment was uncomfortable. The last time she'd seen him, they'd been like two dogs, tugging at Lara as if she were a particularly desirable bone. It made her blush to remember some of the things they'd said.

She still didn't know exactly what had happened between him and Lara. When Lara had come back to Lazy Gables, she'd merely said she didn't want to talk about it. So, though Lara's face was gray and pining, and all Karla's maternal instincts had been activated, Karla had somehow managed to keep quiet.

Oscar had said he was particularly proud of that. He had obviously sensed how hard it was to let her little girl be hurt, and not insist on knowing why.

"Would you like to come in?" She opened the door farther, but then she hesitated. "You do know Lara isn't here? She's still in L.A."

"Yes," he said. "I had heard that. That's what I wanted to talk to you about."

"All right." She let him move past her into the front foyer. "Would you like a cup of coffee? I've just made a fresh pot."

Now that he was inside, in a brighter light, she saw that he looked almost as peaked as Lara had. She wondered what on earth had happened to make these two vibrant young people suddenly so desolate.

"No, thanks, no coffee," he said. "I can't stay long."

"All right," she said again. And then she waited.

"I just wondered if you know when she'll be coming back." He smiled, but the smile didn't touch his eyes. "If she's coming back at all, that is."

"Of course she's coming back," Karla said. Had Lara told him nothing? Had their parting been as difficult as that? "She's got the spring concert at the retirement home next week. She said she wouldn't miss that for the world."

He nodded, but he looked disappointed, somehow. She wondered why. And then she realized…he must have been hoping that *he* would be the magnet that would draw her back, not the folks at the retirement home.

"Is there anything I can do?" She asked the question tentatively. "I know I've been a great deal too much involved with Lara and her life for a very long time. And I've been particularly rough on you. So I hesitate to inject myself into this. But if I could help…"

He smiled at her, another of those mirthless curves of his chiseled lips. He was a handsome devil. *The sinner,* they said. She had heard the stories, and even though she had feared for Lara's happiness, she had also seen why he was so irresistible.

"*Can* I help, Bryce?"

"No. Not unless—" He paused, but after that the words seemed to rush out of him, like steam from an underground geyser. "Not unless you can help me understand why she refused to be honest about her plans. Why she lied to me, why she never told me she was planning to go back to L.A."

Oh, dear. Karla instantly recognized the bewildered pain behind his tight words. The wounded rejection masquerading as anger. She recognized it because she had felt it herself. She'd been so hurt, so furious, the day Lara had finally broken the news that she was leaving show business.

And she had stayed angry for months. She wondered if Bryce could possibly be ready to hear the truth. It had taken Karla months to be willing to listen.

"I think I can tell you," she said. "But I don't think you're going to like what you hear."

He looked at her somberly. "Try me," he said.

"All right. I think she didn't tell you because you had made it too difficult. You had somehow made it clear that your love was conditional, and that if she said or did something you didn't like, such as getting involved with Hollywood again, you would withdraw it."

He narrowed his eyes. "That's ridiculous. I never said any such thing. And it wasn't a question of love, in any event. We—liked being together. It was very special. But it certainly wasn't love."

"Are you sure about that?" She touched his arm. "I know you better than you think I do, Bryce McClintock. I know all about the dumb things people can do because they've been hurt before and don't want to be hurt again."

"I'm sorry, Karla." He frowned and shook his head. "I believe you mean well, but it's not—"

"I know," she said, smiling a little. "It's not love. Well, then maybe you'd better ask yourself what *else* would have driven you here, with your grim face and your stiff back…and your broken heart hanging out there on your sleeve."

THIS MIGHT, Bryce thought, go down as the most bizarre day of his life.

First he'd written that ridiculously large check to Ilsa, hoping to save his brother's marriage, which wasn't his lookout and was probably hopeless in the long run, anyhow. And then he'd made that dumb visit to Karla, like a starving animal trying to sniff out a few crumbs of information to keep him alive. God, what *had* he been thinking? He had never behaved like such a pathetic sad sack before in his life. No wonder she'd assumed he was just another in Lara's trail of broken hearts.

And now, just to top it all off, his fool mutt had gone missing.

No, not *his* mutt, damn it. When had he started calling it *his* mutt?

But it was.

As Bryce grabbed Lucky's leash from the hall stand, he caught a glimpse of himself in the inset mirror. The sight froze him in place.

Who *was* that man? It sure as hell wasn't Bryce McClintock, carefree bastard and happily heartless sinner.

This man looked worried. He looked tired. He looked lonely.

Maybe Lara had been right. Maybe it was time to stop lying to himself. Bizarre or not, these facts seemed to be the new reality: he *did* want Kieran's marriage to succeed, he *did* miss Lara, and the ridiculous dog had, somewhere along the way, become his dog.

And now, according to the message on his answering machine, the dog was at the pound. If Bryce didn't get there by five to redeem him, Lucky would not be sleeping on silk frat-house sheets tonight.

The fact that it would serve the mongrel right for wandering off didn't seem to make a lot of difference. Bryce drove as fast as he could, watching the dashboard clock. He got there at four-fifty-five.

"Sorry, Mr. McClintock," the kid at the front desk said, looking confused. In the background, dogs were barking plaintively. "Mrs. McClintock…the other Mrs. McClintock…well, you know what I mean—"

"Claire. My brother's wife. What about her?"

"She just took the dog. Just like two minutes ago. She paid and everything. If it hadn't been Mrs. Mc-Clintock, I probably wouldn't have—"

Bryce didn't hear the end of that sentence. Leash in hand, he was already heading back out the door of the pound. When he got to the street, he looked up and down, trying to remember if he'd ever heard what kind of car Claire drove. He hadn't ever seen it—but it would have to be expensive. Nothing but the best for The Saint's lovely wife.

As long as you didn't count the having-an-affair-with-the-Swedish-housekeeper thing.

Movement halfway down the block caught his attention, and he began to walk in that direction. It was a late-model minivan, white with gold trim, all the bells and whistles. A woman was bending over the passenger seat.

Suddenly she backed up awkwardly, almost losing her balance, as if she'd been knocked over. And at the same moment a big pile of dirty fur came streaking out of the car and raced down the sidewalk toward Bryce, barking ecstatically.

It was Lucky, of course, and the poor off-balanced woman was Claire. Bryce put his hands down, but Lucky ran so fast he couldn't skid to a stop in time. He collided with Bryce's legs, damn near knocking him over, too.

"Easy, boy," Bryce said, trying to get the dog to stand still long enough to attach the leash. Lucky thought the sight of Bryce was a big thrill right now, but who knew when he might decide it would be fun to go exploring again?

Claire, who was dusting dog-mud off her pretty blue skirt, laughed as she watched Lucky climbing all over Bryce, licking his hands and generally making a fuss.

"He saw you from the car window," she said, "and he just went nuts. I couldn't hold him."

Bryce rolled his eyes. "He's dramatic," he said. "I'm sorry he barreled into you like that."

"It's okay. He's cute. And he sure does adore you." She knelt down and patted Lucky's head. The dog was calmer now, sitting by Bryce's left foot and smiling, his tongue hanging eight inches out of the side of his mouth.

"Yeah, well." Bryce shook his head and pretty much gave up. Like it or not, he was clearly now saddled with the first pet he'd ever owned in his life. With his luck, the dog would probably live to be fifty, and never give Bryce another moment's freedom. He tugged on Lucky's ear. "I kind of like him, too. Thanks for the heads-up, by the way. How did you know he was there?"

Claire smiled. "A friend of mine does volunteer work at the pound, and she recognized him as your dog. She didn't feel comfortable calling you, so she called me. Actually, I was just about to bring him to you, over at the frat house. I was afraid you might not get the message in time, and I didn't want him to be stuck here all night."

"Thanks," he said. "Did you have to pay to get him out? Of course I want to reimburse you—"

"No," she said quickly. "It was nothing, really. After all, we're family."

He wasn't sure how to respond to that. She obviously put a lot more emphasis on "family" than he ever had. But then, she probably didn't have the same kind of family he'd had.

She was still squatting, still patting Lucky self-consciously. She looked up at Bryce with a strangely nervous expression.

"To tell you the truth," she said, "I was going to come by to see you today anyhow. I—I really need to talk to you."

He hoped his self-conscious guilt didn't show on his face. What could she possibly need to talk to *him* about? Oh, God. Had Ilsa spilled her guts to Claire in spite of the generous check Bryce had written? Damn the woman if she had. The check was about three times the cost of an airplane ticket. It was only fair, he'd said. A kind of severance pay, he'd said.

They'd both understood it was hush money. Or at least he *thought* they'd both understood that.

But maybe he was worrying for nothing. Though Claire looked serious, maybe even a little concerned, she didn't look as distraught as surely she would have if she'd just discovered her husband was cheating on her with the housekeeper.

"Okay," he said. "Shall we talk now?"

She rose to her feet and looked around at the nearby stores. "Is there somewhere we could go, somewhere with a little privacy?"

He shook his head. "Not with the dog, I'm afraid." He scanned the businesses, too, and saw no likely candidates. But they were standing at the edge of the downtown park, too, so....

"How about if we walk Lucky around a little bit? The park's not too busy at this hour."

They practically had it all to themselves. It was a little too cold, and a little too close to sundown for many people to be jogging or reading or playing Frisbee. But it was an attractive spot for a walk. The sky behind the park was a dramatic icy blue swabbed with silver clouds, and the trees cast long chilly shadows.

She nodded. "A walk sounds good."

Lucky, though dumb enough to get caught by Heyday's animal control department, was somehow smart enough to recognize the word "walk." He had already begun straining at the leash.

They walked in silence for a few seconds. Claire seemed to watch her feet, and he could tell she was organizing her thoughts, preparing her first sentence. He found himself hoping that it would be something simple, like another concerned invitation to please be a good brother and come eat dinner with the McClintocks.

But given how this day had gone so far, what were the odds?

"Kieran doesn't know I'm here," she said abruptly.

Oh, man. The odds got even slimmer.

She took an audible breath. "It's about Ilsa."

Luckily, he was accustomed to playing cat-and-mouse interrogation games, where the objective was to let the witness divulge as much as possible, while revealing as little as possible at your own end. Otherwise, he might have blurted out something he'd regret.

Lucky was sniffing a tree trunk, which thankfully gave Bryce the chance to busy himself making sure the leash didn't get tangled.

"Okay," he said. "What about Ilsa?"

He was pleased with how natural he sounded. He would have liked to glance at Claire, to see whether she was buying his casual disinterest, but he didn't dare.

"Well, she—I wanted you to know—" Claire made a small, frustrated sound, and then started over. "Kieran said he doesn't want you to find out about it, and I don't like to go against his wishes. But I've seen the damage that can come from keeping secrets. And besides—this involves you, and I think you have the *right* to know."

He did look at her then. It could be about the check he'd given Ilsa, of course. But somehow the things Claire was saying didn't jibe with that. Why would Kieran want to hide from Bryce something that Bryce himself had done?

It didn't make sense. Instinct told him she wasn't talking about the check.

So what *was* she talking about?

"It involves *me?*"

"Yes." She nodded somberly. "I'm so sorry, Bryce. In some ways, I feel as if this is our fault, because she was our housekeeper, and Kieran encouraged her to go back to school. He thought she was bright, and she ought to get a degree so that she could make something of herself."

Bryce tightened Lucky's lead. He needed to focus, not divide his attention between Claire's rather convoluted story and the twisting investigations of a curious dog who found himself in a brand-new place.

"Claire, I don't know what you're talking about. Don't worry about sugarcoating it, or prefacing it with apologies. Just tell me straight."

He had to love this woman. She understood, and she did exactly as he asked. "All right. Ilsa came to Kieran last night, and she told him she's fallen in love with you."

Bryce's mouth fell open. He would have liked to

have been more suave here. He would have liked to be able to say he saw this coming.

But the truth was, he couldn't have predicted this in a million years.

"She said you seduced her, kept her after class, offered to help her with her work, things like that. She said that then, when you were tired of her, you refused to even talk to her anymore. She said she needs to go back home, back to Sweden, but she didn't have enough money. She implied that if she had to stay here, she might end up going to the college and—"

Finally, here at the end, her courage failed her.

He looked at her. "And reporting me?"

"Yes." To his surprise, her eyes were bright with unshed tears. She was either terribly embarrassed for him, or she really believed this might cause him pain. "So Kieran paid her. He paid her a lot, so that she would just leave."

Bryce shook his head, still stunned, still disbelieving. "How much?"

She hesitated. "Five thousand dollars." She put her hand on his wrist and forced him to pause. "It isn't that Kieran believed her, you have to know that. Neither of us believed a word of it. But these things are delicate. Even when rumors aren't true, they can do a lot of harm."

"Oh, Claire." He couldn't help it. He started to laugh. Lucky looked back at him curiously, then returned to his exploration of a light post. The dusk had just reached the point that the electric streetlights had begun to glow, pale and insignificant against the deep blue sky.

"Oh, Claire, if you only knew how funny this really is."

She tilted her head, frowning. "Bryce, I'm not sure you understand how seriously the college would take any allegation—"

"No, no." He took her gentle hand and squeezed it. "That's not it. I understand the implications of all that quite well. It's just that—"

He broke off. "Where's Kieran?"

She flushed. "He's at home with the baby by now, I'd think. He'll be wondering where I am. I'll have to tell him I've talked to you, although I know he won't like it. He was afraid that you'd take it the wrong way. That you'd see it as another proof that he doesn't trust you, or think that he was trying to buy your gratitude and friendship, or—"

Oh, poor Kieran, Bryce thought. He was such a saint he was even ashamed to have his kindness broadcast.

"Claire, come with me. I think my baby brother and I need to have a talk."

THEY TOOK LUCKY BACK to the frat house first. Things were complex enough without a muddy dog hanging around.

When they got to the beautiful old Federal-period mansion in Riverside Park, Kieran was standing on the front porch, spotlighted by the carriage lamps. He was scanning the street, as if he'd been expecting them.

He held a sheet of notepaper in his hand, and when Bryce walked up to him, Kieran just offered it without preamble.

"Does this make sense to you?" he asked.

Bryce took the note.

"Dear B&K," the curly script, written in turquoise ink, began. "By now you guys have probably compared notes. So all I can say is, thanks, boys! Love and kisses, Ilsa."

Bryce began to laugh again. He could almost see Ilsa grinning at them, her crocodile tears long dry. Perfect, colloquial English, too. Damn, the woman was good, wasn't she?

"Well?" Kieran took the note back and was reading it again, as if there might be some hidden code he could find if he looked hard enough. "Does it mean anything to you?"

"Yeah." Bryce put his hand on Kieran's shoulder. "It means we're two identical chumps, and we've been had big-time." He winked at Claire, who had finally begun to smile, too. "Why don't you guys invite me in, and I'll tell you all about it?"

IT DIDN'T TAKE LONG. Claire stayed and listened long enough to hear the basic facts. Then, when the baby monitor began to issue whimpering noises, she trotted upstairs happily to take care of Stephanie.

Within half an hour, now that they were alone, Bryce and Kieran were both laughing until their eyes ran, comparing notes, as Ilsa had predicted they would. In spite of everything, they had to admire the complex double-scam the woman had pulled.

They even shared the verbatim transcripts of her halting, tearful confessions. "I love Kieran so much," Bryce said in a terrible Swedish accent. "I think I will have to have five thousand dollars, or my heart will be breaking."

Probably the clever, devilish fraud wasn't even Swedish. But she was smart. Smarter than they were, because she had seen what they couldn't admit—that they cared about each other in spite of everything. That they were family, whether they admitted it or not.

That, in the end, each of them would do anything to protect the other.

They didn't discuss that part of it. They didn't have to. They knew the truth now. It was in the air, in their smiles, in the easy way they sat together. They had a lot to catch up on, a lot of things to learn about each other, but they somehow knew there would be plenty of time for that.

God, what a day. First a dog. Now a family.

Bryce sat in the comfortable armchair, listening to his brother berate himself for not seeing through the sneaky witch, and wondering what life would be like now. Now that he was no longer alone.

"Gentlemen?" Claire had appeared in the doorway, a sleeping baby cradled in her arms. She grinned. "Or should I say 'boys'?"

Bryce and Kieran exchanged glances and grimaced. They knew this was just the beginning of a long, humiliating tease-fest. Now that Ilsa had conned them out of ten thousand dollars and officially belittled them as "boys," they might as well have bull's-eyes painted on their backsides.

Kieran smiled at his wife. "What? Is it time for dinner?"

"Only if you've ordered pizza," she said, coming

into the room. "I've been bathing Stephanie, not making chateaubriand for you two suckers."

She turned to Bryce. "What I was going to say, before I was so rudely interrupted, is that I've brought your niece down to say hello."

Bryce stood awkwardly. *His niece...*

Claire came closer, and stretched her arms out just a little, moving the sleeping infant in his direction.

"Take her, Bryce," she said. "She's been waiting a long time to meet you."

Numbly he put out his hands. He didn't know anything about babies. He didn't know how to hold them. She'd probably start bawling and wriggling and throwing up all over him.

But she didn't. Claire placed Stephanie in the crook of his arm, and she settled there, her head nestled against his chest, without waking. He looked up at Claire, stupidly shocked by how warm and pliable the baby was. Somehow he had imagined that she'd be more like a hard plastic doll.

But she wasn't a doll. She was a living person. A miniature, intact miracle. He bent his head and studied her face, even though his vision was oddly prismed and imperfect.

God help her, she really was a McClintock. She had Anderson McClintock's straight, haughty nose above Kieran's wide, generous mouth.

Though her eyes were shut, she began to wave her tiny fingers, as if she groped for something. Instinctively he held out his forefinger, and she clamped her hand around it with surprising confidence, as if she'd known it would be there when she needed it.

He tried to speak. But nothing came out, and when he looked at Kieran, his little brother was grinning.

"I know," Kieran said with feeling. "It messes with your mind big-time, doesn't it, Uncle Bryce?"

Uncle Bryce.

Oh, yeah, it messed with his mind all right. But that was nothing compared to what it did to his heart.

CHAPTER SEVENTEEN

WHILE THE GAFFERS WORKED on the lighting, and the walkie-talkies crackled in the background, Lara sat in a chair in the corner of the set, going over her script one last time. She wanted to be sure she knew these lines backward and forward. She couldn't afford to shoot this bit again.

She was determined to be back in Heyday by Saturday. She was not going to miss that spring concert at the retirement home, no matter what.

But it was already Friday, and they'd run into one glitch after another. First, the paperwork had been fouled up, and they'd lost permission to shoot at the location. Then, when they'd finally settled on another location, it had started to rain. Julian, her director, naturally had weather cover scenes on standby, but transitioning would have been time-consuming, too. He gambled that the shower would pass. It finally did, but in the meantime they'd lost a precious hour.

It wasn't that Julian wasn't trying. Because he felt that Lara's involvement in this project was so important, he'd made a hundred small—and large—accommodations for her. He'd accelerated, tightened and completely rearranged the shooting schedule to get her part of it done in only three days.

Unfortunately, even the most talented director in the world couldn't keep equipment trucks from breaking down, or human error from leaving them a battery short. He'd provided meticulous call sheets, but there was always someone who wasn't in the right place at the right time.

Which had apparently just happened again.

"I can not bloody *believe* it! Who was supposed to be watching the bloody schedule?"

Julian's voice was furious, and Lara knew someone's head was going to roll. He stomped over to where she sat. "Take twenty, sweetheart. Jimmy has let the audio wizard go to lunch, and we can't shoot till she gets back."

"Julian." Lara could see that he was frazzled, but she needed to be sure he didn't lose sight of the deadline. Maybe he could settle for something short of a wizard? "My plane leaves at noon tomorrow, whether we're finished here or not. You did agree to that."

"I know, I know." He ran his hand through his balding, stringy hair. He didn't look like much, but Lara knew he had poetry in his soul and kindness in his heart. That's why she hadn't been able to say no to this project.

Julian had written and directed this documentary, which was an exploration of the tragedy of schizophrenia. His sister suffered from the illness, and he wanted the world to understand. He'd found it difficult to get financing—people who were eager to back *The High-*

wayman, with its sexy stars and exciting battle scenes, couldn't quite see their way to underwriting a "downer documentary" like this.

But when Bryce had killed Kenny Boggs, and subsequent investigations showed that Kenny had untreated schizophrenia, it had ironically breathed new life into Julian's project. Suddenly the topic was hot—or at least hot enough to attract the bare-minimum financing.

It might never make a penny, but Julian didn't care. This was the film of Julian's heart. He wanted people to watch it, to be educated about the difficulties of this disease. He had a good documentary, but finally he faced the sad truth. He needed to make it marketable. He needed Lara to sign on as its host.

When she'd said yes, and she'd agreed to do it for the SAG minimum, the odd, wonderful man had actually burst into tears.

Not that you could tell that now, looking at his sour face and knowing what hell awaited the poor guy responsible for the call sheet screwup.

"I'd just like to know who the guy is, that's all." Julian looked sour. He popped an antacid into his mouth and chewed with focus. "The guy back home in Hee-Haw."

"Heyday," she said, smiling.

"Yeah. So he must be some kind of amazing dude to make you give up all this."

She had to laugh. *All this?* She had forgotten how much time was wasted on a movie set. In the months she'd been in Heyday, every minute had been filled with something that felt important.

People, family, horses. Music, learning, loving.

Tree-climbing. Cutting out stars. And smooching at the movies.

Real life. Crazy and hectic and sometimes sad. But always wonderfully rich and real.

This slow-motion pace of wait, wait, wait was like torture after all that happy action. And after months of going without even a dash of lipstick, she squirmed with claustrophobia as two separate makeup artists combed, covered and colored every millimeter of her face, every hair on her head. She wanted to scream every time they stopped the camera to rearrange the curl of hair they'd positioned over her shoulder.

Julian might think this life was heaven. But Lara couldn't wait to get home.

"So," Julian said, still eying her curiously. "Aren't you going to tell me who he is?"

"The guy I'm rushing home to see tomorrow night?" She smiled…not too broadly, of course, because she couldn't afford to smudge her lipstick. "His name is Nelson, and he's seventy-five years old. He's a divine dancer."

Julian looked surprised, but it didn't seem to have occurred to him that she was joking. Lara had forgotten that, around here, pretty, ambitious twenty-something girls married rich seventy-something men fairly frequently.

"Oh, well, lucky Nelson. Just don't dance him into a heart attack." He ate another antacid. "I'd better go talk to Dr. Spinner. He thought he'd be leaving an hour ago, and I need him to shoot another take."

Lara went back to her script. A few minutes later, she stifled a yawn. She wished she could get out of this artificial box, this stage set carefully decorated to look like a warm and inviting living room. But back home in Heyday she had a real living room, and she would give anything to be sitting there right now.

Back home in Heyday.

Back home with Bryce.

For the past several days, she hadn't allowed herself to think of him. She'd built walls to keep the feelings out so that she could concentrate on this project.

But apparently those walls weren't built to last forever. Already they were crumbling, growing porous. Thoughts of Bryce were seeping in through the bare spots, trickling in around the edges. Soon, she feared, there would be a total collapse and a flood of pain and loss.

She wondered what he was doing. Was he thinking of her at all? Maybe not. She remembered the day they had quarreled. He had been so ready to call it quits, so quick to anger. Perhaps that meant he'd already begun to grow bored and was glad to have an excuse to dismiss her.

The thought was so painful she had to press the script up against her chest to contain it. Surely not. Their last night together had been so beautiful.

Maybe there was still hope. She put her script on the floor. She could call him now. She could apologize, make him see how sorry she was that she hadn't been honest. She could make him understand, make him believe her—

No. She picked up the script again. *No.* As tempting

as the thought of him might be, she was *not* going to make that call.

She had just emerged from the long struggle with her mother, in which she couldn't dare to be honest, in which her desires, her truths, had been sublimated to keep her mother happy. She was never going to live that way again.

Even if it meant she would be alone forever, she would not give up control of her life to anyone. Not even to Bryce. She'd fought too hard to get it.

She shut her eyes. She wouldn't give up her independence to have him back, but it was going to be a long, long time before she could think of him without bleeding inwardly. It might be longer than forever, before she could forget.

"Lara! Damn it, Lara!" Julian's annoyance was turned on her now. It reminded her of how frazzled he'd been toward the end of filming *The Highwayman*. "Lara Lynmore," he'd bellowed then, "will you for God's sake get over here and bloody *die* already?"

She laughed, remembering. And, thankfully, the laughter helped make the misty tears go back where they belonged.

"Damn it, Lara Lynmore, we need you front and center. Run!"

She steeled herself, stood carefully, making sure her hair didn't change position, and walked slowly to the sound of Julian's voice.

"Coming, master," she said with a chuckle. "But if I run you'll have to bring makeup back out, and you don't want to do that."

When she reached him, though, he wasn't alone. Standing beside the balding, portly little fussbudget genius of a director was another man.

Tall. Dark. Dangerous.

Bryce McClintock.

She put out a hand and used the back of Julian's director's chair to balance herself.

"Someone to see you," Julian said. "You've got ten minutes." He glared at Bryce. "Look, I don't know why her old bodyguard has suddenly shown up again, but I've got my ideas. I just want you to know there'll be no touching the face or the hair. We're on a deadline here, and it's *her* deadline. If she comes back to the set kissed all to hell, I'm taking it out of her time, not mine."

"I understand," Bryce said, his eyes glinting with laughter. "No touching the face or the hair."

"And remember, if you're really who I think you are, I hate you already."

Bryce narrowed his eyes. "Who do you think I am?"

"I think you're the bastard who stole my favorite leading lady. I think you're Mr. I-have-to-be-in-Hee-Haw-by-Saturday-for-a-reason in the flesh." He didn't wait for an answer from Bryce. He merely gave Lara a wry grin and turned to go.

"Seventy-five, my ass," he grumbled as he walked away.

Lara watched him all the way to the back of the set. She needed those few seconds desperately. Her legs seemed to be shaking slightly, and she was afraid her voice might do the same.

"Lara."

Finally she turned her head and looked at Bryce. She wished, irrationally, that she didn't have all this makeup on. He liked her better without it. Even that first night, months ago, when he was her bodyguard and Kenny Boggs was still alive, he hadn't ever kissed her when she had her makeup on. Their one night in each other's arms had come when she was fresh from the shower....

Thoughts like those weren't relevant right now. But what *was* relevant? What did this mean? Why was he here?

She wanted to hope. Something inside her chest was poised like a bird already, wings outstretched, just waiting for the command to fly.

But she didn't dare give that command. Not yet.

"Hi," she said. "I—I didn't expect to see you here. I thought you hated Los Angeles."

He shook his head. "No. I don't hate Los Angeles. I'm *afraid* of Los Angeles. That's very different, really."

"I—I'm not sure what you mean."

"It's simple." He laughed harshly. "Embarrassing as hell, but in the end, disgustingly simple."

"Well, you'll have to help me understand," she said, still holding on to the chair for support. She loved him so much. It took all her courage not to simply throw herself into his arms. "It doesn't seem simple to me."

"I'm *afraid,* afraid that L.A. might take you away from me. I'm afraid of how glamorous it is. I'm afraid of how much they love you here. I'm afraid of their excitement, their power, their money…all of which they are begging to lay at your feet."

He tilted one corner of his mouth. "I'm afraid of your costars. I'm afraid of the Brads and the Mels and the Colins. Hell, I'm even afraid of Tony."

"Oh, Bryce." She laughed, the wings in her chest beating now, so fast, ready to rise onto a buoyant current of relief. "Surely not Tony."

"Yes, that's how low I've sunk." He tried to smile. "Even the foppish dweeb."

"You don't need to be," she said softly. "Not of him. Not of any of them."

"But I was. And so I tried to set rules. I tried to control you. I tried to make you give up this world and choose me. Only me."

"Oh, Bryce."

He took a deep breath. "When you wouldn't, when I learned that you were coming back to do another film, I just didn't have the courage to live with the fear. Rather than endure it, I drove you away. I thought it would be easier."

She searched his face. He looked weary, with dark circles under his eyes. "And was it?"

"No. It was hell." He reached out and touched her face, very gently, with the tips of his fingers. "I love you, Lara. I didn't want to. Until you were gone, I hadn't even admitted to myself that it *was* love. And do you know why? Because, deep inside, I just couldn't believe that, with all those glittering, seductive choices, you could ever choose me."

"But I already had chosen you," she said. She tightened her grip on the chair. "I chose you from the very beginning. But that wasn't enough—"

"It was more than I deserved," he said. "I've come here to ask you to forgive me, Lara. I've come to tell you that wherever you want to live, whatever you want to do, I love you. Heyday. Los Angeles. Music therapy. Movie star. I don't care. Whatever life you choose, I just want to be a part of it."

Her legs had begun to shake again. "Does that mean you're not afraid anymore?"

He smiled. "Hell, no. I'm more terrified than ever. I don't know anything about this kind of relationship, Lara. I've never let anyone really matter—I've never been willing to give anyone the power to hurt me. But you have the power now, and I can't take it back. I don't want to take it back."

Her eyes were suddenly filled with tears. Julian would kill her—they'd have to redo her face. But she couldn't stop herself. She stumbled toward him, and he held out his arms to catch her.

With a sigh of complete relief, she folded herself against him.

He wrapped his arms around her with a groan. "Lara," he said, as he kissed her hair. "Thank God. Thank God it's not too late."

"Damn you, man, if you touch her hair I'll have you arrested!"

Julian came barreling over, followed by three appalled assistants and one horrified makeup artist.

Lara lifted her head. "It's okay, Julian," she said. "They can always fix it."

"Not in the next ten minutes, they can't, and we're on a deadline, in case you've forgotten. *Your* damn deadline, I might add."

He turned to Bryce. "And I don't know what *you're* looking so smug about, bodyguard. She may be kissing you today, but tomorrow she's got a hot date with a seventy-five-year-old geezer who's probably got fifty million dollars and a hinky heart, which can be a very attractive combination."

Lara shook her head, laughing, but Bryce just held her tighter.

"I'll risk it," he said, projecting such a powerful force that even the makeup artist didn't dare come any closer. He looked down at her, and the love in his eyes took her breath away.

"For you," he said softly, "I think I just might be able to risk anything."

EPILOGUE

ALMOST EVERYONE in Heyday was packed into the auditorium of the retirement home that night.

"Damn, this place is jumping," Oscar said as he, Karla and Bryce found their seats. "Can the old folks handle this much excitement?"

Bryce grinned. "You haven't met these 'old folks.' But for God's sake don't call them that to their faces. They'll knock you flat on your ass."

Kieran and Claire were already seated. Stephanie was sound asleep, draped across Kieran's shoulder, bonelessly molded to him, no more substantive, it seemed, than a rumpled pink towel. Bryce patted the little head and then leaned down to kiss his sister-in-law's cheek.

Kieran growled softly. "Hey. Get your own girl."

Bryce grinned. "That's a good idea, little brother. I think I'll do that."

Kieran raised his eyebrows. "Have you got it with you?"

"Shhh!" Karla leaned over and slapped their knees. "Show some respect, you two. It's starting!"

She was right. The house lights dimmed, and the

stage lights exploded into action, glinting and sparkling off the dozens of foil-covered silver stars hanging from the rafters.

Kieran leaned closer. "You *do* have it," he whispered, "don't you?"

Karla was still glaring, so Bryce just gave Kieran a nod, patting the breast pocket of his jacket. Of course he had it. He and Kieran and Claire had spent all morning at the jeweler's picking out the perfect diamond ring, and now the thing was glowing in his pocket like a radioactive bomb.

He hadn't felt this nervous since he was twelve years old, which was the last time he'd even come close to taking a risk like this. Back then, he'd tried to give Missy Falstaff a tree frog he'd caught, but she'd screamed and knocked the poor little thing away to its death.

He could only hope he'd have better luck tonight. Claire had promised him this ring would please any woman. He hoped she was right. His nerves had been shot from the high-octane emotional buzz of elation and sheer terror. In his panic, he had been ready to buy the biggest, showiest, most expensive diamond in the store, but Claire had gently put her hand on his arm. "Remember who you're buying this for," she'd said with a smile.

And so he had tried to settle down, tried to keep Lara's face in front of him whenever the jeweler pulled out a ring. Finally, one simple ring stood out. Not huge, but full of color and light. Just a clear, steady solitaire, with tiny diamonds spilling on either side down the golden band, like the trails of a comet.

The audience began to go wild. Bryce looked up, and he saw that Lara had appeared on the stage, beautiful beyond description in her white beaded Eliza Doolittle gown, which she'd wear for her own song.

"Hi, everyone," she said, and the roar went up again. Just like that. Two words, one knockout smile…and her fans went mad. "Welcome to our spring concert. We hope you enjoy the show."

It was two hours of great fun and fantastic music, and it was a huge success. A dozen senior citizens, some of whom had amazing talent, some of whom had only enthusiasm, came out and performed for the eager, receptive audience. Vivian managed to say "white cliffs of Dover" correctly for the first time ever, which brought thunderous applause. Then a tiny, wrinkled man brought the audience to tears with a simple, a cappella version of "Edelweiss."

There was no overall theme. Lara had let each performer choose the song he or she loved best. Bryce had at first feared that the result might be a jumble, but now he saw how right Lara had been.

This wasn't just show business—it was therapy. It was a chance for these people to bring the passions of their past into the present, to let those passions live again. And to share them with people who cared.

Even more than that, it was an exercise in humanity. Bryce didn't know, for instance, exactly when and where that tiny man had last heard "Edelweiss," but he felt the remembered love in his performance, the poignant echo of a simpler time. Bryce even thought, for a moment, that he could see the young, vibrant man he once had been, just inside the wrinkles.

And as the man sang, without knowing why, Bryce suddenly remembered a day, long, long ago, when his father had sung him to sleep. He frowned. Blinking, he tried to tighten his heart.

But it was too late. He'd forgotten such a thing had ever happened—but it had. Somewhere, under the years of anger he'd piled on top of his betrayed love, that night had been lying dormant, waiting for him to remember.

Lara and Nelson's *My Fair Lady* song brought the house down, of course, but then suddenly, too soon, it was all over. The audience surged to its feet as one, clapping and stomping and whistling and calling out names.

Bryce felt Kieran's hand on his shoulder. He looked at his brother and nodded, though his throat felt dry, and his hands were oddly numb.

"You can do it," Kieran said.

Claire, who now held Stephanie, who was staring, wide-eyed, clearly curious about all the noise, blew him a kiss with her free hand. "Go get 'em, bad boy," she said with a grin.

He made his way somehow to the back of the stage. The audience was still applauding, the cast still taking curtain calls. Dozens of bouquets had been delivered, and petals of roses and daisies now littered the stage floor.

Lara saw him the minute he appeared at the corner of the curtain. With a glorious smile, she edged over to him and fell into his arms with a sigh.

"We did it!" She lifted her face for a kiss.

"You did it," he said. "You were magnificent."

She sighed happily, settling herself against him. "Thanks for coming," she said. "It was wonderful to look out and see everyone sitting there."

"Well, I had to come," he said. "Because—because I have something to ask you."

She looked up at him. "You do? What is it?"

He wondered if she knew what was coming. He wondered if she knew how terrified he was. This was something he had told himself he would never, ever do. He'd told himself he didn't have the right to do it, not with his genes, not with his history.

And yet now he knew he had no choice. Life without Lara was no life at all. He could only take the leap, and then vow never to make her suffer for his sins.

He fumbled in his coat pocket. Finally his unfeeling fingers closed around the box, and he managed to get it out.

"Lara," he said, his voice strangely hoarse. "Lara, will you marry me?"

She made a soft, incoherent sound. She took the box from his fingers, and he thought perhaps her own were shaking a little, too.

He held his breath—would she like it? Was it too small? It hadn't been bought for a movie star. It had been bought for a woman in love.

But the look on her face when she opened it put his doubts instantly to rest.

"Bryce—" She seemed to have no voice, just a jagged whisper. "It's so beautiful. It's—oh, Bryce, are you sure? I thought you said—"

"I was wrong." He took the ring out of the box. "I was so wrong, Lara. I *am* the marrying kind—as long as the woman I marry is you."

The tears in her eyes sparkled as brightly as the diamond. She held out her hand—yes, he saw with tenderness, she was trembling, too—and let him slip the ring onto her finger.

He kissed her. He could have gone on kissing her forever. But they had stolen all the time her fans would allow.

"Lara! Lara!" The audience was chanting her name and stomping their feet in unison.

She smiled up at him through her tears. "I'll have to go out there," she said. She hesitated. "What would you think if I—I mean, are you sure you won't change your mind?" She pointed to the microphone. "May I tell them?"

"Tell the whole world if you want," he said. "I love you. That will never change."

She kissed him hard, and then she moved gracefully toward the center of the stage. "Hi again," she said into the mike. The audience grew more quiet, though there were still random calls and whistles. "I want to thank everyone for coming tonight, and for making this show so special."

She glanced one last time at Bryce, her eyes asking the question. He nodded. The whole thing still felt a little surreal. Maybe if he heard her announce the words he could begin to believe she really had said yes.

"I'd like to share something with all of you, something that makes tonight even more special for me." She took a deep breath and held up her left hand. The diamond was on fire under the stage lights. "Bryce McClintock just asked me to marry him. And I accepted." She looked at him one more time. "With all my heart, I accept."

Gasps, laughter, applause… People rushed the stage to congratulate her. Nelson, the stylish little choreographer, leaped impulsively onto the piano stool and launched into a lively rendition of "Get Me To The Church On Time." *My Fair Lady* was clearly his favorite musical.

Many of the cast members knew the song, of course, and they began to sing along.

In the midst of all the chaos, Lara held out her hands, and Bryce moved onto the stage to take them.

"I'm getting married in the morning," she said softly, as the others sang the words.

"No," he said, laughing and pulling her into his arms, oblivious of the hundred or more people watching their every move. "You are most definitely *not* getting married in the morning, my love."

She tilted her head back. "I'm not?"

"No way," he said. "My father may have had five weddings, but I'm going to have one, and only one. We are going to take our time and do this thing right."

"Yes, sir." She grinned. "I'm sorry to be impatient. It's just that…suddenly I can't wait to be the sinner's one and only wife."

"The Sinner's Wife." He laughed and bent his head to kiss her one more time. "That sounds like something right out of Hollywood."

"Yes," she said, touching her warm lips to his with a soft and curving smile. "It is, as my agent would say, the role of a lifetime."

* * * * *

*Turn the page for an excerpt from
THE STRANGER,
the final book in* THE HEROES OF HEYDAY
trilogy by Kathleen O'Brien.

*THE STRANGER
(Harlequin Superromance #1266)
is available in April 2005.*

CHAPTER ONE

MALLORY RACKHAM loved many things about owning a bookstore in Heyday, Virginia, but balancing the bank accounts wasn't one of them.

Balance? What a joke! Watching the numbers on her computer screen cling to the "plus" column was as nerve-racking as watching an acrobat bicycle across the high wire without a net.

And she hadn't even entered this month's sales tax payment. She typed a few keys, and, sure enough, the dollar total tumbled off the tightrope and somersaulted straight into the red.

She put her head in her hands and groaned. Apparently living your whole life in Heyday did things to your mind. Heyday had been built around a circus legend, and from the Big Top Diner to the Ringmaster Parade it was a one-theme town. And now she was even going bankrupt in circus metaphors.

"Mallory?" Wally Pierson, the teenager she'd hired to work the cash register in the afternoons, stuck his head through her office door, so she arranged her face in a calm smile. He knew she was doing the books, and of course he knew business had been off lately. Wally's weekly paycheck wasn't huge, but it was important to him. No need to make the kid wonder where his next Whopper was coming from.

"Phone's for you. Some rude guy, won't give his name. Just said to tell you it's about your sister's wedding."

Mindy's wedding. Oh, hell. Mallory had completely forgotten that the check to reserve the room was due to the country club at the end of the month. Her eyes instinctively darted back to the computer screen. If she typed that entry in right now, the whole thing would probably explode in a storm of flying red numbers.

"Another salesman, do you think?" The minute Mindy's engagement had hit the papers, the phone had started ringing. Apparently people assumed that when you married a state senator's son, you had a fortune to spend on satin and lace and geegaws. They seemed to forget that the bride's family paid for the wedding.

"Doesn't sound like a salesman," Wally said, toying with the silver ring in his eyebrow. "Sounds like a weirdo, actually. Voice like Darth Vader."

Great. Just what she needed. Darth Vader peddling pink votives and silver-tasseled chair shawls.

"Thanks, Wally," she said. "I'll handle it."

He ducked out, clearly relieved that she hadn't asked him to get rid of the caller.

"Good morning," Mallory chirped as she pulled the phone toward her. "You've reached the offices of Maxed Out and Dead Broke." But when she picked up the receiver, sanity reasserted itself, and she merely said, "Rackham Books. This is Mallory Rackham."

"Good morning, Miss Rackham," a strange, electronic voice said slowly.

Mallory's hand tightened around the telephone. How bizarre. The voice didn't even sound quite human, and yet it managed to convey all kinds of unpleasant things with those four simple words. Everything from an unwanted familiarity to a subtle threat.

That was ridiculous, of course. A threat of what? She was a small-town bookstore owner, not James Bond. And yet this voice clearly was mechanically altered. Why would anyone do that?

"Who is this?"

"I want you to listen to me carefully. I have some instructions for you."

"Instructions for *me*? Who *is* this?"

He ignored her question. "I want you to go to the bank this afternoon. I want you to get fifty twenty-dollar bills and wrap them in a plastic baggie."

She straightened her back. "Are you crazy? I don't know who you think you are, but—"

"I'm only going to say this once, so you'd better listen." The metallic voice had an implacable sound, a cruel sound. She felt her spine tingle and go soft. She leaned back against her chair and tried to think clearly. Did she recognize anything about this voice? Could it be a joke?

But the hard kernel of anxiety in the pit of her stomach said no.

"Put the baggie in a small brown lunch bag and close it with packing tape. Then take the bag to the Fells Point ferry tomorrow morning."

In spite of her confusion, in spite of her outrage that anyone would talk to her this way, she instinctively reached for a pencil and began to make notes.

"Buy a ticket for the 11:00 a.m. trip," he continued. "When you get on the ferry, go immediately to the front. Put the bag under the first seat, the one closest to the bow. And then get off the boat and go home."

She scribbled, her mind racing. Not because she had any intention of taking orders from an anonymous blackmailer, but because, at the very least, she should have some concrete record to show the police.

"Did you get that, Mallory? Do you know what you're supposed to do?"

"Yes," she said. She put down her pencil. "What I don't know is why you think I would agree to do it."

He chuckled. It was a terrible sound, full of unnatural metallic reverberations, like laughter emanating from a steel casket.

"You'll do it because you're a good sister. You'll do it because you love that spoiled brat Mindy, and you wouldn't want to see anything happen to that classy wedding of hers."

Mallory tightened all over. "Her wedding?"

"Yes. You wouldn't want me to ruin her wedding, would you? Senator Earnshaw's son…Frederick, isn't it? He's such a good catch. So handsome, so—"

"How could you do that?" What was he getting at? What exactly was he threatening to do? "How could you possibly ruin my sister's wedding?"

He laughed again. "Easy," he said. "I'd just tell the senator and his son about Mindy's nasty little secret."

For a second Mallory couldn't answer. She was suddenly aware that her heart was thumping, hard and erratic, like a fish struggling on a wooden dock.

This wasn't possible. This couldn't be happening. No one knew about...*that.* Not even Tyler Balfour, big-time investigative journalist, had discovered Mindy's part in the whole—

"Are you there, Mallory?" The voice slowed, clearly savoring her shock. "Are you thinking about it? About the scandal? Mindy's always been a little weak, hasn't she? Not too stable. God only knows what she'd do if her fairy-tale wedding fell apart."

Mallory opened her mouth, but in place of her normal voice she heard only a strange, thin sound, so she shut it again.

The electronic voice hardened. "Be on that ferry, Mallory. Or I'll have to tell poor Freddy Earnshaw that his lovely bride is nothing but a two-bit prostitute."

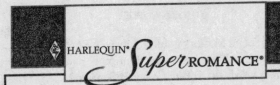

Lost & Found

Somebody's Daughter
by Rebecca Winters
Harlequin Superromance #1259

Twenty-six years ago, baby Kathryn was taken from the
McFarland family. Now Kit Burke has discovered that she
might have been that baby. Will her efforts to track down
her real family lead Kit into their loving arms? Or will
discovering that she is a McFarland mean disaster for
her and the man she loves?

Available February 2005 wherever Harlequin books are sold.

**Remember to look for these Rebecca Winters titles,
available from Harlequin Romance:**

To Catch a Groom (Harlequin Romance #3819)—on sale November 2004
To Win His Heart (Harlequin Romance #3827)—on sale January 2005
To Marry for Duty (Harlequin Romance #3835)—on sale March 2005

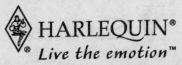

HARLEQUIN®
Live the emotion™

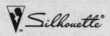

SPECIAL EDITION™

Discover why readers love
Sherryl Woods!

THE ROSE COTTAGE SISTERS

Love and laughter surprise them at their childhood haven.

THREE DOWN THE AISLE

by Sherryl Woods

Stunned when a romance blows up in her face, Melanie D'Angelo reluctantly takes refuge in her grandmother's cottage on the shores of Chesapeake Bay. But when local landscaper Mike Mikelewski arrives with his daughter to fix her grandmother's garden, suddenly Melanie's heart is on the mend as well!

**Silhouette Special Edition #1663
On sale February 2005!**

Meet more Rose Cottage Sisters later this year!

WHAT'S COOKING—Available April 2005
THE LAWS OF ATTRACTION—Available May 2005
FOR THE LOVE OF PETE—Available June 2005

Only from Silhouette Books!

Where love comes alive™

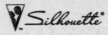

SPECIAL EDITION™

This month, Silhouette Special Edition
brings you the newest
Montana Mavericks story

ALL HE EVER WANTED

(SE #1664)

by reader favorite

Allison Leigh

When young Erik Stevenson fell down an abandoned
mine shaft, he was lucky to be saved by a brave—and
beautiful—rescue worker, Faith Taylor. She was struck by
the feelings that Erik's handsome father, Cameron, awoke
in her scarred heart and soul. But Cameron's heart had
barely recovered from the shock of losing his wife some
time ago. Would he be able to put the past aside—and
find happiness with Faith in his future?

GOLD RUSH GROOMS

Lucky in love—and striking it rich—
beneath the big skies of Montana!

**Don't miss this emotional story—
only from Silhouette Books.**

Available at your favorite retail outlet.

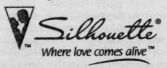

Where love comes alive™

HARLEQUIN *Super*ROMANCE®

A six-book series from Harlequin Superromance

WOMEN in Blue

Six female cops battling crime and corruption on the streets of Houston. Together they can fight the blue wall of silence. But divided, will they fall?

Coming in February 2005, *She Walks the Line* by Roz Denny Fox (Harlequin Superromance #1254)

As a Chinese woman in the Houston Police Department, Mei Lu Ling is a minority twice over. She once worked for her father, a renowned art dealer specializing in Asian artifacts, so her new assignment—tracking art stolen from Chinese museums—is a logical one. But when she's required to work with Cullen Archer, an insurance investigator connected to Interpol, her reaction is more emotional than logical. Because she could easily fall in love with this man…and his adorable twins.

Coming in March 2005, *A Mother's Vow* by K. N. Casper (Harlequin Superromance #1260)

There is corruption in Police Chief Catherine Tanner's department. So when evidence turns up to indicate that her husband may not have died of natural causes, she has to go outside her own precinct to investigate. Ex-cop Jeff Rowan is the most logical person for her to turn to. Unfortunately, Jeff isn't inclined to help Catherine, considering she was the one who fired him.

Available wherever Harlequin books are sold.

Also in the series:
The Partner by Kay David (#1230, October 2004)
The Children's Cop by Sherry Lewis (#1237, November 2004)
The Witness by Linda Style (#1243, December 2004)
Her Little Secret by Anna Adams (#1248, January 2005)

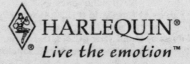